Praise for Regan Black's

Justice Incarnate

"Move over Lara Croft–Jaden Michaels is the quintessential heroine of the twenty-first century, full of heart and totally lethal! Get ready because *Justice Incarnate* is one thrilling ride!"

~Bestselling suspense author Debra Webb

"Love truly conquers all in Regan Black's exciting debut novel!"

~Claudia Dain, 2004 RITA Finalist

"This was a fantastically wonderful story...tension and mystery...built to a perfect level and maintained throughout.... Ms. Black brought her intricate world and the characters to believable life and spun a tale of cliff hanging suspense."

~Coffee Time Romance

Famous Last Words

"...a change of pace... It intrigued me, surprised me, and made me think...an interesting and inventive plot twist... Bravo for coming up with a unique approach to the age old 'he done me wrong now I want revenge' theme."

~Fallen Angels Reviews

"Watch it witch," a raspy voice threatened from the gutter.

Close enough, she thought, in both his advice and labels as she walked on.

"You need an escort."

She ignored the bogus offer, focused on her destination and purpose.

"Wasn't a question," the street rat persisted, falling into step beside her and earning Jaden's full attention.

She knew she could take him, or any other challengers. But something in his stance, his eyes, made her wary on another level. A flash of familiar came and went. A closer look only showed he wasn't stoned and the normal haze of scorn for a stranger was absent.

"I'm good. Just passing through."

"There's a price for that."

She knew all too well there was a price for everything. Just stepping outside could cost anything from a cell card to a life these days.

She turned to face him. "And you're the collector?"

He shrugged and sneered. "Seems like."

"So state your fee or get outta my way." She wanted that diary before her cursed nemesis destroyed it.

"In a hurry, pretty girl? *Hmmm*." He eyed her lazily. "Guess I should tag along and take my cut from whatever you want so bad you'll risk the street to get it."

She thought of killing him.

One sweep of hand to throat and he'd be gurgling in the gutter where no one would give half a damn when they found him in the morning.

She thought of using him.

A bold, sober, and not entirely stupid man might be helpful tonight. Quickly she rearranged her original break-in plan.

JUSTICE INCARNATE

REGAN BLACK

To Susan,
Trading is the best – thanks!"
Live the adventure!
Regan Black

Echelon Press

Echelon Press
56 Sawyer Circle #354
Memphis, TN 38103

First Echelon Press paperback printing: February 2005

Cover Artist: Nathalie Moore
Editor: Kat Thompson

Printed in LaVergne, TN, USA

Dedication

I'm blessed and grateful for every person God put in my path at just the right time to bring my dreams to life. Thanks to you all for the encouraging words and limitless belief. And to the hero of my heart, my Mark: for every time you picked me up, dusted me off, and convoluted my plot plans - I couldn't have done it without you!

Chapter One

"There are a thousand hacking at the branches of evil to one who is striking at the root."

—Henry David Thoreau

Chicago: 2096

Jaden Michaels splashed the last of her best Merlot into the only clean glass in the kitchen. Presentation didn't matter when a woman only needed to rinse the taste of a poor lover from her lips.

And poor he'd been. She'd almost been able to catch up on her sleep as he bounced rhythmically. But the indulgence would've cost her a source of invaluable information.

Bouncy-boy reported to another in the criminal food chain, this one with enough clout to bring her closer to her target.

She swirled the wine in the glass and her mind flashed with timeless, bloody memories. She tossed it back and imagined the day when she could rest. She prayed this life would break the cycle.

The wine at last relieved her of the stale taste of her informant. He needed advice in the sex department, but Jaden wouldn't waste her time. She'd probably serve him better by teaching him to defend himself against the wrath of dissatisfied women. On the off chance one of them would care.

She stripped the sheets from her bed, unwilling to sleep amidst the smells of a sweaty bar fly. Cocooning herself into a clean blanket she closed her eyes, willing her elusive quarry to behave himself tonight.

Then the crying began. The frightened, jittery tears of an innocent child pushed into a new world of horrors. Naturally, he couldn't be less than the demon he was.

The bastard.

Jaden had tried for years to tune out the echoes of pain and terror that sounded in her mind each time he struck. She'd even grown cold enough to sleep through the attacks occasionally, if the new victim happened to be too shocked to do more than whimper. But she knew anyway.

Her body harbored the same residual grief in the morning. It's what fueled her to keep slugging her way through the bottom dwellers, the middlemen, the lieutenants and bodyguards until she could take the head off the beast– permanently.

The cries escalated as the current victim panicked. "No sleep tonight."

She rolled from bed and crossed her apartment to work off her useless fury.

This unbreakable connection between the demonic entity living as the Honorable Stewart Albertson and her would only cease when he did. And he wouldn't cease his perverse brand of torture without her help. Her violent, fatal brand of help.

Jaden punctuated each thought with a kick or punch into the bag. Not a fan of the technical marvel of today's electronic sparring partners, she kept an antique, sand-filled bag of 120 kilos. She liked the challenge it gave her body, the technology would've spoiled her. Besides, if she needed a sparring partner, she could just hit the streets.

She lunged into an uppercut, sending the bag swinging. Then the girl shrieked and Jaden froze. But the bag finished its arc and knocked her to the floor.

"Damn you," she hissed, rubbing her head where the weighted canvas connected. "You'll pay for this Albertson. The moment I find you, this time you'll pay with your soul."

Wasn't that the same thing she'd been vowing for centuries? To make him pay for all the evil he'd committed against her and countless others. The same evil she'd failed to dispatch for all these centuries.

In every life she'd come up against him. Never really knowing him until it was too late. Until she was the girl screaming for mercy. Until she was the woman too terrified to whisper. Until in the lacy light of predawn she recognized an ageless predator; recognized her greater purpose and vowed to expose him. To exact justice.

"For all the good that's done."

Here she sat, a martial artist bested by a sandbag, while he continued to wreak havoc on innocence and purity. Nearby, if the volume in her head was any indicator.

She'd searched the neighboring warehouses and failed to find his current house of horrors. She knew his home address. She'd snuck into his chambers at the courthouse more than once. She'd even had opportunity to cut him down, but had hesitated.

"Coward."

Jaden stood, knowing the lie for what it was. Frustration and fatigue. Moving her body through a soothing yoga routine she reviewed the facts.

Her hesitation had not stemmed from cowardice. Sure, an armed deputy had accompanied him, but death wasn't a scary unknown to her. She'd aborted her rash attack at the sight of his daughter. How much should one child suffer?

"Dunno? How much?"

Jaden whirled, furious that she'd spoken aloud, more so that she hadn't heard the 'friendly' intruder.

"Cleveland." Her heart slowed at the sight of the pale, narrow face. "How'd you get in here?"

"I used the key you gave me."

"I didn't give you a key," Jaden said, glaring at her not-so-reformed burglar friend.

"Does it really matter? I'd never rip from you, kid."

"Thanks. I think."

His bark of laughter made her jump.

"So how much should one child suffer? And why do we wanna know?"

Jaden ground her teeth. "Children shouldn't suffer at all." *Innocence should be guarded, especially in this wide-open, free-for-all time.*

Cleveland gave her a wide berth as he walked through the kitchen toward the wall with a fire escape to the alley. "A little late for that, don't ya think?" He jerked his thumb to indicate all the societal injustices within easy view.

"Whatever. It's late, what d'you want?"

"Got a live one here, Jade."

She shrugged and filled a glass with water, trying not to notice the murky color. She'd lived how many lives? A little pollution wouldn't hurt. Not much anyway.

"C'mon, babe. Show a little interest?"

She swallowed.

"Fine. Spoil my fun. But he's got cold cash and a bunch of frightened mules."

She shrugged.

"Female mules."

Cleveland knew just what button to push. Regardless of the Common Era's perceptions, Jaden acted from a view of right and wrong molded by centuries of experience. Anyone less fortunate deserved her help, but especially the female side of a population. She'd witnessed countless sacrifices made by women determined to survive and protect the next generation.

This era 'juiced' its men with a human growth hormone cocktail for war's sake and women from all walks of life suffered from the physical iniquity. Jaden gave her time and expertise in an effort to balance the scales.

Employing the combat conditioning she'd originally learned at the turn of the twenty-first century, she taught women how to protect themselves regardless of physical differentials.

"What are they afraid of?"

Cleveland barked another laugh. "Him, probably." He walked over and tucked the business card into the strap of her tank top. "Nah, more like the rivals. Someone's making a move and all the little people are worrying."

"Like that'd help."

"Look, if you want more money to stuff your mattress, make the call."

Cleveland left as quietly as he'd come, only this time via the fire escape.

Jaden shook her head. She wanted more money all right. But not to squirrel away. She wanted money to fund her research into the perfect weapon to dispatch one particular evil entity. And paying the rent on time wouldn't hurt, either.

After the interruption, Jaden tried to meditate to clear the girl's pain from her psyche. Successful at last, but unwilling to risk sleep, she resumed her Internet search for legendary weapons.

Swords, axes, stars, and blades of every metal and configuration. Guns small and large, silver bullets valued only because of an early author's imagination. Rare and common poisons delivered in a variety of ways.

She sighed. The piece she needed had to be *somewhere*.

Scrolling through the sludge of information she already knew, a surprising teaser popped up. It advertised a new acquisition on display at the Museum of Natural History.

A bitter laugh spilled from her.

She was on display. Or rather, one of the earlier versions of her. A distinct shiver ran down her spine as she faced her past.

This woman's rare brand of true compassion during the Victorian era hid an alternate personality, not unlike Dr. Jekyll and Mr. Hyde. Though it would seem from her diary that this fair lady sought to avenge wrongs rather than wreak havoc...

Naturally the article continued, for a modest fee, or interested parties could visit the exhibit in person. Jaden didn't need to read on. She knew the darkest of the details intimately. But a personal visit...well, that could be worthwhile. Especially knowing she wasn't the only Chicago resident familiar with the true motives of the long-dead woman on display.

Donning her black catsuit and a cloak to guard against the night chill, Jaden strapped on matched daggers at wrist and ankle. Securing the electronic code-breaking card at the small of her back she felt ready to face the jungle of the street.

She'd had ample time to wonder precisely when her perpetual opponent gained his past life memories. At the moment of attacking her? Or at the moment she struck him down?

In this most recent incarnation, her increased sensitivity forced her to consider that his skills might be changing too.

The new and improved elevated train rumbled along above her, but she preferred the street for moods and tasks like hers tonight. And she'd never quite trusted the el, having seen it constructed all those years ago. Jaden stumbled as the flash of old memories veiled her current reality.

"Watch it witch," a raspy voice threatened from the gutter.

Close enough, she thought, in both his advice and labels as she walked on.

"You need an escort."

She ignored the bogus offer, focused on her destination and purpose.

"Wasn't a question," the street rat persisted, falling into step beside her and earning Jaden's full attention.

She knew she could take him, or any other challengers. But something in his stance, his eyes, made her wary on another level. A flash of familiar came and went. A closer look only showed he wasn't stoned and the normal haze of scorn for a stranger was absent.

"I'm good. Just passing through."

"There's a price for that."

She knew all too well there was a price for everything. Just stepping outside could cost anything from a cell card to a life these days.

She turned to face him. "And you're the collector?"

He shrugged and sneered. "Seems like."

"So state your fee or get outta my way." She wanted that

diary before her cursed nemesis destroyed it.

"In a hurry, pretty girl? *Hmmm*." He eyed her lazily. "Guess I should tag along and take my cut from whatever you want so bad you'll risk the street to get it."

She thought of killing him.

One sweep of hand to throat and he'd be gurgling in the gutter where no one would give half a damn when they found him in the morning.

She thought of using him.

A bold, sober, and not entirely stupid man might be helpful tonight. Quickly she rearranged her original break-in plan.

"If you can keep up, you can claim one item."

"Oh, baby, how can I refuse?"

He ran a grimy finger over her shoulder and she squashed the urge to break his arm, instead resuming her course. He'd soon learn she wasn't on the list of his possible 'rewards'.

As they approached the museum, her companion earned an ounce of Jaden's respect. He was smart enough to keep quiet. But when his steps slowed, putting him directly behind her, she spun around and instinctively dropped into a defensive crouch.

"Ease up, baby." He raised his hands slowly. "I'm just looking for the easy way in."

Jaden stood up, impatient with every moment of delay. "This is my game. You're only along for the ride."

"Don't I know it." He leered at her breasts. "But–"

"Nothing," she finished for him. "I'll get you in, and out if you're quick about your decisions."

"I've decided." He stepped closer and reached for her.

She whipped her foot out, connecting with the inside of his knee. Following him to the ground, she muffled his pained cry with her hand on his mouth and her knee on his chest.

"I pulled that kick. You're not permanently damaged." His eyes grew wide and wild. She tried not to enjoy his panic. "I have business here. I'll open the door. You walk in, choose your piece and get out. We'll have three minutes. If you're not out before me, you'll be on trial by eight and in jail by noon."

At least some things improved with time. The courts and prisons were still over-crowded, but this society dealt with 'Clear Crimes' swiftly. Cops processed evidence in real time, on scene. Finding this street rat in the museum would be enough for an instant conviction and thirty days of behavior modification injections.

"You afraid of needles?"

He shook his head.

"You will be." She hauled him to his feet, granting him a moment to find his balance. "Three minutes."

Following the shadows around the loading docks, Jaden readied her code breaker. She waved the card in front of the scanner and waited.

Infinitely.

Yet another minute ticked by, giving her ample time to cross this particular 'hack-rabbit' off her good list. If his codes were old, or worse, compromised, she'd be hard pressed to avoid a month of needles herself.

If she lived through dispatching her enemy this time, she just might champion prisoner rights and the call to do away with the cruel needles. There were better delivery options...

The lock clicked, whirred and the door slid back on hushed tracks, putting the prized possessions of history at her fingertips.

And gimpy boy's too.

She cringed, inwardly, hoping he was in too much pain to

take anything priceless. She disabled the remaining alarm systems to prevent any surprises from security.

"Better hustle," she advised, dashing off on her own.

Her cape billowing behind her, Jaden loped through the various galleries to the nearest marble stairwell, taking the steps two at a time.

Exercising restraint, she stayed her course despite the siren's call of the Medieval Weapons and Armament gallery. She could always return as an ordinary citizen during standard business hours and pore over each curator's note and battle-scarred blade. Again.

She rounded a corner and praised heaven to see the diary still in place. The dress and trunk, which bore a previous life's initials, didn't warrant more than a fleeting glance. She needed the book. It might hold clues that could save her months of research. And every day saved meant another girl spared.

"Now that's worth my while."

Startled from her private hell, Jaden turned to see her unwelcome companion eyeing a case of jewelry. He could have it. It hadn't done her any good then and she had no need of it now.

"One piece," she reminded him, using a dagger to pry open the diary's case. "Clock's ticking." She smiled at gimpy boy's dread and ran for her freedom.

And her cause.

She paused at the security panel only long enough to reset the alarm systems. Rubber soles squeaked on the marble floor somewhere inside, but she had other business. Outside, she took her first real breath and then made the call.

"I'm certified in a dozen different self-defense methods," the woman stated.

"I only need one," the man replied in bored tones.

"Which is?" she asked.

"The most lethal. Turn."

The conversation went static for two seconds before the detective listening to the wireless tap found it again.

"Uh-huh." She paused. "Hand-to-hand or weapons?"

"Hands only. If I arm 'em, they'll turn."

The detective noted date, time, and frequencies and began speculating on the woman's identity. He signaled his partner to pick up the second headset. They both listened.

"When and where?" the woman asked.

"My place. Late."

"Fine. You'll see me when the money's clear. Turn."

The connection fizzled. The detective scrambled, but lost the continuing conversation.

"Damn. That's it?"

Larry Ferguson was more hopeful than his sour-stomached partner. "It's more than we've had on Slick Micky before."

"Ain't enough," Chuck Loomis groused.

"Let's run it for the DA and see what he thinks." Larry ignored the doom and gloom of his partner and did what he could to buff the recording. If he could find a single locator clue, the DA would jump on it. Better, if he nailed the woman's ID the DA would write the reference Larry needed to get promoted out of this sorry detail.

"Hey, Chuck. Check out this short list of female self defense instructors."

Chuck swiveled around, scanned the list and grunted. Larry hadn't expected anything more. "It's a code, is all."

"I don't think so. She—"

"She knew when and how to change channels. They got

outta your reach fast enough. It's just a new code."

"Maybe."

"Larry, you're a good kid, but let me dash your hopes right now. These days ya got a better chance marrying the chief's daughter than moving up and outta this tin can. Now put the ears back on and find us a real crime we can prevent."

Larry ignored the barb about the youngest *bachelor* chief in Chicago history and resumed his work. "Hot damn!" Larry caught Chuck's dismissive headshake. But Chuck couldn't hear the alarms wailing down at the Museum of Natural History. With a few keystrokes, Larry accessed the security cameras onsite. "Put it in gear, Chuck. I found you a crime scene."

"Yee haw." Chuck yawned as he settled his over-regulation bulk into the driver's seat.

Larry tracked the burglar's progress from gallery to gallery while listening to the chatter of the robotic security drones in pursuit. "He's hurt, Chuck. This collar'll be a breeze."

"Don't count your chickens, kid."

"What the hell's that mean?"

"It's some farm thing my granddad said."

"You've seen a family farm? You are an old-timer."

"Aw, shut up. Where do we pick up this thief?"

"He's made a cut for the northeast exit."

"Where's security?"

"I'll clue 'em in," Larry said while Chuck grumbled about the perils of technology.

He disagreed with Chuck's hardened view of society in general and their job in particular. But his partner had a point about the flaws of the new totally robotic security systems. Twentieth century sci-fi had inspired inventors, but the same stories messed with the lackluster vision of legislators, leaving no loopholes to create a thinking machine.

"You'd think the Museum of *Natural* History would leave a couple humans in the place."

Larry ignored his peevish partner and continued to ready the evidence kit.

Jaden saw the mottled gray police unit barreling down the street and sighed. If she let the street rat take the fall for her burglary, she'd have joined the ranks of the despicable thing she hunted. As she organized her explanation to enable his escape a bright flash came from the Museum side of the street.

Instinct had her tucked and rolling out of danger as the driver of the evidence van fought for control with a laser-melted front tire.

How in the hell did a smart aleck street rat land a police-issue pursuit-stopping device?

When the raucous scrape of metal on asphalt ceased, she came to her feet and stared at the van. It lay on its side with black clouds of electrical smoke rising from the rear. Watching the driver stumble from the wreck, she turned for home. But when his agonized bellow carried above the screeching of the alarms, Jaden felt the pull of the driver's desperation.

Mindful of the diary, she approached. Keeping her hands visible, she moved with caution born of several hard lessons. The cop looked as hopeless as a drowning victim. She didn't intend to let him drag her under.

He ranted and wrestled with the crumpled door, too busy to worry about her.

Jaden didn't need cohesive conversation to understand there was another man trapped inside. Evidence processing equipment was expensive, but not priceless. It gave her weary spirit a lift to see how frantic one man could be to save another.

Leaving him to his battle, she put her dagger to work on

the hinges of the door. Between adrenaline and training, the door gave way and the cop outside pulled the inside man clear of the burning van.

Familiar enough with death, Jaden knew they were too late, and she wished for tears enough to weep over the loss. One bold street rat bent on escape just cost a man's life.

Everything has a price.

The echoing words taunted her. Then she recognized the dead man. "Larry," she gasped.

The surviving partner heard and turned on her. "What do you know about him? About this?"

He grabbed her shoulders and shook her while she tried to recall his name. Chad, Charlie, no–

"Chuck. Chuck, ease up buddy," she said through rattling teeth.

"Who the hell are you?" Chuck demanded.

"Jaden Michaels–"

"The security specialist? This was some miserable test run?"

She wouldn't take the easy way out–couldn't. Not with Larry's blood staining the street. "No, no test. It must've been a real call."

"And you just magically appear during a real call? This was some damned department party. Well I hope they're slaphappy about it. I'm a man short and he was a good one. He had a future."

His fingers bit into her shoulders, taking her body back to another man, a different sort of attack. In a blur, she broke his hold and caught herself before she landed the follow-through punch.

"Take a step back, Chuck. You're upset. When you see the download, you'll feel better." It pained her to lay blame on

Larry, but she offered the most likely scenario. "If Larry wasn't buttoned down, it's no one's fault."

Chuck's face reddened and she saw his pulse accelerate in the jump of a blood vessel in his temple. "I know what a lasered tire feels like. And I know how and where to look for evidence, Michaels. Get the hell outta my face before I do something real stupid."

The adrenaline made her itch for the fight he offered. But pushing her luck here and now put the diary at risk and muddied her true path. She left the messy scene in Chuck's capable hands and replayed the events in her mind.

She hoped the street rat made the best of his good fortune. She'd count her blessings to never cross paths with him again.

The ache began as a slow burn in her stomach and climbed painfully toward her heart with every step away from the collateral damage. She knew her normal cool detachment would eventually return, but prayed it would hurry.

She could've spared the street rat a month of prickly injections by providing a cover story, especially with Larry on the case. Hell, she never should've let the street rat into the museum at all. She'd been around often enough to have developed better judgment.

"Ah, don't beat yourself up."

She gasped. "Quit sneaking up on me, Cleveland."

"Pay more attention," he countered.

"I've paid enough as it is." Jaden made a valiant effort to control her sorry mood. "How'd you find me?"

"Anyone with a scanner could find you, girl."

She knew she paled because Cleveland reached out to steady her. She brushed aside the assistance.

"I meant anyone who knows you and has a scanner."

"Funny." No one really knew her. "What do you want?"

"I'm your escort to your next appointment."

"My next appointment's with my pillow."

"Tempting as that image is," he said, wiggling his brows. "You've got a class first."

"How'd you know anything about that?"

He swung an arm over her shoulder and guided her around a corner away from her own place. "I'm the only trusted soul on the street, my fair Jaden."

"You've been watching the history channel again."

"Nope. But I've been through a museum or two lately. You should go. Get you some culture," he teased.

She glared at him.

"Ouch girl, don't give me the hairy eyeball just 'cuz you screwed up."

She glared more, but at the ground this time. "He wasn't strapped in. Couldn't've been." Completely unlike the Larry she'd worked with for years. "Follow protocol or die, I always say."

"Protocol!" Cleveland laughed. "Keep it up and some day you might convince me you're just that harsh."

He opened his arms and she stepped into his embrace, taking this one moment to grieve the unnecessary loss. She backed away, automatically checking for the diary and daggers. True to his word, Cleveland hadn't ripped her off.

"Told you I wouldn't," he said.

She smiled, feeling better. "Guess there's good reason you're the only trusted soul on the street."

"Yup." He grinned. "You live above it."

She shrugged off the odd compliment. "Whatever. Let's get this gig over. I've got things to do. Like sleep. If you're the escort, show me proof of the transfer."

He pulled the slim black remote from his inside pocket.

The monitor showed the agreed amount ready to transfer to the account of her choosing. She made Cleveland turn away and shielded the keypad with her free hand as she punched in her codes.

"Done," she said, handing the remote back to him. "Lead on, oh trusted one."

He replaced the remote and wrapped her hand around his arm, a chivalrous move she hadn't seen in ages. "Such lovely company in the past. Wouldn't you agree?"

She made herself chuckle. She hoped the past would be her friend and provide the answer to get her soul 'unstuck'. She was tired of battle and desperate to break the cycle. She couldn't fail to banish the evil this time. She wasn't sure she had the strength to live again.

Chapter Two

Time stamp: 1884:

My research has uncovered an intriguing reference during the Norman Conquest of 1066. Though I care little if William created the feudal system or simply reorganized the establishment, the interspersed tales of a particularly evil land baron were extraordinary.

Claims of his prowess on the battlefield pale against his depraved preference for young girls. It was much too familiar, an almost verbatim accounting of my most disturbing dreams. As was the subsequent telling of his gruesome death at the hands of a woman I assume to be one of his victims.

–From the diary of Gabriella Stamford

Jaden battled exhaustion with a cold soda infused with an excessive level of caffeine. Thank God for the humanitarians industrious enough to buck the current government health department. The relatively new bureaucracy took obscene delight in regulating everything from alcohol and fat to nicotine and sugar.

She supposed she should be grateful. More regulations led to more contraband. For a woman working both sides of the line, it meant more profit to use for her own method of sheltering the population.

She took a hard look at the group of mules practicing each move with a desperation born of fear. All women, though size, shape and age varied. They obviously respected and feared Slick Micky, the man who'd hired her too, but she didn't think he was the source of the anxiety shivering in each pair of eyes.

"Wait. I know the urge is to pull away." She stepped between two students. "But you must lean in closer or the move will be ineffective." She demonstrated the escape again, in slow motion, until both nodded. "Try again."

This time the smaller woman got it right, evading her larger partner and jumping with elation. "I did it!"

Jaden smiled and moved on to the next cluster of students.

Slick Micky waited until she finished to pull her aside. "Will they remember this on the street?" he muttered.

"They should, with practice."

"Of course you'll want to lead those practices."

"I can, if you'd like."

"I can't lose too many nights of work for this. Or there won't be cash to pay you."

His frustration came through clear enough, but Jaden struggled with how much to advise the known criminal. "I'm not all about money. What's their cargo?"

Micky's eyes narrowed, then relaxed. "I don't mess with hard stuff. If my mules do, they're out. I have standards."

Don't we all, she thought, then spoke to advise another sparring pair.

"They are catching on," Micky said with grudging satisfaction.

Jaden only waited.

"Sugar, nicotine and caffeine." He raised his palm as if taking an oath. "That's it."

She wanted to laugh. One of the most renowned criminals on the street ran the lightest of contraband. "Not even the better alcohol?"

"You're surprised."

"Yes. But why interfere with those runs? Even the government looks the other way on sugar and caffeine most of the time."

"The government's not the problem."

"Someone wants your routes?"

He shook his head. "I thought so at first."

They finished the circuit of the room and Jaden interrupted the conversation to finish the class with a brief stretching series to prevent sore muscles. Then she left them with a word of encouragement before Micky stepped up to give his orders.

She edged toward the door, ready to head back to her own warehouse several blocks closer to the edge of respectability. At least she'd managed to improve the décor beyond the bare bulbs and cold cement floors of Micky's distribution hub.

"Hang on a minute."

Jaden wanted to refuse, but the caffeine had kicked in and sleep wouldn't be an option for at least another hour. "Yeah?"

Micky jerked his head toward his office and Jaden obliged.

When the door closed he faced her across a desk scarred and stained from cigarette burns.

"It's not the routes. Well, not entirely."

She considered him. "Then what. Entirely?"

"It's the girls."

Her opinion of Slick Micky dropped considerably with those three words.

"Just what else are you running?" She didn't care about

accusing tones or causing personal offense. She would *not* allow any abuse to continue.

"I told you what I run. Someone else is picking off my runners. Sometimes the cargo too, but that's rare."

After careful study, she believed him. "How many girls have you lost?"

"Four last month. And two more just last week."

Okay, the man did have a problem. And just how deep she'd get dragged into it was hers. "Why tell me?"

"Cleveland says you might have a vested interest."

She arched a brow and crossed her arms. What did Cleveland know about her hunt for the esteemed Judge Stewart Albertson?

"One girl escaped."

"Good for her."

"After she saw the man giving the orders."

Jaden felt her heart skip, knew the flush on her cheeks gave away her curiosity. She felt herself leaning in, eager for the information, praying it was the break she needed. "And?"

"She says he's too big for me. Won't talk unless I promise to drop it. Cleveland says you'd get it outta her."

"Interrogation's not my specialty." She turned to walk out. She didn't have time, energy or inclination to be used for anyone's vengeance but her own.

"Maybe not. But I hear Judge Albertson's your hobby."

Her hand froze, an inch off the doorknob. "Gossip's cheap."

"And truth's free," he shot back. "My girls know my reach. I'm up against someone well funded and very well connected. My rep's been enough to keep my cargo and routes safe for years. No one else would scare her this bad."

Jaden doubted that. There were plenty of scary people on

and off the street. "Why blame a pillar of the community?"

Micky laughed, heartless and cold. "Pillar, my ass. Down here we all know how it plays. Maybe the fancy suits and big verdicts fool your kinda–"

"Watch it, Slick."

He raised a hand in surrender. "Talk to her. Just cuz he's too smooth to get jail time doesn't mean he's not at the top of the food chain."

Jaden nodded. He was preaching to the choir. "Show me the girl." She'd recognize Albertson's personal handiwork. If the girl bore his mark, she might consider the rest of her information.

She followed Micky through a hidden door in the back wall of his office and accepted the weight of his trust as it settled on her shoulders. The dim lighting near the floor revealed a narrow hallway and the echo of their steps told her the ceiling was a long, long way up.

Micky disappeared suddenly, until Jaden reached the intersection and saw him on her left, stopped in front of a plain metal door. This hall was broader, though no better lit, and reminded her of an old hotel. So the expert smuggler had more than a few secrets himself. Not the least of which was that he seemed genuine about the care he gave his mules.

The door opened a mere crack after Micky's second knock, and nearly snapped shut before his foot stopped it.

"I brought a visitor, honey," he said in surprisingly gentle tones. "She can help."

A strangled sound came from the dark room, either doubt or quiet hysteria, but certainly not confidence.

Micky signaled Jaden closer. "She just taught the family some self-defense moves. You can trust her."

"She'll only tell you and you'll go get yourself killed.

Without you, we're all gutter food. I'm not worth all that."

Jaden willed herself to breathe. She'd heard that voice. Before it had become the dead and dispassionate version it was tonight. She didn't need to see the mark to know this girl had been in Albertson's clutches.

"Look." Jaden turned slightly and peeled back the flap of false skin behind her right ear. When she heard the sharp inhale, she knew the girl could see the vile, infinity-shaped scar from her own encounter with Albertson twenty years ago. She pressed the patch back into place and resisted the urge to roll her freshly tensed shoulders. This girl could be the break. The one witness to blow Albertson straight into hell.

The girl widened the opening and Jaden took a twitchy step inside, wishing she'd forgone the mega dose of caffeine, and shut the door in Micky's face.

Chief Brian Thomas sat in his office with his right foot propped on his desk and an ice pack on his swollen knee. He'd ditched the contacts and scruffy jacket. Phone card clipped to his pocket, he toyed with his 'prize' while his mentor's affable voice filled his ear.

"Tell me again why I shouldn't have my men out looking for this thief?" Thomas asked.

"Because you're doing me a favor," Albertson said. "The item she stole is of no consequence. What'd she look like?"

"The ghost of Christmas future."

"Beg pardon?"

Thomas moved, then gritted his teeth when his knee complained. "All black. Head to toe. With a cape." He didn't even know her hair color and her eyes had been shadowed as well. Of course she could've disguised her features as he had.

"Ah, yes. The proverbial Bat Girl."

Thomas laughed. "Maybe. The evidence crew lost a man during the response. My men will want to see justice done."

"I'm sorry to hear that. But she won't get away with it."

Thomas caught himself caressing the necklace he'd hastily removed from the display. It took more effort than it should have to lay it down. When he did, his hands felt empty, his chest hollow.

Weird.

"Brian?"

"Yeah, sorry. I'm tired."

"I understand. These are odd hours you're keeping on my behalf. If the media should find this story, let them know you think the crime is of a personal bent."

"So you've got yourself a stalker." Thomas gave a low wolf whistle. "Sure you don't want a team on you?"

"Absolutely not."

Thomas blinked, startled by the vehement reply. "Too bad. She looked professional."

"But what sort of profession?"

Thomas fought back an instinctive defense of the thief, but Albertson's hearty belly laugh sounded first. When he caught his breath the judge said, "She can't touch me."

"If you say so," Thomas replied. His hands were back on the cool gold surrounding the fiery opal of the antique necklace. The filigreed heart-shaped setting would've drawn much attention to the cleavage of the young lady wearing it. "Anything else?"

"No. You've done well and I thank you."

The judge disconnected before Thomas could ask anything else. It seemed he'd have to wait for more answers about the threat this burglar posed. Not unusual, but still irritating.

His desktop monitor lit up with an incoming call. Then another. The primary questions of both callers filled the text fields while pictures of impatient reporters popped up above the words.

The media had found the story all right. With a reluctant touch, he slid the necklace into the lockbox in his desk, and then prepared to enter the gauntlet of question and answer.

The burly man storming into his office stopped him.

"Chuck, have a seat."

"I'll stand." He tossed his silver shield at Thomas. "I won't spend another minute in the hell-hole you've got here."

Deliberate, precise motions moved the ice pack and brought Thomas to his feet. "You'll control yourself and follow orders."

"I won't take orders from a man who'd sacrifice his own."

"You've crossed a line here, Loomis."

"That's the pot callin' the kettle black, I'd say."

Thomas shook his head and then recalled the antiquated saying. "What's set you off?"

Chuck tapped a thick index finger on the desk. "Tonight's little exercise crossed the line, Chief." He sneered at the title. "Wait'll the boys hear Larry died in the name of a lousy test run. Neither you or the city'll survive the Blue Flu."

"Test run? Flu?" Baffled, Thomas dropped back into his chair. "Start over. And use English this time."

"I saw the Michaels woman." Chuck bit out each word. "She's tested response times and codes and the like before."

And suddenly it clicked. The mystery thief was 'the Michaels woman'. Jaden Michaels, a security specialist with a tendency to favor the underdog. She had some sort of girl-power school in town and did some freelance with the police force occasionally, but they'd never met in person.

"Chuck," he applied his calm buddy tone. "We weren't running tests tonight. If you got a call—it was real."

He glared at Thomas. "So real the museum says nothin's gone."

Thomas sat up straight, ignoring the jab of pain climbing his leg when his foot hit the floor. "Nothing?"

"Nope. They just spewed nonsense about false alarms and sent me on my merry way." He swiped that beefy hand over his face and cleared his throat. Twice. "After they took away...the body...I looked around for the laser gun. It wasn't on her, but I'll be damned if I know where she ditched it. Larry'd been trying to link a call we were tracing with the museum break in. When the laser flashed I dodged but it caught the tire. Now how'd she get a hold of that except from someone skimmin' from us?"

Thomas understood every layer of Chuck's agony. "I'll look into it. Personally." *Won't have to look far.* "I've already seen the video. Larry bounced out of the seat. He just wasn't buttoned down when the vehicle rolled. An unfortunate accident, that's all."

"Bull." Chuck upended an evidence bag and a charred buckle and webbing clattered onto the desk. The bitter smell of burnt flesh and fried circuits hung in the air between them.

Thomas pressed his fingers to his temples in an attempt to stop the relentless pounding. He didn't need to deal with equipment failure, even if it would soothe his conscience.

"Go home. Get some rest. And keep the badge." Chuck nodded, and then just stared down at him like a lost puppy. "Take tomorrow off, Chuck. I'll handle Michaels."

"Yessir." At the door, Chuck paused. "Check the tapes. Larry's last entries should lead you right to her."

"Got it," Thomas said and dismissed the grieving officer.

What the hell was going on?

He had a judge who didn't care about a display he'd personally funded, a museum denying all trouble, a good cop dead, a security specialist posing as a thief, a chat room buzzing with reporters, a bum knee and the devil's own headache.

"Lord love a duck," he groaned and washed a couple of painkillers down with a hefty gulp of antacid.

Jaden woke a half hour before the day's first class. Her body ached from last night's scuffle at the museum and the impromptu class for Micky. She looked forward to working out the kinks in warm-up. She programmed the shower for high efficiency and tried not to remember a past life when she'd indulged in long hot soaks in a massive marble tub. Having a wealth of diverse experiences in the subconscious wasn't always a gift.

She loathed having to wait another whole day to dig into the diary and fit together the girl's account from last night, but she wouldn't put off the women who sought her instruction. The classes filled a void for her and her students. Whether simply providing fitness and a confidence boost or a life saving tool, she made sure everyone got her money's worth.

"Aren't you the picture of perfection," Cleveland said, walking through the studio door in time to join her for lunch.

She blotted her sweaty face with a towel. "Your timing's suspect."

"No way. I brought food."

She eyed the white sacks, smelled the heady aroma of marinara sauce and sighed. "We feast while some poor child goes hungry."

He laughed and began filling the plates she'd handed him.

"The kid two blocks over is fine. I bought for him too."

"Who? Quinn?" She grabbed two bottles of water, tossed the towel in the direction of the workout room and sat down to the nearest full plate. "Cool. He doesn't get the first shot at a hot meal very often."

"I don't know." Cleveland pinned her with a look. "He mentioned something about two days running."

Jaden felt color creep up her neck, but refused comment. "Why're you here?" she asked around a mouthful of fettuccine.

"I worry," he said.

"Bad for your health. I'm a big girl."

"Lookin' to chew on a bigger bone."

She stopped eating. Could Cleveland be like her? Another soul reliving life until he got it right. "Just what do you think you know?"

"Enough to point you in the right direction. Last night paid off, right?"

"Financially." She weighed the risks and went for it. "Other areas, I'm not so sure. Met a girl marked up recently."

"Dead or alive?"

"Depends on your definition."

Judging by the haunted eyes and hollow voice, she'd have to say dead. But if life meant merely a beating heart and independent breathing, alive would be the verdict.

"So how you gonna take down the untouchable?"

"Excuse me?"

"I know what Judge Albertson's capable of."

"What makes you think I do?" Jaden tried to avoid his penetrating gaze, but she couldn't avoid the finger on his neck, tracing a faint scar behind his left ear she'd never noticed before.

"Let's say we have some things in common."

Her appetite gone, she pushed the plate aside and crossed her arms over her chest. "What gave me away?"

"Nothing," Cleveland admitted. "I just knew what to look for and where to look for it. My sister didn't make it. Killed herself halfway through counseling."

Jaden wasn't sure she could take any more victim stories right now. Or ever. Last night had been bad. The judge was escalating and she had to find a way to stop him.

Permanently.

"Look, Jaden, all I'm sayin' is, whatever you need—count me in."

"This is a solo gig, Cleveland."

"Maybe it shouldn't be." He stood and with a flippant salute, was out the door.

Unsettled, Jaden switched on the wall-mounted video panel. She left it tuned to her favorite of the myriad 24/7 news networks and caught the tail end of the police chief's press conference.

"We're investigating the cause of death. We suspect the officer will be cleared of any wrong doing and the criminals apprehended soon."

She studied the image, grabbed the remote and keyed the request for a closer camera angle. The image changed, zooming in on the chief's face.

"I'll be damned," she muttered to the air around her. The facial structure reminded her of last night's street rat, but the eyes were the wrong color.

No, she corrected. Today they were the right color. The unique, deceptively easy-going pewter gray. The color they'd been when she'd fallen in love with him. A millennium ago.

"So you have a lead?" a reporter called from off camera.

"We're working from surveillance material in the evidence

vehicle, the surviving officer's testimony and other resources."

"Meaning informants?" another voice cried out.

"Meaning *other resources*." The chief gave a benign smile and stepped back from the podium. He turned and walked away with a pronounced limp.

"Other resources my butt," Jaden hissed at the image on screen. "Bet that's really hurting you today." She couldn't help her smug smile. But it faded as she tried to sort out why the police chief would be posing as a street rat.

She pushed it to the back of her mind and went to greet the next class. She demonstrated, they followed, she encouraged, they panted. And still at the end of class, her mind hadn't unraveled the mystery. The chief was surely in the judge's pocket, so why not arrest her when he had the chance?

Then, in the final pose of the cool down it hit her. Other resources. If Chuck tagged her with a tracking device, he could lead them straight to her. It was time to make a dive for the bottom of the societal pool until she planned her attack.

"Jaden?"

She turned to see her part-time assistant, Brenda Calhoun, threading her way through the departing class. "Hi there. You want to take the afternoon schedule?"

"Sure." Brenda wrung her hands, and then swung her arms back into a stretch. "Um, my court date's tomorrow. You asked me to remind you."

Jaden groaned inside. She couldn't dive when she had to appear as a witness for Brenda. "Thanks. I have it on my office calendar."

"I appreciate it. Your set of photos is all that's left of that night."

"What?" Jaden reeled from the shock like she'd been punched.

"The hospital records went missing."

"Who's presiding tomorrow?"

"Judge A."

"I see." *Did she ever.* The whole twisted picture.

Brenda's ex-boyfriend had been a bailiff in Judge Albertson's courtroom. He'd apparently served him well, if the Judge was pulling favors like this. "Awful small case for Judge A to be looking at."

"That's what my advocate-advisor said."

Jaden wanted to groan. A battered woman, not nearly recovered, with only the aid of an advocate-advisor. She didn't stand a chance against a false accusation judgment. And Albertson loved to hand those out like candy on Halloween.

"What do you need if you lose?"

Brenda paled. Jaden hated making her think about the worst-case scenario, but it was a likely outcome.

"I-I'm not sure."

In a display far too rare these days, Jaden's heart softened. She led Brenda away from the classroom to her apartment upstairs. In the kitchen she began brewing her personal blend of comforting tea.

When Brenda's hands were wrapped around a warm mug, Jaden tried to make it as painless as possible. "You have to think about it. Has he made any threats?"

"Not while the TRO's been in effect."

"Brenda, a temporary restraint is only *temporary*."

"I know, I know." She looked at Jaden with frightened blue eyes filled with tears. "But I like my job. Jobs," she smiled and glanced in the direction of the classroom. "I have real friends, a real life again."

"Any family who could keep an eye out for you?"

"Not in town."

"Where?" Jaden pushed. "You have to consider running. If the court rules you've accused falsely you won't have any legal support."

The tears fell and Brenda wiped at them, but it didn't stem the tide.

Uncomfortable, Jaden reached out, hoping the touch would calm Brenda. The girl needed to start thinking clearly again.

"You think I'll lose," she whispered.

"It's likely."

"But you have the pictures."

She had more, but wouldn't mention it yet. "Pictures or not, Brenda, it doesn't look good."

"Can you help?" Brenda whispered at last.

"I can testify." Regretfully, at the moment it was all she could do.

She'd gladly kill Judge Albertson with her bare hands in front of a thousand witnesses. But she'd been there and done that. Instead of a T-shirt, she'd been awarded a lethal bullet.

And had been given yet another life to try again.

"I can get you out of town. If you lose, we'll both have to disappear."

"But your school, the students." Brenda's head landed in her hands. "Oh, Jaden. I'm sorry I ever got you into this."

Jaden stood to pace, her racing mind demanding a physical outlet. "Trust me. I was hip deep before we ever met."

"What?"

"Never mind. If the case goes bad tomorrow, I'll see you safely out of town. In the meantime, teach this next class. And when you get home, pack a bag and be alert."

Brenda nodded, with a little more confidence, then headed

off to follow Jaden's orders, leaving Jaden with cold tea and boiling thoughts.

Nothing she knew added up to anything she could use to eliminate the judge legally. Albertson's reach was increasing. In all the lives she'd known him, he'd never been sloppy about the people he chose to use, whether for his own perverse delight or to increase his power within a community. Which meant Chief Thomas was a vital link. Again.

"Great," she muttered to the empty kitchen. "He's even named for a doubter this time."

The control panel chimed, announcing the arrival of more students. Jaden shoved back from the table and went to make some calls. Whether or not Chief Thomas would kill her in the days to come, she first had to arrange for Brenda to survive tomorrow.

Chapter Three

"The more corrupt the state, the more numerous the laws."

—Tacitus

Jaden resented the chime of midnight and her complete sleeplessness. Shoving fingers through her hair, she loosened the braid she'd woven minutes earlier.

So far, the diary revealed nothing of value. No new or vital tidbit of information she'd forgotten in the living of a dozen lives. She locked it back in her safe.

With a gusty sigh, she let herself long for the sort of rest that was impossible in her current state of existence. She ached for eternity's blissful peace.

Irritable, she strode through the kitchen and down the hall to pound her stress into the punching bag.

She could feel the Judge on the far edge of her conscious mind, and knew without doubt the outcome of Brenda's case. With no authenticated video or still shots of the damage her ex-boyfriend caused, Brenda was doomed to serve time as a false accuser.

A swift kick sent the bag out and Jaden caught it in a hard hug on the return. Her first instinct was to make contact with her one link inside the system, but Larry had died en route to a crime scene starring her as the criminal.

Correction—he'd died when the police chief posing as a street rat lasered the tire. That eased the burden a bit.

Larry believed in his oath to protect society and his fellow officers. She combined two uppercuts with a right hook and smiled as she considered the hero's homecoming Larry must be enjoying in the eternity she desperately wanted for herself.

A yellow light above the doorway diverted her attention. She held her position at the bag and waited for a follow up signal or sound. She expected a grind or hiss of a lock being tumbled or bypassed. She didn't expect footsteps on the roof, or the sound of windows shattering in her classroom downstairs.

She thought first of the diary, then the photos in her floor safe. Then her mind emptied as she prepared to defend her home, and possibly her life.

"Clear."

"Here, too." The first guttural voice was answered by an equally deep and dispassionate reply.

She waited, pressed flat against the wall, for the rest to check in. None did. Her lips curved. Her against two put the odds heavy in her favor.

She listened to the footfalls to determine the intent of the intruders. Hearing the quiet whir of her computer told her they were most likely after Brenda's pictures.

"Found it. What about you?"

Two searchers. Two targets. But was she the second target or the diary? Somehow the Judge knew what she was about, knew who she was this time. As far as she could recall, he'd never come directly after her before.

Jaden had to move before the computer revealed the diary's location.

With a rude burst every light in the place came on at full

power. The man at the computer had found the master controls. Soon he'd activate the infrared to show the location of everyone in the house, blowing her element of surprise. It was a standard security system and relatively pointless. Any hack with the most basic password finder could seize control with little effort.

This was precisely why she'd personally rewritten a new code and layered it over the standard system.

With heavy footsteps beating a quick pace to her position, Jaden dropped to a crouch and ran, using the wall as a shield.

"The east side. Hidden access."

The informed shout gave her pause and made her decision easier. Changing direction, she leaped for the nearest control panel, entering her contingency code.

Jaden heard the soft hum and click as her commands took effect, but the following whistle of a passing bullet earned her full attention.

The lights snapped out, just as she'd programmed, and the cursing of the intruder at her computer told her he couldn't stop the cascade of automatic responses.

"Retire the side and let's get out of here."

The unmistakable sound of a revolver being loaded reached Jaden's ears. She knew only one enforcer still using a revolver.

"What about the package?"

"Working on it. If ya had better aim, we wouldn't need it."

In the silence she felt the signals. Signals she would use if she were the hunter. Taking the only strategic advantage left, she rolled out of the open door toward her nearest opponent and slid into his knee with a single, bone-crunching kick. His shot went high and wide.

His agonized screams ended with her merciful knock out sweep to his neck. Now armed with his weapon, an old-school automatic, she maneuvered through the darkness to find his boss.

Keyed to every nuance of sound in her home, Jaden heard the move he'd assumed to be silent. She aimed the mac-10 at her opponent, squeezed off a warning shot and gave the voice command to bring the lights up halfway.

"Stand up," she called to the intruder. "Hands high and let me see the gun."

Even in the dim light the man's polished revolver gleamed.

"Triple Threat Tony," she said, using the nickname he'd given himself years ago. "What brings you by?"

"Just business, Ms. Jaden." The revolver's business end still targeted her ceiling.

It might've sounded like any other mundane conversation, but she kept the gun trained on him. Tony would've ruled the Wild West with his talent for speed and accuracy with a firearm. She didn't dare relax.

"So, how much am I worth?"

"Not you, hon. Not you. Couple trivial items is all. That's all I need."

"Tony, I'm not deaf. You told your worthless buddy over there to kill me. And trivial's a matter of perspective."

"True, hon. That's true. Give me a break, huh? I knew his aim would give you a fair chance."

Jaden glanced at the time display just over Tony's left shoulder. "Look, you've got about one more minute before cops are crawling all over this place. Tell me who's paying you and I'll give you a head start."

"Can't do that."

"Can your pal?"

"He's not dead?"

"Tony," she scolded. "You know better."

He shrugged, and she took it as an apology of sorts.

"He doesn't know nothin'. Worthless, just like you said."

"C'mon, Tony. Give me a line on the money."

"Sorry, sweetie." The wail of sirens grew closer. "Time's up." Tony dropped his arm and got off a shot, forcing Jaden to dive sideways while firing his buddy's weapon. As she lay there, her first concern was how Tony had missed. Then, willing her breathing to slow, she counted back the shots fired. Three.

Three?

"God, no!" She leaped up and vaulted the counter to see Tony lying in a puddle of blood, his hand still wrapped around the gun at his temple. "No! Tony!"

"Police! Step back, ma'am," a new voice boomed behind her.

She didn't. Instead she swiped the tears from her eyes and looked for where her shot lodged. In the fridge, of all places. She shook her head.

"I'm fine."

"Good for you. Care to explain?"

"A break in. Hacked my system. I engaged the backup."

The officer didn't seem to care. "With two dead, the paperwork'll kill me."

"Two?"

"Yeah, two. You didn't pop this guy here?"

Jaden shook her head again, understanding the impact of the three shots. Tony had killed his partner, then himself. With an outdated silver revolver. *What wasted skill.*

For Jaden, it confirmed the obvious. The Judge wanted those pictures buried and Jaden with them. Failure was clearly not an option Tony cared to explore.

"Wouldn't put it past her."

Jaden turned to see the glowering face of Chuck Loomis. "The ballistics will clear me."

"Good thing we've got us a shiny new van," Chuck said with a sneer.

I miss Larry too, she thought as Loomis pulled gunshot residue from her hands and labeled the sample.

"Why are you using guns anyway? Thought you were the hands only expert."

"She's both."

The new voice belonged to the Chief of Police, a.k.a. the 'street rat'. Turning, Jaden noted the slight limp and would've bet her best code-breaking card the bruise was dark, purple and painful.

She extended her hand in an effort to head off further hostilities. "Jaden Michaels. What brings the Chief out on a routine call?"

"You consider two dead men routine?"

Apparently he hadn't spent much time on the streets of his city. "Not at all. Nor is breaking and entering. They compromised my security system and came gunning for me."

"Yet here you stand without a scratch."

"A woman's got a right to defend herself." *And others who can't.*

His arms folded across his chest and she wondered how dense she could be. His arrogance, intensity, his every movement should have alerted her to his real identity, regardless of the shabby disguise he'd used on the street.

"You run a tidy profit on that theory I'd bet."

"I get by," she said.

His bark of laughter startled her and when he walked

away, inviting himself for a full tour, having to follow him grated her nerves.

"This place is tricked out beyond a typical 'getting-by' income." He fingered the control panel in her private workout room, eyes widening as it responded negatively to his touch. "Well beyond."

"Touch sensors aren't that pricey."

His eyes narrowed and Jaden felt the years melt away. Long ago those storm gray eyes gave her that same look of disbelief. The disbelief that had cost her life then and several times over in the years since. *Jaden, meet your executioner. Again.*

The burst of awareness stole her breath and she stumbled toward the nearest chair.

"Are you okay?"

"No." Any idiot could see she wasn't.

His hand pushed her head between her knees. "Breathe," he ordered, and then called for water.

"Leave me be," she muttered in the general direction of her crotch. But he ignored her.

When the water arrived, he helped her sit up and sip slowly. Then he began to question her.

"Did they steal anything?"

"I stopped them."

"So what'd you do to earn a bad contract?"

"Guess I helped the wrong woman."

"Maybe so. One of my officers swore you were the best hand-to-hand teacher in the district. We'll need your student roster."

"No."

His eyes went wide.

"No, thank you." Jaden scooted out from under his

hovering to stand up on her own.

Based on their history, trusting him ended badly, fatally, for her. It amazed her that he seemed the one piece of the puzzle completely oblivious to the horrendous connection she shared with him and Albertson. Regardless, she didn't have time to explain to him, or anyone else, how and why she intended to fulfill her mission.

"Chief Thomas, I can deal with this threat without exposing my students to more trouble."

"We're trained to keep them safe, Ms. Michaels."

"They're safe now. I see no reason to change what's working. If you'll excuse me, I'll provide my DNA sample to help your men on their way." Then she could blow up her warehouse and retreat to an alternate hideout.

"In a hurry?"

She forced herself to sound casual. "Just a busy day tomorrow." She checked the clock. "Today. Whatever."

A piercing wail sliced through her mind and she reached for the nearest stability. But it wasn't the wall or even a chair. It was the police chief.

He held her forearms in a secure grip, her own hands instinctively gripping him in turn. When her knees buckled under the second scream, Jaden gazed up at the man she'd once loved with utter abandon.

"What's happening to you?" he asked.

His brow furrowed with confusion or concern, she couldn't tell. And he couldn't see. Even touching her, he didn't know her, didn't see the truth.

"Ms. Michaels?"

He knelt, searching her face, but the tragedy unfolding on the fringes of her consciousness stole her voice.

She had to end the Judge's reign of terror, but her strength was failing. She struggled for breath, no longer aware of her fingers digging into the chief's arms, oblivious to both her white knuckles and his hiss of pain.

She braced for the next wave, but instead of crushing her, the pain eased. Instead of exhaustion, she felt a shimmer of renewed energy.

Opening her eyes she filled her vision with him and understood. Cleveland was right, she needed help. But why did the source reside in the one man who'd never once in over a thousand years believed her?

"Thank you," she murmured, her touch lighter now.

"What happened?" he ordered.

"You tell me." She didn't dare volunteer anything. Who knew what he'd reveal to the Judge or use against her in the current case.

"You paled, cried out, and fell."

"*Mmm-Hmmm.*"

Chief Thomas released her suddenly. The cold loneliness returned with a wicked rush, but the Judge was done, leaving her to bear only her own burdens for the moment.

Thomas shook his head, rubbed at his arms. "You've got a strong grip."

"Guess so." She stood, the moment gone and with it her desire to have any partner in this venture.

"That's all?"

"I said thanks."

"But what...what caused you to...to do that?"

"Low blood sugar I guess." She stepped back, and away, eager to resume her original plans.

His hand landed on her shoulder and spun her back to face him. She wanted to lash out, but wanted to serve time for assaulting an officer of the law even less.

"Yes?" she managed.

"You're lying." His eyes locked with hers. "I know you, now. The thief." His voice dropped to a whisper. "This was a trick. A little bait and switch."

"No." She wished. "How's the knee?"

"Chuck! Get over here; I've got charges to press."

Funny, she did too. But of a much different nature. "Don't do this. You don't get it." Loomis crossed the room. "Where's the trinket you lifted?"

He held up a palm to stop the approaching detective. "Fine," he growled. "Fill me in."

She calculated her options and the price. "As soon as you clear everyone out." Maybe then, with no distractions, she could make him see the truth.

He scowled at her and she sympathized, momentarily, with his confusion. Then he snapped orders to the evidence crew to clean up and list the case as closed—with her name cleared. Larry's partner didn't care for this development, but all his protests were cut off without further discussion.

When the apartment was clear, she gently probed the issue at hand. "You've known Judge Albertson long?"

"Most of my life."

"He's like a father, a mentor, right?"

"Yes," he admitted, with a frown.

She ignored the doubt stamped on his face and the skeptical set of his mouth. "I'm testifying in his courtroom tomorrow."

"What sort of case?" He shoved his hands into his jacket pockets. "Breaking and entering, maybe?"

"While I've testified on the validity of certain security systems–"

"Which you test by defying them."

She dipped her head, then met his ferocious gaze. She loosened the leash on her street temper. "Who're you to judge me?" Her chin jutted and her finger stabbed at his chest. "You followed me in. You took out one of your own."

"Not without regret."

"I should hope not." Jaden turned away. She'd let it matter too much. Let Cleveland fill her head with stupid ideas about teamwork. Innocents were counting on her. Time to get on with it.

"All right, talk. Why me?"

Hell, if she knew that, life would be too easy. "I thought you might be more reasonable than your officers."

"Loomis is pretty unhappy."

"So am I," she lashed out. "Of all the people your little stunt had to cost, that's the one man I needed."

"Oh, this'll be good." His hands came out of his pockets and folded across his chest.

She remembered that pose. It wasn't a good sign. She tried to dial down her emotions. "Larry kept important evidence safe."

"Safe from what?"

"From people who wanted it gone."

"Evidence doesn't bow to the whim of 'people'."

"It shouldn't. But–"

"But nothing. Our department has protocol and procedures. We've worked hard to reclaim the integrity of law enforcement. Give me something concrete or stop insinuating otherwise."

"I give up." Exasperated, Jaden hitched her thumb at the door. "Go away. I've got to sleep if I'll be worth anything in court. Check into the Brenda Calhoun case. Then, should you care to broaden your mind, stop by your buddy's courtroom."

* * *

Jaden heard the question, but looked straight at the Judge rather than the advocate. He needed to see her courage wouldn't falter.

"Answer the question, Ms. Michaels," Judge Albertson prompted.

"The woman arrived, bruised and bleeding, begging for help."

"And you took pictures?" the Judge interjected in a patronizing voice laced with doubt.

"Yes. After I called the police. Ms. Calhoun gave her statement to them and the evidence crew collected information–"

"And took pictures," the judge interrupted again.

Stay calm. "Yes. Then I escorted Brenda to the hospital for treatment."

"Did they also take pictures at the hospital?" the defense-advocate inquired.

"Yes." Hell must've frozen over, she was wishing for an attorney. These proceedings were tedious under the wrong judge, and Albertson was as wrong as they came.

"Yet only your set of pictures remains?"

"Apparently."

"Pictures any four-year-old could create on his home computer."

The judge waved the defense-advocate to his seat and assumed the questioning himself.

"No," Jaden said quietly.

"No?"

"No. You can scan my programs. I don't have photo enhancement software. You can review the pictures themselves and you'll see no trace of tampering."

"So where are these pictures?" Judge Albertson snapped.

Jaden paused, looking for the verbal trap. His henchmen had failed to kill her and the evidence. What did he hope to gain by staring at the proof himself?

She pulled a slender tube out from her portfolio. The courtroom door opened and Chief Thomas walked in. After last night, he was the last person she expected here.

Jaden unscrewed the cap off the tube and set several flat disks on the rail between her seat and the Judge's dais. Pressing the power button on, she brought each hologram to life. Close-ups of Brenda's bleeding, swollen face shimmered in the air between Jaden and the judge.

His face went red. "You said pictures," he snapped.

"Yes. I have those too." She reached into her portfolio and extended the envelope containing the dozen or so prints.

He hesitated, then accepted, his eyes hot with temper. All courtrooms were wired with a constant feed to the news services and anyone interested could tune in to any case.

In light of the incontrovertible proof she'd just presented, the Judge would have to send his friend to behavior modification. Brenda would be free to get on with her life. An angry look passed between the Judge and Brenda's ex. The accused looked away.

Jaden waited until the Judge ordered her to light the last disk. It wasn't a still. It was a recording of Brenda's testimony as given to the evidence crew.

"Ms. Michaels, is this a stunt to earn an interview for a detective's position?"

"No sir. I merely wanted to help one of my students."

"You consider yourself better equipped than the legal system we have in place?"

She couldn't believe he'd opened that door. To her, of all

people. "I believe our law enforcement faces the same challenges it has in the past. Corruption and over work. I merely wanted to see justice served."

Judge Albertson brought his robe-shrouded bulk out of his chair. "Chambers, Ms. Michaels," he bellowed. "Bailiff take those things to the lab for verification."

Jaden watched the bailiff scurry to gather up the disks, then followed the judge behind the bench to his chambers.

The door slid closed behind Jaden and she heard the lock engage. A perfect opportunity to take down a demon incarnate. But without an escape route, more importantly, without the answer of how to break the curse, she wouldn't act.

And he knew it.

"Well done. You're clearly committed to this girl."

"I'm committed to all of your victims."

"You've grown up. Filled out too much for my tastes."

"Lucky me."

He leaned back into his chair and laced his fingers over his broad girth.

"I'm ready. Go ahead."

She frowned at him. "Ready for what?"

"Come on, you've got a knife in your shoe. A gun on your thigh, right?"

"Neither would've survived the search at the door."

"Oh, something quieter this time? Poison maybe, or a garrote?"

"So you hauled me in here to kill you? How absurd."

"But you're so good at it." He leaned forward and the chair groaned under the burden. He slid a small plastic card across his desk. "Here's the pass card for the back door. Once you're out of the building you can go wherever you please. You'd have purged the world of me and my evil intentions."

He chuckled like a narrator for an old horror flick, but Jaden ignored it, trying to calculate what brought this on.

He wanted something. Something she already had. He'd never before invited her vengeance. But what could it be, what was worth the risk?

"Why?" she asked bluntly.

"Seems you've always had an axe to grind."

She clasped her hands behind her. "The axe didn't work."

He guffawed. "Well in the long run, I suppose not. We've been around this all before. Here's your opportunity, Ms. Michaels. Take your best shot."

It was tempting. Beyond tempting–it was the end all, the ultimate goal right here in her grasp, yet it didn't feel right.

"Why?" she asked again.

"So curious. Just do it and let's call it done. I'm tired, you're tired. Let's finish it."

He had lived longer than any other time they'd met. She felt it then, caught the slight glimmer in his eyes. He had a plan. Somehow he knew her strength was waning. If she gave in to the instant gratification now, it would only be tougher next time.

"What's your verdict on this case?"

"Simple. A juiced man forgot his own strength in the throes of passion and the woman cried abuse. She's alive and well enough, isn't she? She's moved on–why isn't he entitled to the same?"

"Maybe because he broke her jaw, her nose, her arm, not to mention the law."

"Dearheart, do you recall the good ol' days when laws made sense? When a man had the right to keep his lady in line without fear of the establishment?"

She looked heavenward, pretending to think. "*Hmm.*

Yes." Her eyes came back to his. "I think they called it the Dark Ages."

He guffawed once more and his enormous belly jiggled, making the robes ripple like a black lake.

"So if you won't kill me, dare I ask a favor?"

"You've dared more without asking."

"Ah, you're bitter." He waggled a finger at her. "That's never good. In this life form or any other."

She held her tongue, wishing she could cut his out.

"Stop this witch hunt, dearheart. Aside from mistakes I made with you and your sister–"

"You're referring, of course, to the sister who died as a direct result of your depravity." The only sister she'd had in how many families? The sister she'd treasured and lost because of the beast in front of her. Her vision hazed and she itched to strike out.

He inclined his head, in admission or invitation she couldn't say. She struggled for control. He was up to something.

"...a sorrowful time indeed," he was saying. "However, all that's behind me." He shifted to open the top drawer of his desk.

Jaden braced herself to defend or evade depending on the weapon he withdrew. And she nearly fell to her knees in grief at the sight of the sparkling bracelet dangling from his stocky finger.

She remembered each of the nine, modest square cut diamonds. She recalled the delighted look on her sister's face at the birthday party that became her last. She still felt the pulse of rage when her sister's small body had been found– without a scrap of ornamentation.

She hated the idea that they had this in common. This

need to connect and collect items from their previous incarnations.

"I'd truly appreciate it if you'd let the past go." He laid the bracelet on the desk between them. "It's the only way to a healthy future."

The urge to seize the bauble and destroy the beast threatened to overpower her sense of purpose. "Convict your buddy out there and I'll think about it," she managed at last.

"Always defending the underdog. Dearheart, I'm only a man."

"You're the foulest of men and the most horrendous of monsters. I will kill you. When the time suits *me*. You can wait and wonder. And rot."

"Well, then, I guess we're done here. Don't say I haven't tried for peaceful reconciliation, Ms. Michaels."

They both knew his very nature made him incapable of peace. "I look forward to your verdict."

She left, bypassing his security to show him just how easily she could get to him when she was ready. The low chuckle behind her only fueled the revenge burning in her heart. She'd find the right weapon, and next time they met, he wouldn't have time to ask for his death.

Chapter Four

Time Stamp: 1066

Slipping out into the cool spring night I see the soaring star. Everyone speaks of it, though usually in whispers that it portends death and worse. For me, 'tis a beautiful mystery how the sky so reflects my joy! I spread my arms and soar with it, for I am soon to be wed to my beloved.

Clouds scud over the new star. I am not alone. Captured in a violent embrace, I struggle and cry out, to no avail. Overpowered, smothered, I am used and left ruined by a man above reproach—the baron himself. Staring I watch the star emerge to continue its celestial journey and I am painfully aware my own life's course has been changed forever.

Brian stewed in his thoughts until Jaden exited Albertson's chambers. Tension clouded her eyes and stretched her mouth thin. It wasn't unusual for a judge to speak privately with a witness. Especially in a case where false accusation carried such a high penalty.

He shifted to lean against the back wall. The charges she'd tossed around last night still weighed on his mind. And her haunted sea-green eyes and tousled honeyed hair left his nerves ragged.

He'd spent the night in his office reviewing old cases looking for any trend of missing evidence. At first glance, nothing seemed wrong. Burglaries, car theft, fraud, and murders had all been processed without delay or questionable tactics.

He went back further, kept digging until the insidious pattern emerged. Rape, mugging, and the occasional domestic dispute frequently settled out of court when evidence disappeared. Evidence the crews swore they gathered and filed. Yet crime scene photos were lost, DNA compromised, and testimony tossed on the basis of coercion. Except in cases processed by Larry. Most of those ended up in court and resulted in heavy sentences.

But only a few had been Judge Albertson cases and none of them connected to Jaden Michaels. So he'd hopped the el for two full circuits of the city to think it all through. But when the news monitors in the train car announced that the Judge had ordered verification of holograms brought to court by Michaels, Brian changed his plans.

Now, as Jaden's eyes met his, it felt as if she stared straight through to his soul. Deeper, if there was such a place. The woman acted as if she knew what he was about better than he did. Unease swept over him, raising the hair on the back of his neck. Was she mystery or threat? Did he really want to know?

Jaden took her place next to Brenda on the pew-like bench, thinking of the last time she'd been to a church. Weeks ago. She should go again, for Larry's sake if no better reason occurred. Neither she nor Brenda spoke, unified in their apprehension as they waited for the bailiff to return. Mentally, she worked through various, hopefully unnecessary, escapes.

Then the bailiff appeared from a side door, crossed the courtroom and disappeared into the Judge's chambers. Jaden's mind blanked and her body tensed for action.

Judge Albertson mounted the dais and raised his gavel. His eyes locked on Jaden before shifting to give Billy a quick nod. She knew before he spoke the words: Brenda would have to run.

"The lab has found nothing fraudulent with the hologram," the Judge began. "I sentence the defendant to five years incarceration with behavior modification in a maximum security facility. Effective immediately."

Brenda clutched Jaden's hand and gave a watery smile of gratitude. Jaden knew relief was premature.

"However." The judge cleared his throat. "The manner of presentation of the evidence in this case compels me to make an example for the future integrity of the law. I'm obligated to place the woman who pressed charges and all advocates and witnesses on her behalf under house arrest for a period not less than thirty days. Also effective immediately." His black eyes landed on Jaden with a sharp, satisfied glint.

She met the gaze even as she plotted her way around it.

The court authority led a confused Brenda, a protesting advocate, an unaffected defendant, and a much-too-calm Jaden out of the courtroom through the back hallways.

Once the procession reached street level, Felon Transport took over, ordering silence as they waited on separate vehicles for the ride to their respective destinations.

Seeing Brenda gulp back a sob, Jaden sought a way to reassure the stunned woman before the transport shuttled her away.

"Officer," Chief Thomas said. "I need a word with Ms. Michaels."

Jaden saw him flash his shield, then nod for her to approach. She ignored him.

"We need to talk." He took her elbow, moving them away from Brenda and the officer.

She disagreed. No point. Doubt and confusion were etched on his whole being.

"What happened in there?" he persisted.

She shrugged. "Justice was served."

"I meant in chambers."

"More of the same, Thomas. You wouldn't believe me anyway."

"Call me Brian," he said softly. "Try me."

She studied him then, assessing the risk of driving him away at what might be a crucial point in their lives. In one deep breath, she spilled it all.

He stared.

"He asked you to kill him?"

"Yes."

"Must be the cancer."

"Cancer?" She huffed. "Most cancers are eradicated." And just what would happen to her if Albertson died of natural causes? Would it mean an easy end for her too? "He wouldn't have told you."

"Contrary to your low opinion of me, we go way back. He's a good friend. And he trusts me."

"Your loss." She started back toward the waiting transport officer.

"Isn't it yours?" he said, catching up. "You challenge my department's integrity and now you don't care about the answers."

She jerked her thumb back to the courthouse behind them. "Clearly I don't need the judge's buddy on my team."

"Don't you? Don't you need to replace Larry?"

"Hardly. I don't want a spy. Or double agent as it'd apply to you. I need an ally." She bit hard on her cheek. Where had that come from? Sure Cleveland suggested it, but as a single opinion she hadn't given the idea real credit. After all, she'd handled her fate on her own every other time. "For all the good it's done," she muttered.

"Say again?"

"Why the interest? Last night you weren't buying my story about the Judge making evidence evaporate."

"I'm still not convinced." He stopped her as she tried to spin away. "But I know you believe it. Looking into some old cases proved something's wrong. I can help you. With my resources and your witnesses, we'll be able to clear the air."

She jerked out of his grip and the odd effect his touch had on her. "I don't want to clear the air, I want to save lives."

"So do I, but for some reason, I want to protect yours in the process."

She knew the reason; she could pinpoint exactly where his instinct to protect took root in his soul. Yet, she couldn't tell him, it was too impossible for him to comprehend. Yet...

"Last night, your touch gave me strength."

He blinked. "I guess that's one way to put it."

"And you feel well now?"

"Yeah. Sure."

Her car pulled up and the transport officer called to them. "There's my ride. Come see me when you've resigned."

"What?"

"You can't help if your loyalties are divided."

"I can't help if I'm out of the loop," he shot back.

She sighed. He'd never trust. Not her, not her guidance and never her mission. He was too close to the Judge. He'd always been too close to the devil, making him blind to his tactics.

"Who says I need anything from you at all?"

"You did last night."

There was that. "An error in judgment. Forget we met. I've got things to do," she said, as the officer dragged her away.

Topping the list was seeing Brenda would be safe.

"I'll put a detail on your girl," he called after her.

She had no way to acknowledge the comment, but that didn't matter. Cleveland was wrong. Fulfilling a destiny was an individual sport.

So was escape. As an art form, it had been easier when handcuffs weren't electronic and vehicles had simple locks rather than the timed devices of this era. Or so the police wanted to believe.

Jaden had learned one lesson above all others through the course of her lives: adapt. Two blocks and she had the combination cuffs unlocked. Another block and she'd worked her briefcase into a better position to access her code key. When the van stopped at the front of her building, she was ready.

The driver pressed buttons on the panel, paused, and then exited the car, coming around to her door.

She heard the whir of the timed locks releasing and when the officer swung the door open, she seized his wrist. With a twist and sharp yank he was in the backseat, sprawled over her. A quick blow to his neck put him out long enough to slip away and jam the time locks.

The standard GPS and a few keystrokes would soon inform the monitoring station at the courthouse of the completion of Judge Albertson's orders.

There had to be some reason why the Judge had baited

her. Something he knew that she'd yet to recall. She knew there were gaps in her ageless memory. What didn't he want her to find?

Walking around to the back of her building, she slid her code key through what appeared to be a worn and abandoned lock. Instead of taking the stairs up to her apartment, she bypassed her empty classroom and slipped through a door no one else knew about.

Descending the dark, narrow staircase, Jaden felt as if she were on a controlled drop into a deep well. The only light came from the penlight she'd flipped on as soon as the door closed behind her.

Slowing, in anticipation of the bottom, she relished the quiet, cool damp of her secret basement. She waved her key in front of the panel she couldn't see and the room lit up. She tossed her briefcase, the extra holograph projector and her code key on the desk as she moved toward an antique wardrobe.

Occasionally she found humor in using the same pieces over and over. Value, she supposed, though it didn't make her smile today. The judge was right, she was tired. Stripping out of the skirt and jacket she'd worn for Brenda's case, she donned a stretchy tracksuit of heathered blue. Comfort clothes, for body and spirit, she thought with a small smile now.

Testifying had taken its toll. No. Being in the presence of evil had done it. She spun the lock on the old combination safe door and enjoyed the sight of her journals, the museum diary, her alternate IDs and the few gadgets she considered useful in this era. Yesterday's intruders could've searched for days and never uncovered her emergency system that emptied the safe upstairs into this one.

She read the entries, marveling at how little her handwriting had changed over the course of time. Interesting as that was, she dug into the pages, finding herself moved by the entries of a girl in love, in misery, and then set on a course she'd been running for far too long.

The yellowed pages revealed a happy childhood, but her innocent faith in love was dashed when her fiancé's superior officer molested her. Ruined her. Unable to convince her betrothed of the truth, she'd been tossed to the outskirts of good society and forced to make her own way.

Jaden stood and walked off the impatience.

She remembered the rest. Hearing her father talk of specific crimes against prostitutes, she'd taken the ultimate risk for a woman of that time and investigated on her own, suspecting the man who'd molested her. Getting to know the women who'd survived, she'd managed to begin an underground escape route to give them a chance against the predator. When her parents died, she used her inheritance to fund a safe haven for those abused women.

It had been unheard of to care for prostitutes to the degree she had. It had been unheard of, as well, to poison a royal officer. Somehow he'd lived long enough to put the authorities onto her.

That life had ended slowly, in prison, making it impossible to help anyone else. Jaden gazed at the diary. It couldn't be useless. She'd studied legends of various weapons. She'd examined in depth the myths of good versus evil. The key was somewhere in the past.

Before she could wonder what would happen if she simply gave in and gave up on exposing the Judge for the devil he was, the screaming started. Terror and confusion coursed through her veins followed by the unthinkable.

Her cozy hideaway vanished, her vision compromised by the current victim. She didn't waste time wondering what was happening; she simply took the new gift and tried to determine where the Judge had taken the helpless girl.

The steel construction of the large room showed when the girl looked around wildly. She tensed, with the girl, when heavy hands squeezed budding breasts. She jumped, as the girl did, when a door flew open. And though tears blurred the view, Jaden could see it was Billy, Brenda's ex, coming toward Albertson.

The girl lurched as the Judge shoved her at Billy. "Take her to holding. I'll catch up."

Jaden's vision was restored when the contact broke.

He'd already seen to Billy's release. Or escape. No difference. With renewed fervor, she studied the diary. This monster had to be stopped. And all his minions with him.

In her flurry of determination, Jaden blocked out everything but the words she'd penned so long ago. And there it became crystal clear. Thomas, as he was known now, as he'd been known to her at the first. Thomas must side with her, must understand the true nature of the Judge. He must accept her word as fact, despite the lack of evidence. How had she missed this simple fact in all the other attempts?

"Stupid," she scolded herself. "Impossible. Bizarre." She pushed the diary away, rejecting the concept. It slid off her desk to land on the floor. Regretting her temper, she picked it up, only to find the fabric covering torn loose from the back and several smaller pages peeking out.

One fact was clear immediately: the writing was not hers.

Jaden willed her hands to stop shaking as she gingerly extracted the papers from their hiding place. Her skin chilled as she read each page.

They came to me, each of them with their stories so like yours. My darling, what have I done? I was a coward not to see. I am unworthy of your faith in me.

I shall work tirelessly for your release as I continue your efforts on behalf of the unfortunate.

He is too strong, too well guarded. Every path I take leads to another, lesser man, merely taking orders.

The pages went on like this. Similar notes of efforts failed and victories nearly too small to mention. And on the last page Jaden read:

Word reached me today of your death. I have failed you in life, but my insistence has at last earned your peaceful rest with your parents. My love for you endures. I pray your forgiveness and that our souls may one day unite as our bodies were denied.

Jaden looked to the ceiling and pleaded with celestial powers she'd never understand and didn't want to. "Why him? It's impossible. He's impossible!" She let the shout build and released her frustration with it.

Spent, she fisted her hands in her hair. "Why not a gun or special sword buried in a rock? Why not a simple silver bullet?"

An explosion rocked the warehouse above, sending an avalanche down on her. Not the answer she wanted.

Jaden blinked gritty eyes and listened to a strange whimpering sound. Her attempt to move resulted in a gasp of pain and she understood the whimpers weren't from another victim, but from her own bruised lips.

Pain radiated from her head to her toes, but she counted her blessings that she could feel both and all the parts in between. It took what she assumed to be several minutes to recall where she was. The death-lock of her fingers around a small book clarified the situation.

Siren sounds faded in and out and she knew she had to get to safety. The defenses she'd installed on her building would soon kick in.

The acrid smell of burning wood and melting steel stung her eyes, but she stuffed the few things worth saving into a backpack. Voices above made her pause at the stairwell. Not up to a fight, she waited until they faded.

Alone again, she snuck out of the burning building, not indulging in regret.

"I've got you." Thomas's hands landed on her and she felt better instantly. Of course better was a relative term.

She elbowed him and made a dash for the alley. Except the dash felt more like a stumble and bruised her pride.

"What's the rush?"

It would take a supreme physical effort to drag him out of harm's way. "Too close," she rasped through seared lungs.

"The fire crew's on it. What happened?"

"He tried to kill me." On sheer will she moved away from the building, refusing to look back. If he was too stupid to follow, oh, well.

"Judge A didn't do this."

Jaden decided she'd never be desperate enough to ask for help from this man who consistently failed her. "Of course not." She allowed him the superior smirk and struggled forward; shamelessly relieved she wasn't hauling him too. "He hired it done and we both know it."

"We don't both know it."

"I'm done arguing with you." Her temper surged past reason. "Judge A is a demon, sent to create as much hell and havoc as possible before I kill him. It's the same every damn time." She shoved away from him, and cursed her waning strength. She resisted Brian's efforts to help or hinder, she didn't know his intent, just that his hands kept seeking her body.

"Back up the bus, gorgeous."

She was about to tell him where to shove his outdated euphemisms when the rumbling tipped her off. "Oh, shit." She grabbed at him and his surprise allowed her to push him down and away from the debris field about to rain on them.

"What the—" was all he got out before he lost his breath when she landed on him.

The windows of her warehouse blew out as the rest of the building neatly folded in on itself, sending a spike of fire heavenward. Dust and bits of her life covered them in a fine powder.

"Bastard," she shouted at the smoldering remains.

"Call me Brian," Thomas muttered beneath her.

"Not you. You're conscious?"

"You could sound happier about it."

Jaden shook her head. Then she laughed. "He doesn't know he missed me. I can be happy with that."

She stood, again refreshed from the contact with Thomas, and tried to resume her escape from the alley, the police and the evidence crews due to arrive any second.

"You need my help," he said, following her.

"From what little you know it might look that way. But I'm okay alone. Really."

"What I know might surprise you..."

Jaden knew he was still talking. His lips would hardly be moving otherwise. But she couldn't hear his words over the screams in her head. *This chick has a set of pipes*. She refused to let her knees buckle until she was out of the alley and into the dim light of the pathway.

On trembling legs, she kept moving. Or tried to. But her

vision was marred by the wild gaze of the terrified girl. She could well relate to the feeling of Albertson's approach. Too easily, she understood the gut-loosening intimidation caused by the soft-spoken delivery of evil words.

With one hand on the nearest wall, Jaden forced herself to move forward, while focusing on the girl's surroundings.

She seized on the few details available. A pattern of long, rectangular windows in groups of three. Light poured through them, telling Jaden more than it told the victim. Albertson staged his vile games on a set as false as he was.

If this girl survived, and held the courage to tell, she'd say her assault took place during daylight hours when the Judge would be safely behind his bench. Her story discredited, he'd remain above suspicion and she'd get a month of injections.

"Bastard," she said aloud.

Thomas gave her a hard shake. "An evidence van just turned the corner. Let's go give your statement."

Though still seeing with the girl's eyes, the poor creature had lapsed into a shocked silence, which allowed Jaden to hear again. "Can't," she said on a ragged breath. "I'm not serving thirty days anywhere but home."

"Home's gone."

"Right. Well, bye." She began to formulate an alternate plan. "See ya around."

She felt him hesitate, then go. She walked a bit further, until she felt the corner of the rusty dumpster. Slumping into what she hoped looked like a pitiful ball of homelessness, she waited for the excitement to pass.

When running feet skidded to a stop beside her she played the part as best she could. Soon, though, she felt Thomas's touch.

"Call me Brian and I'll get you outta here."

"Okay, Brian." She reached out. "But why help me now?"

"Later. Tell me what's wrong," he ordered.

"I'm sorta blind at the moment."

"The explosion?"

It was a convenient excuse. "Sure. Did anyone see you?"

"Counting you?" he teased, easing her arm over his shoulders. With his free hand around her waist he snugged her close.

It troubled her to enjoy it so much. But it restored her vision and her energy level soared. She felt alive, awakened, as if she could conquer anything.

"My statement would've been worthless."

"Yup," he agreed. "Nothing to say. The place just blew."

"Gas lines suck," she snickered.

"And it's an old place."

Appalled at the easy camaraderie, Jaden snapped back to business. "Why did you come back?"

"That whole protect and serve thing. Once you're safe I'll go back–"

His radio card crackled with news of an officer shot while responding to a murder-suicide scene across town. The address was Brenda's.

She stopped walking and pulled away from him. "You came back." She tapped the pocket holding the radio card. "Because of this." The answer was clear enough in his eyes. And the solution crystallized in her mind.

"Did anyone see you?" she demanded.

"No."

"Good." She yanked the stressed cow-safe fake leather jacket from his body and pulled his badge from the waistband of his jeans. She drew the dagger and nicked his hand before he could protest, smearing blood on his badge. Next, she sliced out a strip of the jacket's lining, handing it to him for a bandage. Digging in her backpack for a lighter, she set the jacket on fire.

"What the hell? Stop that!" He stomped out the flames and then tried to reclaim his property.

But she was focused and quicker now. "Stay here." She snuck closer to the demolished warehouse and tossed in the evidence of his 'death'.

"My condolences," she said, returning.

"You're outta control, Michaels."

"Since we're both dead now, Brian, call me Jaden."

"Neither of us is dead," he pointed out with a surly tone.

"Think what you can learn if we play it that way."

"You're crazed. You need to be in a hospital."

"I've heard that one before." Though never from him. She sniffed at the insult. "Look at it as undercover work. If I'm an insane stalker with a grudge against your buddy, you'll have all the access and evidence you need. It won't go to court and you can resume your life a hero among saints." *Just like every other time.*

He stared, studied really, his gray eyes weighing all the possibilities. "What's the plan?"

"Develop our ghostly skills, I guess." She tried to smile, but it troubled her that the Judge knew so much. If he'd found this place, he'd soon find her alternate hideout. Resigned, she turned away toward the next best thing to home.

Slick Micky's.

There she could trade her teaching skills for a few key favors and get on with the research to complete her mission to destroy Albertson.

Chapter Five

Time Stamp: 1066

From the shadows of the balcony I watched him training. He moved with grace and speed and my heart broke for all that I'd been denied. My family could take no action against the baron and my betrothed could not accept another man's seed swelling my stomach.

At the sound of scrabbling on the stones, I turned my head.

"A thousand pardons," the girl rasped as she tried to scurry away.

She stumbled over her gown and I rushed to her aid. I barely recognized the swollen face of the nurse's young daughter. "Who did this?" I demanded. Though she refused to answer, I saw the mark and knew the baron was to blame.

With God as my witness, I vowed to set this wicked world to rights.

"You're new," said the guard at the door.

Jaden shrugged. "He'll wanna see me."

The guard harrumphed and eyed Brian. "Not him. No way."

"Him who?" Jaden asked. "He's dead."

Before the guard could take a poke, Brian sidestepped. "Figuratively."

"Literally too. Just watch the news," Jaden suggested with a saucy smile for the guard.

"Whatever. I'll ring you through door one."

"Great."

Door one buzzed, swung open, and Jaden stepped forward without hesitation. Brian followed. The door clanged shut behind him, then the lights in the small room came up, stopping just short of too bright.

Jaden waved at the camera in the corner and jerked her thumb at Thomas. "He's cool. We're both dead and I need a place for a day or two."

"It'll cost," Micky's voice declared from the speaker.

"One class," she agreed.

"Two."

She rolled her eyes. "Okay. But if you or your girls talk you've made an enemy."

"Same goes," Micky replied, before an entire wall of the room slid away to reveal a warehouse full of young women packing smuggler's bags with pure, refined sugar.

She heard Thomas–Brian–suck in his breath at the sight of such criminal activity. "Oh, relax, you've dined with worse."

"So you've said."

"Maybe just once in this dance of ours, you'll simply take my word."

His furrowed brow said it all. He had no clue to the true origin of their relationship.

Then Micky descended from his office and embraced her. Quite an unusual display from the man, and at only their second personal meeting. Jaden noticed he looked nothing like the confident, cocky smuggler she'd met earlier.

"What's happened?"

"Two more girls gone. This morning. The cargo dumped in the gutter."

"Which you recovered, naturally," Brian said.

Micky gave Brian a calculating glance. "Naturally. Who is this?" he asked Jaden.

"Man of a thousand faces. He's—"

"The chief," Micky snarled as recognition dawned. He turned on Jaden. "You've exposed the heart of my business to a man who can take it down with a word?"

Put that way, maybe she should've left Brian to manage the second explosion on his own.

"The media thinks he's dead. Take a look." She pointed over his shoulder. The monitors he had at the end of the room were running the story now. Micky strode over, punched a button for volume and paused. His head swiveled back to Brian, then toward the monitor once more. Jaden waited until he signaled them to join him upstairs.

"Come on," she whispered to Brian. "And behave yourself."

"I knew about him, y'know."

"And let his business run unhindered?" she asked, climbing the stairs.

"Unhindered doesn't mean unmonitored. He's breaking the law, but it's a stupid law."

She felt him lean in, felt his words against her neck. She hated herself for the instant shiver of excitement. Attraction had plenty to do with it, but loving him once had doomed her forever. A woman should learn her lesson and move on.

She stopped at the landing, just outside the office doorway and gaped at him.

"Can you really say that?"

"Sure. Especially now that I'm dead."

His grin was sharp and fast. And electric.

"Well then, dead men tell no tales," she reminded him, struggling to regain her objectivity.

"Got it. You talk I'll observe."

"Deal." For a second, hope bloomed again. Then she remembered who she was dealing with and common sense nipped it.

Stepping inside, she focused on Micky. "So what's the big upset?"

"I've lost another one. Dead this time. Used and dead and tossed back."

"Tossed back?" Jaden and Brian asked simultaneously. Jaden scowled at Brian who acknowledged his mistake with a dip of his chin.

Micky continued, oblivious to their subtle exchange. "Tossed back. At the back door, of all places."

"Back door?" Jaden inquired, alone this time, though she could see Brian thinking the same.

"The private entrance for my girls. Only they know about it. Only they have access."

"Then someone's talked."

"I assume so."

"Have all the missing girls been–accounted for?" Brian asked.

Can't fight nature, Jaden thought. Brian's nature was inquisitive, even with his narrow mind.

"No. Three have never been heard from again."

"Have you reported this? Given descriptions?" Brian asked.

Jaden nudged him with an elbow. "Pretty talkative for an observer." She turned back to Micky. "But he's got a point."

"Are you kidding? Filing a report is financial suicide for me. And I think this bastard knows it."

"You mean your mules are targeted because you won't complain."

Micky shot a look at Brian that said more about his estimation of the chief's intelligence than an IQ test. "Yeah."

"So we've got a serial killer or rapist on the hunt."

"That's only the tip of the iceberg," Jaden grumbled. "There's more here."

"More what?"

"More to it," she snapped at Brian, tired of his consistent interruptions. She knew her enemy, knew his patterns and this had a different feel.

To his credit, Brian let her think. Her last life was usually the easiest to recall, down to the smallest details about society. "Last time he dabbled in video. Cambodian girls I think."

"What?" Micky asked.

She ignored him. "Chinese girls were priceless, and largely unavailable. Their female population was already dying."

"How do you know all this?"

The memory faded and she met his quizzical gaze. "Experience."

"You mean research."

"I say what I mean, thank you," she snipped, not liking the reaction but helpless to stop it. "But research isn't a bad idea. I'll need access to old reports. Both police and news."

Brian shrugged. "Good luck. I'm dead, remember?"

"I've got news files here," Micky offered.

"And with the right computer I can hack police files," she thought aloud. "Micky if you want your girls protected, I'm gonna need to set up shop. My place is gone."

"And I'm dead."

"Oh, get off it." She elbowed Brian again. "Being dead might be the most helpful thing for all of us. The Judge will be upset about taking you out. Unless he did it on purpose. Who told you to follow me? Or did you decide to answer the initial call on your own?"

Brian scowled. "The Judge asked me to follow up and make sure you didn't try anything with the transport officer. Not unusual considering how the case went down."

She quirked a brow, daring him to *not* make the obvious connection.

"You undermined his authority," Brian defended.

"Yeah? And what did you do?"

Brian just stared so she resumed her preference of ignoring him. "Micky, can I check out the rooms of the missing girls?" He nodded. "And do you have a place with a computer we could call home for a day or two? We need to do some planning."

"I've only got one free place."

"With three missing girls?"

"Most of them share."

Jaden knew it wasn't true, but she held her tongue. It was likely Micky had wired a suite just for business visitors. In his position she'd want to keep the 'former' police chief under surveillance too.

"We'll deal with it." Her look squashed any unnecessary commentary from Brian.

Leaving Micky's office from the opposite door, they headed into the building Micky used for housing. He led them to a suite two levels up from where Jaden had met the survivor just days ago.

"Nice digs," Brian said, stepping into a spacious room

decked out with real furniture and a state of the art entertainment system.

"Enjoy your stay," Micky deadpanned as he handed over a key card.

Once they were alone, Jaden jumped into the real issue. "I know you're not buying into why I'm gunning for your boss–"

"Friend. Boss would be unethical." He flopped onto the couch.

"So you're an ethical guy."

"I like to think so."

Once upon a time, she'd thought so too. "Good. Fine. Whatever. Are you gonna listen and cooperate or not?"

"Are those my only options?" He rubbed his knee absently.

"Let's get this straight. I have one, sole purpose in this sorry existence: to take down a monster hurting innocent girls and unfortunate women. Will you help, in the name of upholding the oath you took a few years ago?"

"My oath to protect and serve includes everyone, not just a select few."

She expected to feel steam burst from her ears. Of all the callous, insensitive things he could say. "Answer the question and we can move forward."

"I'll answer when you explain what old files have to do with this case."

She sighed and took pity on his lack of memory-aided comprehension. "I'll be looking for trends within the missing girls. He has preferences."

"*He*, meaning Albertson."

She knelt on the floor and took over the task of massaging his knee. "Whether you believe it or not."

Brian threw up his hands. "What started your obsessive

vendetta against Albertson?"

With practiced control, Jaden answered only the question asked. "He raped me. Then he marked me so he'd be sure not to use me again." She watched Brian's eyes widen in shock. Then soften as he considered her. She could handle anything. Anything but pity from him.

She stood up and began to investigate their temporary quarters. Within moments she found wiring for a miniscule video camera. Expecting Micky to be the cutting-edge wireless type, she kept looking.

"How old were you?"

She didn't bother pretending to misunderstand his question. "Thirteen." She scanned the corners where walls met ceiling. Nothing.

"You want me to pull your report and reopen the case?"

"You won't find a report." But she had found the wireless video tap. She stuck out her tongue and disabled it with an efficiency Cleveland would appreciate.

"Your parents didn't file any of this? They didn't take you to the hospital for treatment?"

The search over, she turned her full attention back to Brian. "Sure they did. A week after the fact when I made it home."

"You were kidnapped?"

His incredulous expression made her want to kick out his knee all over again. "My story's only important if you can prove it. There are no records. Except maybe my suicide attempt. I don't think he erased that one."

"I can't picture you as a suicide."

"Weak moment." She shrugged. "Good thing for both of us I didn't or he'd win this round."

"This round?"

"Oh, forget it." She'd get into that later. If she decided he was worth the effort. She settled into the chair near the couch. "Let's just agree I hate him and you adore him. How about you explain that to me."

"I don't adore him." Brian scowled and came to his feet. "He's a respected member of the law enforcement community."

She snorted. "He's the devil's own assistant."

"An opinion I'd expect from any victim."

"I haven't been a victim in—" She opted not to do the math. "I told you why I'm in the market to kill him. You tell me why I shouldn't."

"He's my father?"

"That's not even funny." But his somber face made her wonder if she'd severely miscalculated this life's challenges.

"Okay, not really. But he's a father figure. When my own father was doing time in Leavenworth prison, he stepped in. I guess he just stayed 'in' after that. Then my dad died and..." He began pacing.

"How?"

Brian stopped moving and blinked at her.

"How did your dad die?" she clarified.

"Transport vehicles were automated back then. It malfunctioned."

"His release was unexpected?"

"Three, no, four months early."

"And you managed to make chief with that big old skeleton in your closet because of a friend like the Judge."

"Hold on!" His hands fisted. "I earned my position."

"I'm sure you think so." Jaden took over the pacing.

If Albertson had the foresight to imbed himself in Brian's life then maybe Cleveland was right. Maybe the key was turning Brian to her side of the battle. Her fingers went to her neck, slid over her heart and paused at her midsection. All points of deadly impact in the past. But how to make him see the truth and get him on board with her version of the Judge?

"To be fair, I'm sure you did. And I'm just as sure he's using you. It's his method. He saw an opening, saw a need and filled it to his benefit."

"But he hasn't asked for anything."

"No?"

Brian's hands sought his jacket pockets before he recalled it was long gone. "Once in a blue moon he asks me to write a leniency recommendation. But–"

"But he watched out for you once and you've chalked it up to his benevolence."

Brian gave a somber nod.

"What about the evidence?"

"When?"

"You dug into it, right?"

"Well, yeah," he confessed.

"And?" Jaden prompted when he said no more.

"And I saw a pattern. Not one I can connect directly to Albertson, though."

"Of course not." It wouldn't be that easy. "What did you see?"

"Missing evidence, harsh judgments, and several false accuser sentences."

"And that tells you?"

"Oh, my God." Brian scrubbed at his face. "The museum."

"What about it?" Baffled she turned to face him.

"He funded the display you robbed."

"I didn't rob it, I retrieved what was mine. You robbed it. What'd you take?"

"I'm not sure." His fingers tingled. He'd have to go back for the necklace before the cleaning crew emptied his desk.

"He asked me to suppress news of your break in."

"Our break in."

"I was undercover," he said with a wink. "My point is he didn't ask for anything dark, mysterious or illegal."

"Suppressing evidence isn't illegal?" she exclaimed.

"Suppressing *news* isn't illegal. It's a common practice in law enforcement. I'd think you'd be grateful he didn't want to press charges."

"When will you get it? Pressing charges against me would be counterproductive for *him*. Whatever he's after, he wants me out here to see it happen. To know I can't do anything to stop him."

"What can you do to stop him?"

"Only death will interrupt him."

"Interrupt?"

"I've killed him a dozen times over. Then you kill me and we start again."

Brian gaped at her, taking a step back and sinking onto the couch. This was too weird. "You've lost your mind," he finally whispered.

"Not at all. I'm sane as they come. You're the problem. You've blocked your memories." And she refused to envy him for it. "You didn't believe me the first time. You've never believed me since. I don't know why I even hope you'll see the light now."

The tears streaking her face unnerved him and surprised her, if her swiping at them was any indication.

"Hold on a minute." On instinct alone, he stood and moved closer to offer comfort.

"No. Go away." She batted at him. "Go back to your

cushy job and your horrible friend and I'll take care of it like I always do. But this time, when you have a choice between taking my life and taking my word at least pause for a second and *think* about it!"

She stormed out of the suite. He thought about following, but she was too mad. Opting for action in the face of an unknown number of hours waiting for her return, Brian began planning how best to break into his own office to recover the necklace.

A tour of the stocked suite revealed not only a fridge full of food, legal and not, but closets filled with an eclectic assortment of clothing. Micky could always open a boutique if smuggling sugar didn't work out.

One call to Micky's assistant resulted in a wig and some basic makeup delivered within minutes. Considering the resources, he knew he'd be pushing it to walk into his own office in broad daylight with nothing more than a poor impersonation of a cross-dressing hooker.

Habit had him reaching for his security access card. "Damn." Another reach proved he didn't have a cell card to contact his favorite informant either. "She had to torch the coat."

When the door chime sounded, Brian was ready to run his plan by Jaden. But the female on the other side of the door was a stranger. A skinny, despondent stranger who seemed just as surprised to see him.

"I thought she'd be here," she said.

"Thought you were her," he admitted. "Can I help you?" She visibly shivered, as if the offer petrified her. Years of victim-sensitivity training kicked in. "We can leave the door open."

She nodded and stepped just over the threshold, gripping

the doorjamb with a white knuckled hand. "I-I just wanted to talk. She gets it."

"Okay." Brian hooked his thumbs in his back pockets and waited.

"She says since he marked me I'm safe. But I wish...I wish he'd killed me too," she finished in a rush.

"Too?"

"Yeah. They're the lucky ones. And I'm too chicken to do it myself."

"So you're thinking suicide?"

She gulped, looked away. "I wanted to talk to her."

"How?"

"I-I've got pills."

"Too slow and no guarantees. Around here someone would find you in plenty of time."

The eyes drowning in the dark, hollow circles filled, telling him she agreed. "I thought maybe–"

"You thought Jaden had a weapon? Or maybe even enough pity to do the job for you?" Tears flowed down her cheeks, but he wasn't done. "Show me this mark."

She trembled, but pulled her hair back from her neck.

He didn't have to terrify her by coming closer. The imprint just behind and below her left ear was all too visible. He stared at the angry red, infinity-shaped branding and as much as he wanted to deny it, he recognized the pattern.

"Rape?"

Her eyes hit the floor.

"Humiliation. Torture," he added.

More tears squeezed through the wet lashes.

"And you'd let him have your life too?"

Her eyes popped open, met his.

He was pleased by the faint glimmer of defiance.

"What good is it to me now? To anyone?"

"You tell me. No one else has that answer. Not even Jaden."

"She recorded my statement. She knows how it feels."

"Whatever." Brian shrugged. "Have a seat. Wait for her." He turned away, pretending to ignore her as he waited for her next move.

"I'm useless," she said, still rooted at the doorway. "I can't even step onto the street anymore."

"That limits your options."

She hissed at him. "You're an ass."

He laughed. "Sticks and stones."

"Huh?"

"Never mind. What's your name?"

"Leigh."

"Well, Leigh, what d'ya know about makeup?"

"Enough."

"I don't know squat," he lied. "Care to lend me a hand while you wait?" He caught the wary gaze and sent her an easy smile. "You can leave the door open."

Out of sight at the end of the hall, Jaden marveled at his technique with the fragile girl. Maybe the man had one redeeming quality after all. But it was one thing to help a victim take a step toward true survival and renewed life. Quite another to help a timeless survivor bent on defeating an evil you called friend.

Chapter Six

Time Stamp: 1542

The tapestry quivers as if stirred by the air, though he room is stifling. Still, I follow milady's orders, shutting the windows tight and keeping the fire ablaze. Tending her every whim has become tedious and hot work these last days. She sulks, eating little and crying much. I worry for her, though whatever causes her distress is beyond my place to ask. Loosening my gown, I fan the stale air into my shift, wishing I could dispense with it as well.

Settling onto my pallet near the window, I am sorely tempted to open it for some small relief. Then the tapestry falls to the floor and several men burst into the chamber, knives glinting in the moonlight. I cry out to alert milady, but they've bound her before I can be of any help. Tears flood her face while I plead for her life and I am near grateful to be seized as well. Whatever happens, she will need me, of that I am sure.

Satisfied in his disguise as one of Micky's mules, Brian stepped into the hallway and made his way back to the first junction they'd passed on the way in. With a steady stride despite the heeled boots, he followed his innate sense of direction and worked his way toward the back of the warehouse building. Falling in with a group of girls, he found himself in what looked like an old college dorm. With less style.

"You're new?" a woman asked.

Not trusting his voice, Brian only nodded. At first glance, he would've pegged her around fifteen years old. But her voice and a closer look revealed a woman in her twenties.

"Don't be shy. C'mon join some face time."

He shook his head and kept moving. Another open door proved the girls were as close as family. The open-door policy proved their contentment with the situation. The bits of conversation filtering into the hallway convinced him he was better off a man. Any public discussion of a bikini wax should be outlawed.

Outside, Brian fell into the rhythm of the street and absorbed the pulse of his city. He'd always felt this raw edge is where the city really came alive. Down here, facing life and death on every corner, you earned a different viewpoint. You appreciated the smallest blessings and learned to let the rest roll off. And you got damn good at recognizing the good and bad in those around you.

If he were completely honest with himself, he'd have to say meeting Jaden on the street, he'd known she was more than the thief she'd presented. And in her apartment, the courthouse, the alley, he'd seen integrity in her eyes.

He wanted to see insanity, at the least. He wanted to see anything but the weary determination that called out to him to believe.

But believe *what*?

He could believe the Judge wasn't perfect. He could admit the man was power hungry—but capable of the travesties she implied?

He didn't *want* to believe that. He didn't want to accept he'd been duped or used all these years. But he also knew that crimes didn't get solved if he boxed himself in with emotions.

"Going somewhere, beautiful?" Jaden asked, materializing at his side.

No sense wasting time wondering how she'd found him. "Yeah. I need to pick up something from my dear departed brother."

He noticed she'd scuffed herself up a bit so they both looked like they'd just come off a hard shift at a local sweatshop. With rounded shoulders and a worn sling bag, she'd blend into the ever-shifting background easily enough.

"So you're trying to be the sister the Chief never mentioned?"

"Would you mention me?" He smiled.

Jaden found herself smiling back. Looking him over, she decided no one would give him more than a passing glance. The boots explained his height, the wig and makeup were overdone. He stood out, yet his police buddies would label him a gender freak and ignore him. Not a bad plan.

"So you're along as my supportive friend?"

She wanted to be honest, but it didn't seem quite right to nail him with his earliest failures. Especially when he was dressed as a girl. "If we're friends, we'll have to discuss cramps and men. You sure you're up for it?"

"On second thought..."

She laughed. "What's your plan? Get arrested for solicitation?"

"Something like that."

"Why not make it easy and use your access card? They haven't cleared it yet."

"It was in my jacket." He shot her a look. "Hey, how would you know if it's cleared?"

"I know quite a bit about codes, processors and the habits of the police force."

"Why and how?"

"Survival 101, girlfriend: know the enemy."

"Odd outlook for a rogue security specialist."

"You mean *dead* rogue security specialist. I suppose the dead part's been my real problem all along," she muttered.

"Meaning?"

She shook her head. "Later." She pointed toward the police station a few blocks over. "What's your plan?"

He stopped and she watched his eyes fog in thought. "I'll walk in, explain how my brother, the chief, called me about something and go from there."

"Your plan's doomed."

"Really?" He crossed his arms over his fake breasts. "You got something better?"

She lifted one shoulder. "I don't even know what you're after."

"I need to pick up something from my desk."

"What sort of something?"

"Just something I picked up."

"Oh! That little bauble from the museum gift shop?" she said more loudly than necessary.

His eyes darted around, searching out eavesdroppers or worse. But the street was empty.

"Nervous?" she teased.

"No."

"Then, why the jitters?" She stilled the fake red nails drumming against his opposite arm.

He froze, staring first at her hand, then her face. His eyes captivated her, transporting her to another time and place before the dark reality of her recycled lives began.

"Who are you, Jaden Michaels?"

His question yanked her back to the present dilemma. "Just a woman on a mission, girlfriend. Let's do this thing."

Who am I? She sulked as they angled toward the alley between the station and the holding cells. *Who am I?* If just once he'd remember maybe they'd be done with all this. But no, Mr. Jigsaw here, needed to fit all the pieces of the puzzle together. Trouble was he'd never adapted to the evolving picture.

"Okay. Let me do the talking," he said.

"Why don't you let me take us in?"

He stared at her.

She laughed, nudged him and kept moving. "You're blowing our cover. Girls like us would be looking for a night out, not a heart to heart on the street. Thought you were good with the whole deep-undercover thing."

At the next corner, she turned to double back to the side entrance nearest his office.

"I am." He bit out the words. "I know what I'm doing."

"Uh-huh." She eyed the lock system. "Now be prepared. It's likely to be eulogy central in there. Don't let it go to your head and forget what you came for."

"No chance."

She slid an access card through the lock and pushed the door open. "Then let's get going and get gone."

Brian followed instead of arguing. Until the high heels biting his feet clacked loudly against the floor. In front of him, Jaden's heels were silent. "How do you do that?" he hissed.

She tossed a feminine, superior glance over her shoulder

and continued toward his office.

He opened his mouth, but familiar voices from the detective's bullpen made him forget any smart-ass comeback. What was Judge Albertson doing here?

"Has the suspect been apprehended?" the Judge asked.

Jaden froze, listening intently for the reply.

"You mean the escapee?" Loomis snarled.

"Whomever! Transport will come under investigation for this fiasco," the Judge shouted.

"It was your damned verdict. None of this shoulda happened."

"You will not speak to me like that!"

Jaden twitched and Brian yanked her back before she could lunge into the bullpen. Exposing themselves now wasn't the way.

Flicking the ridiculous bauble hanging from his ear he made his point. His disguise wasn't up to direct scrutiny. Her eyes dark with irritated resignation, she gave a clipped nod and they ducked into his darkened office together.

She stayed at the door, crouching beneath the window to keep watch and listen to the flaring tempers. If circumstances were different, he'd allow himself to notice the fine cut of her legs, the smooth stretch of skin that on any other woman might have him itching to touch.

But stuck in both harsh reality and female costume, Brian focused on recovering the necklace. Using the master code rather than his personal code, he unlocked the desk drawer. Within seconds the opal and his spare gun were tucked safely away in the mammoth shoulder bag. On reflex, he skimmed the reports lying on his desk and snagged a redlined file before pulling Jaden away from her post.

Back on the street, the raging argument in their wake, a

much-too-quiet Jaden matched his quick pace as he aimed for the nearest el platform.

"We'll switch trains a couple times before we head back."

"Better off walking," she countered, refusing to even climb the stairs.

"Not as women."

"Afraid you can't handle yourself in heels?" She strolled away with an ease he envied.

"I'm doing fine," he called after her. But he'd never try this stunt again. He tugged his oversized purse back onto his shoulder and thought back over those reports. "I'm sorry about your friend," he said when he'd caught up with her.

"Brenda?"

He'd meant Larry, but he followed her lead. "She lived in Pierview, right?"

"Yeah. That was the murder-suicide call?"

He nodded.

"And the evidence points to Brenda's ex, today's defendant, right?"

He nodded again. "You're not surprised."

"Not a bit. And if you are, you're not the police chief the masses adore. Especially after watching my place go up in flames."

"All right, your place made me think. But your attitude tells me you know something about the scene at Brenda's."

"Yup. I know Judge A ordered it."

Brian shook his wigged head. "So now you're psychic– and me without a hotline."

"I'd normally be happy to kick your butt for that comment. But seeing how Brenda's only as dead as the two of us, I'll let it pass."

"H-how's that?" Brian sputtered, catching his heel in the

cracked sidewalk.

"I changed her ID. The transport officer took her to a safe house. By now I suspect she's halfway to Cuba."

"You can't do that. You have no–"

"Authority?" She quirked a high and mighty brow. "I've got all the authority I need."

"I was going to say proof. And what about the bodies? The evidence?"

"Oh, build a bridge, girlfriend. If you really searched the records you've seen evidence manipulated. You know the proof was real in Brenda's case. And isn't gathering more proof your top priority right now?"

"No." He twisted in his skirt. "Right now, I'd kill for my boxers."

"Boxers? I was sure the chief wore briefs."

He didn't have a chance to reply. A blow to his back knocked him face-first to the pavement. Gasping for air, he struggled to keep his wits, and his purse, with him. Gathering the bag to his midsection, he rolled away from the would-be thief.

Brian anticipated the next advance and dodged. Coming to his feet, he spun and jumped his attacker, landing on top of him and stealing the mugger's air. Denying the savage urge, he rendered his attacker unconscious with one quick blow, instead of pummeling the bald head to the concrete.

He looked around for Jaden, fearing the worst, only to see her sparring with a second thug. And sparring was the word. Her relaxed stance and easy block of the each advance contradicted the life or death reality of the scene.

Suddenly a kick connected with her side and she doubled over, bringing Brian to his senses. Gaining his feet despite the tight skirt, he came to her aid. This wasn't some bizarre pay-per-view video. This was all too real. Before he could help, he realized Jaden had feigned the weakness to draw her opponent closer for the debilitating combination of elbow to solar plexus and hammer fist to neck.

The immediate crisis over, Brian dug into his bag for plastic restraints to confine the assailants.

"Where'd you get those," Jaden asked, dusting the fight off her palms.

"Office." He bent over, hands on thighs, trying to catch a deep breath. He couldn't get the image of an injured Jaden out of his head. He didn't want to dwell on why he felt such a desperate rush to protect her. Not even thinking of the business at hand swept his mind clear, though he tried.

"We need to ID these two." He nudged the unconscious thugs lying between them with his toe. "And decide how to contact the nearest precinct." He took a step and turned his ankle. "Well, damn. The heel's broken."

Jaden found the broken piece and toyed with it. "Y'know, you make one really lousy woman."

"Well, praise God for small favors."

Her mouth fell open and those lovely amber eyes went wide. He swiveled around, braced for another attack, when the most remarkable thing happened.

She laughed.

"What's so funny?" he demanded.

Jaden's face ached with the grin she couldn't stop. His disguise wouldn't fool anyone now. The wig and skirt were well off center, the makeup and shoes ruined.

"Give me your other shoe." She held out her hand, waiting. When he handed it over she broke the heel off and handed it back.

"The rest of the walk will be easier."

"Thoughtful looks good on you," he muttered, forcing his feet back into the mangled footwear.

"Don't tell anyone."

"Real kindness would be taking the el." He sent her a hangdog look.

"Rome wasn't built in a day, Suzie Q." She walked away.

"What about these two?"

She shrugged. "Let the neighborhood deal with its own. We've got a lead to follow."

"What lead?" He fell into step with her and leaned over her shoulder.

She fluttered the scrap of paper, worn from folding and unfolding. "Check this out. It's a map of sorts."

"Ah, hell. You made us targets?"

"You're a very bright girl, aren't you?" she said, studying the map, trying to decipher symbols along the side. Then she glanced back up to see his face dark with temper. "Oh, ease up. We conquered."

"Some warning would've been nice," he groused. "You could let me in on your plans."

"I think that skirt's gone to your head. You know how undercover work goes. Besides, trouble's never too far away."

"In your case, I agree completely."

She refused to let him get under her skin. He'd be out of the picture soon anyway. Providing she could persuade him to let her go as soon as she'd killed the Judge.

Jaden stuffed the map into her pocket and they continued on toward Micky's. She mulled over what she'd heard in the station house and what they'd dealt with on the street. "You handled yourself well, Brian."

"For a desk jockey?"

"Where'd you pick that one up, a retro site?" To her surprise, he gave his answer some thought.

"I'm not sure. My slang's always been a little behind the times."

Jaden ordered the eager sensation near her heart to stop. Just because he used outdated euphemisms didn't mean he'd be receptive to the notion of having lived, loved and let her down, repeatedly, over the past millennia or so.

Rounding the corner to Micky's place, she stilled, struck by a memory of this same neighborhood in the early nineteen hundreds.

"Want me to carry that for you?"

"The map?"

"No." He smiled and alarms went off in her head. "The chip on your shoulder."

She flicked an imaginary speck of dirt from the point in question. "Nah, I'm good."

And just that simply, she ditched the sweetness of nostalgia for the bitter present and stormed through the gates of Micky's fortress.

They reached the suite, thankfully without having to chat with Micky or any of his girls. She was in no mood for anything that didn't further her mission.

"So what'd we steal?" she asked when the suite door closed behind Brian.

He gently set the purse aside. "We *recovered* a necklace."

Her curiosity reared up. "From the museum? Can I see it?"

"Here?" He stripped off the wig and unzipped the skirt.

"We're safe enough." She wiggled her fingers eagerly. "Have you had it appraised?"

"Obviously not."

"Because?" She mentally crossed her fingers. Maybe he remembered having it commissioned all those lives ago.

"It *is* technically stolen property."

She slumped back onto the couch and closed her eyes. She couldn't bear to look at her past, likely present and future executioner anymore.

"Besides," Brian continued, "I don't really care what it's worth. I feel a sort of connection to it. I like it."

She peeked, watching him from beneath her lashes. She saw him stash the velvet bag way back into a drawer before heading to the bathroom.

"So you'll want to return it to its rightful owner?"

"Yeah. I'll get on that just as soon as my manhood's restored."

She chuckled, but kept her eyes shut until she heard the door close and the ionic shower begin. Then she went straight for the necklace.

And taking it in her hands again, she felt the years slip away. Once more she was young and in love. She could smell summer roses. The sunshine danced on the water, every diamond-drop a tiny reflection of the abundant hope within her heart.

But surrounding the warm edges of that glory crept the familiar haze of fear for her future, both mortal and eternal.

Brian stepped out of the bathroom, content once more in boxers and the more masculine jeans and T-shirt. He considered himself as prepped as ever for the next verbal attack from Jaden when the look on her face stopped him cold.

She held the necklace with reverence and longing. Her face glowed with what, on any other woman, he'd label as love. Clearly she was caught up in a daydream. As awful as the day had been, he hesitated to steal the moment from her. But when her expression changed to vivid, gripping sorrow, he intervened.

"Here. Let me."

"I just wanted to see it."

Her thready voice troubled him more than the grief in her eyes. "I know. I have to look at it, too." He had to hold it or struggle with his twitchy hands and rapid heart rate.

She blinked, and the word vulnerable popped into his mind. A word wildly unsuited to Jaden. "It's okay," he soothed. "Weird, but okay. We'll figure it out."

"Figure what out?"

"This whole bizarre situation–"

She was glaring at him now and the vulnerability evaporated under the quick head of steam building with her temper. "Calm down, Jaden" he soothed as she came to her feet, necklace swinging from her locked fist.

"Why him?" she asked with a calm voice completely at odds with her flashing eyes.

"I'm not tracking."

"What draws you to him? What keeps you close when you know he's no good?"

"First of all, I know no such thing. There's no evidence to point to the Judge for the crimes against these girls."

"'These girls' aren't good enough for you? These girls want lives, families. These girls are trying to survive in a whacked society set against them. These girls are brave enough to keep surviving and you don't give a damn simply because they're mules?"

He waited to be certain her outburst was spent. "Quit twisting my point. There's no evidence, Jaden. And from a security stand point–is the Judge a likely threat?" He saw the fury blaze across her face and braced himself. But her expression mellowed into resignation.

"I don't want to fight with you," he continued. "I want to figure this out so we can restore your life. And mine." And why did he feel better thinking those lives should be intertwined?

Because she was a danger to herself, if no one else. Going off half-cocked against the likes of the Judge. Going out of her way to prove him wrong, to embarrass him in his own courtroom. She'd been baiting him—oh shit—could she be right? Could the Judge be pissed off enough to blow her place?

"That should be enough. You'll have your evidence and I'll prove I can play nice with others."

He hadn't heard a word she'd said.

"Well, coming sheriff?"

"That's Chief to you."

She gave a half smile and a shrug. "Same diff."

"Haven't heard that one in forever."

"Me neither. Put that away and let's rock."

He stashed the necklace and then rummaged through the purse for the gun and ammunition. There was no telling what she'd planned while he'd been shuffling facts in his head.

It seemed safe to bet on danger.

Jaden pushed open the discreet door between Micky's office and his security center. "Let's start here." She ignored the panel of monitors, hoping Brian would do the same. "I've matched up routes and schedules with attacks." She approached the table covered with her research and lit up the small computer that held Micky's personal notes.

"Any trends yet?"

She shook her head. "Not anything obvious, but–"

"Random may be the pattern," he finished for her.

"Right.   Micky's mules--girls," she amended pointedly, "work their routes alone.   Just one more thing tucked into a purse or backpack."

"Then who busted the route? And how?"

"You know anything's for sale. But if you're at the top of the pyramid, you can see it all."

"I thought Micky topped this food chain."

"Micky thought so too."   Jaden looked up from the maps and notes on the table.   "Why haven't you ever busted him? Not even a single inspection under false pretense."

"Despite your glowing opinion, Ms. Michaels, my department doesn't operate that way."

She snorted.   "Of course it does. Micky runs sugar and nicotine, both banned substances, yet you've never hauled him in."

Brian shuffled his feet and became too interested in the paperwork. "He's not hurting anyone."

"Tell that to the Health Coalition."

"I have."

A trembling began in her knees, making Jaden glad for the nearby chair. She collapsed into it just as whimpers of a young new victim played an ominous backdrop to this revelation.

"When?"

"Four or five years a–"

She launched herself from the chair to his arms.

"Whoa, Bessie."

She wished she could laugh at his archaic turn of phrase. But her priority was holding on to him, to separate herself from the victim's agony. She heard him muttering nonsense in her ear, felt his hands soothe the bunched muscles along her spine and reveled in it a moment, before cursing her weakness.

"Sorry." She leaned back a bit, and then dared a full step more. But she kept her fingers twined with his as she resumed her seat.

"Can I have this back?" He tried to extricate his hand.

"No. Not yet." She checked the wall clock. "Five minutes, maybe ten."

"Explain," he ordered.

"Eventually."

With her free hand she scrolled through Micky's notes on his routes. "Trouble began about eighteen months ago."

"No connection there."

"I see a clear connection. Right there." She pointed.

Behind her, Brian snorted. "So Micky sees the Judge dining with the Health Chairman, so what? It's a free country."

"Used to be freer."

"That's not a word."

"Self appointed chief of the grammar police, now?" Aggravated, she tossed his hand back before checking the time. But her mind was her own, her eyes and ears only subject to the immediate irritants of the man next to her.

"If you won't dig into the Judge, please dig into the Health Chairman. He's the highest ranking official in the state."

"Leo Kristoff's clean."

"Not after dining with the Judge," she sneered.

"Hey, I've shared many a meal with Albertson." Brian held up a surrendering hand. "I know. I dug into the Judge's case file and saw your point."

She folded her arms across her chest. "But it didn't matter."

"It didn't convince me Albertson's the bad guy."

She sniffed.

He scowled. "Get up." He helped her to her feet, a bit

roughly, but when she saw what he was up to she forgot to be offended.

Relief washed through her as Brian used the computer to hack into the police system. After several minutes he'd found and accessed files Chairman Kristoff had surely paid dearly to bury.

The current guru of good health had been caught during a bust of a specific back room of a mid-town restaurant. A room known to cater to the more disreputable desires of man.

"A dirty little town you run, sheriff."

"We all have a little grime under our nails."

Wasted breath to argue the truth. Before she opened her mouth, he said it for her.

"Even the judge."

"No way," she gushed.

"Way." He tapped the screen.

Her eyes widened. Only six months ago, Kristoff had been accused of contributing to the delinquency of a minor. Except the victim wasn't under eighteen. The case was thrown out of Albertson's courtroom–after the accuser was sentenced to two weeks of injections for attempted slander of the Chairman.

"But you'll say coincidence and hang me for murder in about two weeks."

"And here I thought you knew the system. You won't swing–you'll get a nice civilized injection."

"So will you, if we're caught. Now that you believe me, log off and let's get moving."

"Hold on. I believe Albertson's meetings are questionable, I believe you think he hurt you, but–"

"You don't believe in past lives, eternal purpose or much else I have to say. Got it."

His hand landed on her arm with just enough persuasion to keep her still. "Get this. I believe in justice and in the system designed to uphold it. If Albertson's abusing his power, I want him out as much as you do."

"That's not possible," she quipped, impatient to finish her task. Even to the apparently unalterable end.

"You don't believe me?"

She didn't care for his challenging tone. "I have reason to doubt you."

"Same goes." He came to his feet, crowding her.

Three ways to take him down came to mind immediately. All of them evaporated under the assault of his lips on hers. She matched his daring and raised with her passion. Pent up from centuries of abject longing, she poured herself into him.

He broke the kiss, but his mouth hovered so his words brushed her lips. "Trust me, Jaden."

How absurd that her heart should want to leap from her chest. This was a physical ploy, nothing more. She knew it. She understood the game better than most.

Too bad she couldn't recall the rules.

Chapter Seven

Time Stamp: 1215

I sank the dagger deep into his inconsistent blubber and seethed. For he laughed at me even as his blood pooled at my feet. Then his black soul slipped free.

Alas, the deed was again fruitless. I knew it before the cold sting of forged steel severed my head. The demon still held the advantage.

My lifeless body lay twisted and foreign beneath me as my soul rose, already fashioning apology and plea. For failure served no one and meant only more pain. When would my mission be fulfilled?

He'd give a year's salary to read her mind. Even the nastiest interrogation methods wouldn't pry open a steely mind set on keeping secrets. And Jaden clearly had secrets.

He wanted to know if that kiss had left her reeling. If her response had been as unstoppable as his instigation. He'd tried to tell himself he'd applied the kiss like a tool. A basic way to determine if a woman juiced HgH to keep up with the men. But the telltale copper taste was absent from her mobile mouth. Brian stifled a groan and thought of cold, dead, two-headed fish to alleviate the rush of hormones to his groin.

They were back on the street at her insistence, tailing a

mule–girl–on her way to a night job cocktailing on Wacker Street. Brian had more appreciation for his jeans and high tops after his stint in a skirt, but he still missed the familiarity of his jacket. Following Jaden's suggestion, he'd donned a Cubs ball cap, the better to play dead by.

He slid a glance over his 'partner', now a redhead thanks to a pixie-cut wig. With her tinted glasses, flowing dress and sandals, she looked nothing like the Jaden he expected. The only give, and only someone very close would notice, was her wary, take-it-all-in way of watching the world.

People continued to crowd into the restaurant district on this sultry near-summer evening. Left to his own, this would be a night he'd grill a steak and catch the game, but he supposed those easy nights were as dead as he supposedly was. His useless reverie died when Jaden tensed beside him.

"Another headache?" he asked. She'd had several; all shorter-lived than the one she'd experienced the night they met in her place.

"No." Her eyes were set on a corner at the end of the block. "Hang back a minute. Please?"

The manners were shocking enough. But he nodded and watched her approach a lanky man and a kid. They shied away at first, then whatever she said ended in a group hug. The scene made him all the more curious about the woman and her self-proclaimed mission. Disobeying her request, he joined them.

"Who's this?" the lanky man asked.

The kid blinked huge, suspicious eyes while Jaden surprised him by telling the truth. "The recently deceased Police Chief Thomas."

The man raised a brow, but stuck out his hand. "Cleveland."

Brian found the grip firm and the message in the hard eyes clear. Cleveland wanted Jaden kept safe. An easier task with a more pliable woman, but Brian suspected this guy knew the score.

"What's the trouble?" Brian asked.

"Quinn's sister is missing," Jaden replied.

"How long?"

"Since morning."

Brian nodded, slipping quickly into detective mode. "How old is she?"

Jaden's eyes flashed with gratitude. She'd caught his optimistic use of 'is'. First please, now thanks, what next?

"Twelve," the boy said.

Brian took a knee to look the kid in the eye. "Where were you and what were you doing?"

The boy swallowed, but answered with a sturdy voice. "We were stocking fruit for Caldwell's Deli. He trades an hour's work for breakfast, but you've gotta be the first one there and you can't bruise the apples."

Brian smiled at the kid's industry and waited for the details.

"Katie went to get another crate of reds and never came back."

Brian stood and shook his head. "We can call it in–"

"It's been nearly twelve hours," Jaden protested. "Cleveland, keep Quinn at your place. We'll meet there after I take a look around."

So much for manners and teamwork. Brian tugged Jaden back a step for an ounce of privacy. "What are you thinking? We're supposed to be tailing Maria."

"She's safe enough."

"Really?" Brian crossed his arms. "How'd you come to

that conclusion?"

She glared at him. "Her hair's black. Katie's a blonde and a preteen. Double jeopardy."

Brian opened his mouth but Jaden's voice came out.

"Look, he's a friend. They've got no one else. You go ahead and keep an eye on Maria. I'll get the girl back and we'll meet up later."

"No."

Her brows arched over those stupid blue glasses.

"No," he repeated. "It's foolish to split up. If you say Maria's safe, we'll go for the girl. Where do we start?"

The stunned expression on all three faces made him want to bruise more than a few apples. Why the hell did being a cop make him subhuman? He settled for issuing Jaden a challenge instead. "What? Not up to a rescue in sandals?"

"Anytime, anywhere, any dress code," she countered with her normal fire.

"Good luck," Cleveland said, fading into the dim alley with the kid.

When they were out of earshot Brian asked, "Where to, Sherlock?"

"Caldwell's, Watson." She led them down the block.

"You've got a hunch."

"Uh-huh."

"Will this hunch get me killed?"

She thought it over as they crossed the next street. "It might."

"You could sound a tad more upset by the possibility."

"No I can't. I have to consider the option that you being dead would make my life easier."

So now he was some 'thing' she was using for whatever purpose she deemed fit? While that might be a fun diversion behind closed doors, here on the street it gave him pause.

"But considering everything," she continued, "I think it's important that you live."

"How reassuring."

She gave a low laugh, a sound he thought might also have a whole new meaning behind closed doors. Then her hand landed on his arm and gripped hard.

"What is it?"

"Katie's a diversion. Call Micky."

"Come again?" He looked around for whatever alerted her as he pulled his cell card from his back pocket. He spoke the order and waited for the connection to go through. The sign on the nearest door marked it Caldwell's, but she walked past it toward the alley entrance. He heard a scuffle of rats, then an irritated groan.

"Diversion from what?" he asked.

She shushed him, released her hold and closed her eyes. When she looked at him again, her determination was clear. "Is he on?"

Brian handed over the wireless earpiece and watched her give orders to Micky. At least she bossed everyone equally. "Check on your girls." Pause. "Then make other arrangements. Turn." Pause. "Two hours."

She disconnected and looked up at him. "Maria will have to wait and hang on. I'm not letting the child suffer."

"Let me call the authorities."

Jaden shook her head and walked into the darkness.

Brian followed, frustrated, but determined in his own right. He just wished he understood what they were really up against. So far she'd offered him nothing concrete to implicate the Judge, though she'd set plenty of shadows into motion in his brain.

"Oh, poor baby." Jaden's voice came from a small circle of light breaking up the dark.

When she moved to the side, he saw a young girl taped into a chair. Eyes wide, face stained with tears, Brian felt the swell of disgust for whoever put her there.

He reached for his knife, but Jaden beat him to it, preparing to slice away the child's bindings.

"Stop!" he called. Her hand stilled. "She's wired to something."

The girl gave the tiniest nod, the move filled with sorrow and defeat.

"So she is. Your pal sure loves his explosives."

"You–"

"Save it until we get her out of here."

Brian dropped to the ground and studied the wiring. In the soft plastique explosive, he saw the imprint of a unique ring and hated the doubt rising like bile in his throat. The Judge, as he knew him, couldn't be doing this.

"Easy enough," Jaden said from the opposite side of the bomb.

He jumped to his feet. "Hold on a sec."

"We don't have the luxury. I'm a security expert, remember? I've seen this before and can deal with it."

"What if it's a dummy fuse?"

"Then you don't have to sweat who recognized you in drag." To the girl she said, "Don't worry, hon. It's almost over."

Before Brian could prescribe caution, she used the dagger to separate wires from plastique. He braced, but discovering they survived, he helped Jaden cut Katie free and scooped her up. The girl's bony frame cut into him as she clung to her newfound safety.

"Where to?" he asked, willing the surge of emotion out of his voice.

Jaden reached over, lifting her dress to dry the girl's face. "Cleveland."

For a moment he thought she meant the city.

Then she snaked an arm around his waist and nudged him deeper into the alley, away from the street. "We'll take the back way."

"What about the diversionists?"

"If we're lucky, we'll bump into them."

Her voice was granite. He'd never met a woman so eager for a fight. Then again, he'd never met a woman so certain she was meant to single-handedly save the female population from an elusive predator, either.

And too bad watching her was such a turn on. The thrill might get him killed for real next time.

No thugs showed up on the way to Cleveland's place. Too bad. Jaden still itched for a fight, needing to unload the remnants of adrenaline in her system on someone or something.

"Here we are," she said, covering her finger with her dress to press the antiquated buzzer.

"Paranoid, even for you," Brian accused.

For a moment she entertained an image of sparring with Brian. Horizontal or vertical—didn't matter, giving her crystalline awareness of the depth of her danger. Swallowing a retort, she smoothed a hand over the sleeping girl's hair.

The door swung open and they stepped off the raw edge of the street into a surprisingly posh lobby.

"Whoa," Brian said.

"I second that," she agreed. "Who knew thieves lived like

kings?"

"Do they live with conveniences like elevators?"

"You wish." Jaden laughed as she started up the stairs. His grumbling wasn't all an act, though Katie was underfed, she had to be getting heavy by now.

Cleveland stood silent at the third floor landing. Behind him, Quinn shifted from foot to foot, shameless worry stamped on his face.

"Is she d-dead?" Quinn asked.

"Not at all," Brian said, his voice a strong counterpoint to the quaking boy's. "I bet she'd like some water and a blanket. Can you find those?"

Quinn dashed off.

Jaden stilled, impressed with Brian's thoughtfulness, while Cleveland ushered him inside to settle Katie on the couch.

"Coming?" Cleveland called back.

"Yeah. Sure." She entered, and then stalled out again. "Haven't seen one of these in awhile," she murmured to Cleveland, as she crossed the Aubusson carpet in the foyer.

"It took a small fortune, but I liked it."

Jaden grinned. "Don't you mean *you* took a small fortune?"

"One day girl, you'll stop giving me crap over the rep I earned as a kid."

"Sure thing, Cleve." She hugged him hard. "Can you help me clean her up?"

He nodded, his eyes troubled. "The kit's all ready. On the counter." His hand on her arm stilled her. "How bad?"

"Nothing that will scar," Jaden said with a meaningful stroke of her ear.

Cleveland exhaled his relief and mumbled a prayer Jaden found appropriate.

She smiled, gently imposing herself between the siblings. As she eased the blanket back to clean Katie's wounds, Quinn made himself scarce and Jaden blanched.

On Katie's wrist was the diamond bracelet the Judge had baited her with in his chambers. Message received. And proof that Katie's peril had been a diversion. Judge Albertson knew far too much about Jaden's movements and weaknesses. She put the troubling development out of her mind, Katie needed her now.

Not once did the girl fuss about the sting of the antiseptic swab or the wound-sealing laser. Even set on the lightest mode for minor surface skin repair, patients complained of the heat. Jaden made a mental note to find out how Cleveland had acquired the special issue medical tool.

"How's our girl?" Brian asked handing Jaden a tall glass filled with a golden, bubbling liquid.

"She's a champ. Nearly good as new."

But who knew if she'd ever be safe again. Jaden had to find a way to draw the Judge away from people she'd come to think of as family.

"Do we have to go now?" Quinn asked.

Cleveland joined them, setting down a sterling silver bucket filled with ice and a bottle of whatever beverage he'd served. Then he wrapped an arm around the boy's shoulder.

"I figure you'd better hang with me awhile."

"No parents?" Brian whispered in Jaden's ear.

She shook her head, as much to gain space as to answer him. Then she made the mistake of sipping her drink, and swore softly as the alcohol burned her lip.

She cursed again, this time mentally, as Brian's intense focus landed on her face.

"What's this?" he asked, taking her chin in his hand.

"Pretty bad bite."

"Pretty big bomb," she muttered, unwilling to admit any further frailties.

He reached over and drew an ice cube from the bucket. Gently, he stroked her lip with the ice and she felt her knees weaken in response. She liked it much better when he was doubtful and impossible. She couldn't afford the additional hazard of being attracted to him. Again.

Who was she kidding? She was into him, wanting him already. And after that kiss she knew it wouldn't be a simple itch she could scratch and walk away from. Giving in to the physical wouldn't be enough and broaching the emotional was out of the question.

And based on that damned bracelet, when she faked his death she'd sent him straight to the top of the Judge's hit list.

"Such storms," he murmured.

"Huh?"

"In your eyes, Jaden. Such storms in your eyes."

She snapped them shut, willing him to go away. When he did, she let her tongue roll over her lip, tracing the path of his touch, catching the lingering taste of him.

Behind her, Brian asked the girl questions about the people who'd taken her. Jaden moved to a safer distance across the room. Under the guise of studying some incredible art, most likely original, and several equally valuable porcelain figures, she listened to Katie's answers.

To his credit Brian didn't ask leading questions and he appeared to take all her replies at face value. Jaden appreciated that, for Katie's sake.

To Jaden it was all too obvious who was behind the attack and when the name circling around her mind was echoed aloud, she started.

"Didn't mean to scare you," Cleveland apologized.

"No problem." Jaden stepped out onto the balcony to prevent the children from overhearing. "Are you really going to keep the kids?"

"Why not? I've got room to spare and no one else cares about 'em."

She nodded. It was sad, but typical in this neighborhood. Hell, it had been typical in all sorts of neighborhoods throughout time.

"You can't blame yourself," he said.

"I can if I'm unable to stop him." She turned to face her friend, and then realized the mistake. From this angle she could see Brian interacting with the kids. No, interacting was sterile. He was nurturing, assuring, showing kindness to two small strangers. She struggled to find solid ground. "You've got room all right. And it's filled with perfect replicas."

Cleveland only gave her that priceless wink. "So the kids don't have to worry about breaking anything."

"Uh-huh." She bumped his shoulder and risked another glance into the apartment. Quinn hovered between Brian and Katie, then seemed to convince Brian to take a tour of Cleveland's unique collections.

"You could call child services."

"Could, but they'd just run away. Quinn didn't find the system appealing. Neither did Katie."

"Who did what to them?"

"Let it go, Jade. You've got your own battles to fight. I'll handle theirs."

She raised the glass, carefully sipped around her sore lip and savored the warm slide of the drink on her throat.

"You'll teach them to thieve and pillage," she teased.

"Everyone needs a skill set."

She heard a silly giggle pop out of her mouth and wanted to know what sort of drink he'd given her. But then the apartment erupted into a flurry of excitement that surged out to meet them.

"Check this, Jaden!" Quinn exclaimed. He shoved a small flat rectangle toward her. "How cool is that? You look just like her! Who is it, Cleveland?"

Jaden stared into a small portrait from the nineteenth century.

"Brian says it's a flake–"

"Fluke," his sister corrected.

Jaden knew better. It was no fluke that the diary, necklace and now this had turned up here and now. For a moment she studied Cleveland, asking silently about the acquisition. It had been tucked away in her apartment just a week ago.

"And here I trusted you not to rip from me," she whispered.

"I could hardly let this one go by," he confessed with a sheepish smirk.

She felt a ridiculous urge to thank him, but before the words tumbled out, Brian's voice broke the mood.

"Thanks for the hospitality. We'll be going." He handed Jaden's glass to Katie and gripped her elbow with convincing force.

"Sure thing," Cleveland called after them. "Take care, girl."

The door prevented her from even trying to reply. She turned her attention to Brian. "What's the hurry, Sheriff?"

He stopped at the next landing and used his grip to spin her around to face him. The motion carried her into his chest. She didn't care for his strong-arm tactics or her body's response.

"I've been patient. Now I want answers."

"Yes, sir."

He shoved the small-framed portrait at her. "What sick game are you playing?"

"Release me."

"No."

"No?" With little effort she could kill him in seconds.

"I could kill you just as easily. And be happier for it, I'm sure."

Had she spoken aloud?

"The fury's all over your face," he continued, startling her more. "Answers. Why commission something like this?"

She tried to put herself in his place. Bizarre didn't begin to cover it. She sighed. "It's not a fake or a fluke. Or an ancestor. That's me about two hundred years ago."

The bare truth earned her release as his hands fell to his sides and his jaw dropped open.

"I found it in an online estate sale. The dated signature puts it about a week before you hanged me for murder."

Brian's mouth moved, but nothing intelligible came out.

She couldn't blame him for slipping into a stupor. It was hardly fair for him to be cheated of even a few sketchy facts when she, and probably Albertson, had nearly full recall. After all, he was an integral character in their recurring drama. He alone was denied the 'gift' of awareness. Whatever the reason, it was a cruel twist of their intertwined fates.

"You. You called me sheriff."

She barely made out his graveled whisper. Tucking the portrait into her pocket, she linked her hand with his. "Never again." She guided him, one slow step at a time. "I promise."

What else could she offer but inadequate words? She knew she was promising an end to more than a bad nickname.

She intended, one way or another, to be sure they never relived this cycle again.

From Brian's back pocket, the cell card chirped the arrival of a text message. He surprised her by recouping enough to read aloud the three words on display. "Maria is missing."

Chapter Eight

A statement by the Rev. J. Horsley, chaplain at Clerkenwell to W.T. Stead of the Pall Mall Gazette, July 1885:

"There is a monster now walking about who acts as clerk in a highly respectable establishment. He is fifty years of age. For years it has been his villainous amusement to decoy and ruin children. A very short time ago sixteen cases were proved against him before a magistrate on the Surrey side of the river.

The children were all fearfully injured, possibly for life. Fourteen of the girls were thirteen years old, and were therefore beyond the protected age and it could not be proved that they were not consenting parties.

The wife of the scoundrel told the officer who had the case in charge that it was her opinion that her husband ought to be burned. Yet, by the English law we cannot touch this monster of depravity, or so much as inflict a small fine on him."

–Article found in the diary of Gabriella Stamford.

Micky jumped on them the moment they entered the warehouse. "Following her was your idea!"

Jaden only nodded. The fighting spirit completely vacant from her eyes.

"And she vanishes into thin air."

"Naturally," Brian agreed.

Micky turned a violent shade of red. "She carries two grand in pure Columbian caffeine and you lost her. Get the hell out."

Brian smothered Jaden's mumbled consent with a vehement denial. "We are staying. One setback has you giving up? Some smuggler," Brian scoffed. "A crisis on the street, one likely connected to this whole mess, detained us. We made a choice, but we also made a commitment." He sent Jaden his best smile. "Class in the morning?"

"Sure."

Brian glanced back to Micky. "Tell your girls to be ready at eight." He strode off, Jaden in tow, before Micky could muster a contradiction.

"That's better," Jaden said when the door closed behind them. "Thanks."

"Hold that thought." Brian considered it a triumph that he didn't just flay her on the spot. Now he set his temper free. "Let me see that portrait."

He studied every nuance of her as she pulled it from her pocket. Steady hands, steady gaze, not a twitch or a sigh. She was good.

He indulged his curiosity with a long look into the picture of those same intense green eyes, the high, elegant cheekbones and the full lips. Then he tossed it onto the table. "It has to be fake. Just admit it and we'll move on."

Her only answer was a silent caress of the polished frame.

"Enough, Jaden! Or whoever you are. Why bring me into whatever this is?"

With a sad smile, she stood and moved to the kitchen, giving the photo a place of honor on a shelf on the way. He watched her rinse dishes, load the dishwasher and then program it to run.

Gathering her sandals and his watch, she went to the bedroom, returning after a moment with a small, worn book. The woman's calm efficiency was infuriating.

The initial shock of her story had burned away with the long walk and Micky's absurd reaction about Maria. Like the man hadn't been losing mules fast enough on his own.

Brian wanted answers, real answers. He wanted to argue, to sink his teeth into a real fight. Instead she sat there reading as if she didn't have a care in the world.

"Just talk to me," he said, sliding into the chair across from her. "You dragged me into it and I'm not going anywhere till it's finished."

"What is 'it'?"

His mouth opened for a swift reply, but the words dried up. "I don't know," he confessed.

"And that bothers you most of all."

So she did see straight through him. He suppressed the urge to shift under his crawling skin. "Yes."

"What will convince you?"

"Tell you what," he countered. "You start at the beginning and I'll tell you when I'm sold."

"Which beginning?"

He came to his feet, shoving hands into his back pockets and filling his chest with air. "Pick a beginning."

"Once upon a time?" She put what appeared to be a diary into his hands. "You can read it yourself. When you're done I'll explain the picture."

He could hardly argue, especially since she'd already left the room. Against his better judgment, he squashed the idea that they were wasting time and began to read through the entries of a young lady clearly in love.

The tale wasn't so different from others he'd heard from the period, except that this was headed for a tragic ending for the star-crossed lovers.

The bastard wasn't worth her time, Brian decided reading how the young military officer refused to accept the lady's version of events.

Brian could sympathize with her disgrace and commend the lady's efforts on behalf of those less fortunate. He supposed he understood why she'd chosen to help prostitutes when she bore a similar, though unjustified, label herself.

Then the dates hit him. Jack the Ripper had been running tame on those very streets.

Brian was well versed in criminal history. Even now, experts examined the DNA and diaries like this one from the period trying to close those unsolved crimes. The lady of this diary was a true hero, committing her resources to save women no one reputable would be concerned about.

A particularly poignant passage jumped out. She'd seen her love in Vauxhall and come home in tears for what never could be. That's when recognition dawned.

Brian dropped the diary, scrambling to pull the opal from hiding. He flipped it over and read the inscription.

To my beloved Gabriella, My heart is ever yours, Byron

The opal pendant and the diary were from the same couple. And both must've been in the museum that night.

"Jaden?" he roared, turning. Then jolted to find her watching him from the couch.

"You've figured it out?"

"You can't be serious. Reincarnation is impossible. A hoax proved in...in..."

"In 2030, I believe. Some scientist came up with a

theory."

"Based on DNA combinations and the creation story."

"Oh, that's right. The first time the Bible was credited in a scientific study." She waved a hand in a dismissive, feminine, manner. He might've smiled if he'd found any humor in this.

"Boil it down Jaden." He slumped into the couch, keeping a cushion-width between them. "Just tell me what I need to know."

Her smile bloomed across her face and she toyed with several loose pages. "Finish the diary first."

"But the whole concept's impossible."

He turned the page, read about a murder plot and was quickly lost in the period and the lady's plight once more. Though, he couldn't help but commiserate with the victim.

Sure Gabriella had reason to despise the man who'd ruined her life, but Brian disapproved of vigilantes. And that's all she was—a well-bred English lady lost to the madness of grief and sorrow.

"She had no proof he assaulted other women." The look and sigh made him feel like a failing schoolboy. "Only the vague descriptions."

"Not vague. Each description matched the others. You have to see —" Her temper flashed and he silently commended her for controlling it this time. "I'm not the one who's blind, Brian," she said at last. "Read through those last loose pages."

He did. And it made sense, finally. This was an analogy of their current situation. That woman had wanted her lover to believe her, had been crushed, emotionally, socially, when he hadn't. He and Jaden weren't lovers but this was an effective way to lure him to her side, to her cause. But—

"I never wrote this."

"Of course you did." She stood, slipping back into the

best cure for her nerves: movement. "It's your handwriting, right?"

"It can't be. It's a forgery." He clung to the denial.

She paused, mid-stretch, and he could practically see her clever mind working over his statement. "Okay, we'll go with that for a moment. What does it mean that your best bud put a museum exhibit together full of fraudulent pieces?"

"That necklace is real. The museum staff authenticates everything."

She nodded, much too calmly. "And the names match those of the diary, correct?"

The hair on the back of his neck came to attention.

"I didn't write this."

"Then your pal made a pay off to get the diary in?"

"No."

She was laughing at him. It didn't show anywhere but her eyes. "Then what do you come up with?"

"It's a mistake. A misunderstanding."

"We agree there." She turned, bending at the waist, her golden braid brushing the floor. "Your mistake."

His mind fogged with how that flexible body would feel wrapped around him. Then he realized it must be a calculated part of her game. "No," he managed.

"Okay. I'll bite." She came upright with a cocky toss of her head. "What's your explanation?"

"Forgery isn't a new concept."

"So everything before your eyes, in your hands, is false?"

Damn her for making him sound like a fool. Even to himself. "What you're proposing is impossible."

"Used to be impossible to walk on the moon. Or the ceiling. Yet with the right equipment, neither is out of reach today."

"So how are you equipped, Jaden?" He was almost sorry he asked when the myriad expressions swept her face. He recognized humor and sorrow. And something fleeting he didn't want to label.

"I'm not sure how it works, and I don't know why—not entirely. I only know that every 'first' time he molests me I remember the others. Even before he strikes, I'm usually plagued with odd dreams and a sense of unrest. Never really fitting in. Then, when he attacks, I know." She tapped her fingers over her heart. "In here. The pieces fall into place and I know it's my job to stop the pain he causes."

"By killing him."

"I always try going through the justice system. He always circumvents it. And now he *is* the judge, with the police chief in his pocket."

He came to his feet to pace. The suite was too small, the air too thin, his chest too tight.

"I'm not in his pocket. I didn't know you before a few days ago. If I recall, we met over two dead bodies in your apartment."

"We met on the street for an evening of robbery," she said, pinning him with a sharp look. "And just why was that?"

He reluctantly considered the possibility that he'd been sent, used, that night. The whip-crack of self-doubt looked for a scapegoat and Jaden made a neat and nearby target.

"I'm beginning to believe part of your story," he confessed. At her single arched brow he finished, "The part where I put you out of my misery."

"Would you like to clarify that, Mr. Thomas?"

If looks were lethal, he'd be sitting in the hot seat of judgment about now. But this was the fight he'd been after. Angry, she might provide more truth than fairy tales. Angry, she might distract him from the gnawing fear that he had cause to buy into her story.

"Sure thing, Ms. Michaels. You said I hanged you two hundred years ago."

"Yes."

He advanced. She held her ground. This would be good. "Why would I do a thing like that?"

"Duty."

"It was my duty to go around hanging women?"

"It was your duty, as sheriff, to see a murderer swing for her crime."

He circled her as she answered. She didn't flinch. He came back around to face her. "Who'd ya kill?"

Her eyes hardened. "The town preacher."

Brian took an automatic step back. "Why the hell would you do that?"

"I found him raping an eight-year-old girl from his orphanage. I strangled him with my apron."

Game over.

"Shit. You're serious."

"Don't believe *me*, Thomas," she hissed. "Find an archive for Cedar Hill, Iowa. I was the devil's tool against a good man. A fine, upstanding man of God." The words were ground out between clenched teeth. "A good man with a taste for young, untried flesh and a master of manipulation."

She pressed in closer, eyes flashing. "Let me tell you how I know. In that life, I grew up in the orphanage he founded, helpless as the rest." Her hands fisted and he braced his jaw for a punch, but she whirled away. "Tell me how good is a man who promises a lonely girl a family if she'll just show a gift for obedience?"

"A gift for...oh, Lord, no."

"Don't say it!" she cried, spinning back to pummel him in the chest. He let her pound, knowing he deserved much worse. "It's too damned late now! I did everything I could and he wouldn't stop. I stayed and worked with that bastard. Tried to intervene. He wouldn't stop." Her fists slowed and she dropped her head to his shoulder. "He fooled everyone. Even you. And he wouldn't stop."

He wrapped her in his arms and denied himself the luxury of apologies. "You insisted on wearing your best dress. And refused your last meal."

Her head snapped up. "H-how? Do you remember?"

He shook his head. Tenderly, he dried her tears with his thumbs and went with the most convenient explanation, for now. "I just know my criminal history."

Jaden watched Brian sleeping on the couch, still marveling at the tenderness he'd shown by tucking her into bed. It seemed like days should've passed rather than mere hours.

She believed he knew his criminal history. Just as she believed there was more to it. She'd seen the clouds in his eyes before he'd shut her out.

And she'd been turning over the recent antics of the Judge. She understood his desire to eliminate her, but what good could come of eliminating Brian? Or had his presence at the explosion truly been an accident?

In the time she'd been awake, she'd skimmed the diary and letters again, finding no indication that Brian had memories of their shared history during that incarnation. She'd also made a list of Internet searches she wanted to try, providing she could grab a few minutes alone with a computer.

She sipped from her over-the-limit coffee with sheer gratitude and studied his restful face. Had she always found him handsome? No. There had been lives she hadn't known him at all until he struck the deathblow. Of course there had been lives in which she dreamed of the earthly pleasures of husband and family. Those dreams had starred the man with the penetrating pewter eyes.

Her watch hummed against her wrist, reminding her of the eight o'clock class. She rose, set a thermal mug of coffee within his reach and left, wondering which sort of ending her life would bear this time.

Brian came awake to the heavenly scent of coffee. Real coffee. Listening, he realized he was alone and decided Jaden's gift for stealth must serve her well in the security industry. Sitting up he scrubbed at his face, then scalded his tongue on the coffee.

She hadn't been gone long.

His stomach growled, but he ignored it in favor of checking on the necklace. Holding it, Jaden's face filled his mind, but it wasn't a recent memory. The woman was dressed in costume from a long dead era, the same era as the display they'd robbed. Gabriella.

Brian blinked the disturbing images away, replaced the necklace and headed to the bathroom. But his brain wouldn't be distracted with mundane routines. What had she said last night about suffering from strange dreams and restlessness?

It was the perfect opening and he'd let it pass. He understood the disconnection she felt. And the dreams, well, his could only be counted as nightmares. Rather than use the information to bond with her, he'd chosen silence. To deceive.

For a man sworn to uphold the law, he was getting damned good at deception.

He'd even overcome his guilty conscience where the

necklace was concerned. If the owner, Judge Albertson, didn't care about it and the museum wasn't wasting manpower on an investigation was it really 'stolen property'?

The old adage about trees falling unheard in the woods popped into his mind, unbidden and unwelcome.

The soft hum of the ionic shower ceased and Brian cursed the impossibly short setting. Slick Micky was sure miserly for a smuggler. It might be smart to look closer at the operation, though, seeing how his career in law enforcement might be over.

Brian slid back into his own jeans, but raided the closet for a new shirt. He wondered if it was like the small hotel refrigerators from years ago. Would Micky charge a ridiculous fee when Brian 'checked out' to resume his real life?

And how soon could that be arranged, he wondered. With a glance toward the opal's hiding place, Brian dug out the redlined evidence report he'd stolen from his own desk.

He'd asked for a rush on the charred webbing of Larry's restraints and now he was grateful. He hadn't killed his own man after all. It had been an act of sophisticated sabotage. He knew enough to recognize a Special Forces op. And he knew just who to call for a quiet inside favor. Reading through Loomis's notes confirming remnants of the same rare chemical solvent in the van, Brian still couldn't figure who would gain from Larry's death.

Jaden would surely blame the Judge Albertson. But maybe an overlooked detail in one of her cases could help him find another answer. Time to find her.

Striding down deserted hallways, Brian followed his instincts to Micky's office, but sounds from the main warehouse floor piqued his curiosity. At the door, he smiled at the scene below.

Jaden stood in front of forty or fifty women demonstrating combos of kicks and punches for purely aerobic benefit. They'd been at it for some time if the sweat was any indicator. She had the lithe, graceful and well-controlled body of a prime athlete. He watched her muscles bunch and stretch, coil and release and cursed the testosterone heating his blood. There wasn't room on this assignment for lust. He had to preserve the remote, undercover mentality. Anything less and he'd be lost with no hope of return.

"A woman on a mission," Micky said, beside him.

"Looks like."

"I appreciate it. My girls need the confidence out there."

"I'd think rough work would breed enough attitude to carry them through."

Micky's mouth thinned. "It's not rough work. I give these girls a roof if they need it, two meals a day and enough cash to function comfortably."

"And all they're giving is their lives." He wondered what got into him. Jaden's lecture or his own conscience?

"It's safe work," Micky snapped back. "They go to work, make a drop and come home. Maria was one of my best."

Before Brian could ask anything specific about the threat to the smugglers, Jaden's voice filled the room.

"Now, let's work on how to break away from an attacker." Her eyes landed on Brian, then slid down and over to Micky. "A little help, Slick?"

Micky made a quick descent to the front of the room to good-natured jeers and applause.

In Brian's estimation Micky didn't make a very convincing threat, so he slowly worked his way down the stairs and around the class.

"One. Elbow jab back." The mules repeated the move on

imaginary opponents.

"Two. Weight on back foot."

Compliance across the room.

"Three. Turn and drive knee to groin."

He winced, but agreed with her choice. A woman needed every advantage to buy a moment to escape or call for help. And no matter what sort of hormonal cocktail a man juiced himself with, his balls were always vulnerable.

"Okay. Now grab your purses."

General shuffling, chatter and water intake swirled around Brian.

"Your assistance, Mr. Thomas?"

He looked up at her, smiled and vaulted to her slightly elevated position, accepting the dare flashing in her eyes.

"Let's make this count," she said with a half grin. Then, donning a shoulder bag she turned to the class. "If you're approached from behind—"

Brian stepped into place and held her with one arm at her waist, the other on the bag.

"Let him think he has the bag." She relaxed her body.

Brian's mind blanked with the sudden pliant feel of her. He inhaled the contrast of honest sweat and her rose scented hair. Then he landed hard on his stomach, gasping for breath. He blinked, but the class was still there, laughing. Twisting around he saw her, triumphant foot planted between his shoulder blades, eyes blazing with humor and awareness.

"Can I get a rematch?" he managed after a moment.

She simply sparkled. "Maybe later."

He welcomed her assistance as he got to his feet. "Too bad I didn't know that little maneuver when I was toting a purse," he muttered for her benefit alone.

"Oh, you held your own."

"High praise from you."

"Yup." She straightened his collar. "Now outta here. I've got a class to cool down."

A wave of relief and a smattering of applause accompanied his return to the relative safety of Micky's office. He had a system to hack if his body would stop humming and let him sit still.

Dropping onto the stool in front of the computer Micky had brought in for him, Brian began the task. While he waited for the black screen to change to something informative, he scrubbed at his face.

The woman had assaulted his senses more than his body in the brief demo. And if the look in her eye was any indication, she knew, and enjoyed making him edgy. But there'd been something more in her gaze.

Brian recognized it as passion. Not sexual, this passion was deeper than the mere physical. The same passion he felt for upholding the law, she felt for arming these women to protect themselves. The same passion that drove him to play dead to prove Albertson's innocence drove her to evade authorities to prove the opposite.

Brian pressed his hands into his gritty eyes. It wasn't the sort of epiphany that gave a lawman comfort.

The speakers chimed and he brought the first search results on the screen into focus and sighed. It would take hours to unravel the long list of corporate dealings to find if Albertson himself owned anything outright.

Then a property address jumped out at him. Brian keyed in a more specific title search and gaped. What use could a judge make of a former steel mill in the ghost town of Gary? Based on Jaden's accusations, he wasn't sure he wanted to know.

"Well, damn."

"Another knock down?" Jaden teased from the doorway.

"You could say that." He waved her over, no point trying to hide this. "Just promise you'll take me with you when you go."

He watched her face, tired from exertion, light up with anticipation as the information sank in.

"In Gary?" she breathed.

"Apparently." He relished one minor consolation. "We'll have to take the el."

She groaned. "A car would give us a better egress."

"Throwing big security words around won't change my mind. We're going in together and we're taking the el."

"Whatever." She shrugged, but the casual gesture didn't fool him. "Check his court schedule. I can't go before tomorrow. I'm pinning the tail on Lorine today."

"Beg pardon?"

She grinned. "Just following your out-dated speech patterns. Thought it sounded better than 'tailing a mule'."

"I'll go with you."

"No."

Her whole body stiffened, making Brian realize her protective walls weren't so invisible. Again he regretted last night's missed 'bonding' opportunity. "I thought we were working together."

"We were. Are." She moved toward the door. "You work here today. I'll work out there." Halfway out the door she added, "Unless you're in a skirt-wearing mood?"

"No." He shuddered for effect and earned a quick laugh. "Be careful," he called, but she'd already gone.

In the scramble that was currently his brain, he decided to take his own advice. He couldn't be too careful or leave anything to chance.

Pulling the diary out of hiding, he scanned Byron's pages and a sample of his current handwriting and sent them to a buddy in forensics for analysis.

Yes, he'd be careful. And thorough. He entered web addresses from memory, ones well used in his hobby, and began a search for historical evidence to support her wild claims and his nightmares.

Chapter Nine

Time Stamp: 1888

Another brutal murder has interrupted the normal chaos of the East End. The papers and police appear unable or unwilling to apprehend the vicious killer. As a spinster of questionable acquaintance, I will hardly be believed, though I've tried to point them in the right direction with my letters.

It seems once more, I must be the final authority. The escape routes for those less fortunate in the East End are firmly established and will carry on if the demon's minions continue to work without him. I pray that will not be the case and that by taking off the head, the whole beast will die away.

For now, I must formulate my plan to bring and end to his reign of terror. Again.

–From the diary of Gabriella Stamford

Jaden sat across the table from Lorine, a twenty-something 'runaway' trying to save up for a move to a quiet suburb with decent schools for her toddler son. The boy was a book-loving three-year-old with big brown eyes and chubby cheeks. His blond hair was whisper soft and he showed a gift for charming ladies already. Having never achieved motherhood, children intrigued Jaden.

"Do you take him to work with you?"

"No. Micky's set-up is fine."

Jaden made a note to find out about Micky's childcare 'set-up' when she returned. "I'd like to follow you today. On your route, around work."

Lorine's eyes narrowed. "Am I bait?"

"Not anymore than the rest of us. I'm just checking the route looking for the most likely ambush sites. When we know how they're thinking we can take better measures."

"They're thinking we're fun to k-i-l-l."

"Then it's time for a change," Jaden countered with a smile for the boy. "He's wonderful. Very smart."

"He gets smart from me." Motherly pride lit her eyes. "I'm not gonna let him turn into his daddy," Lorine vowed. "However God made his DNA, that's how it'll stay."

"The juicing for war was supposed to be temporary."

"Leave anything to Health Chairman Kristoff and you're gonna have side effects. Guar-an-teed."

"Not a Leo Kristoff fan?" Jaden tested.

"Hell no." She bit her lip and shot a furtive glance to be sure her word choice had flown over her son's head. "But you can't pick your relatives."

"Excuse me?"

"Leo's my mom's oldest brother. He's been an a-s-s since the cradle, according to the family."

"Hey Lorine!" Another young woman with a child in tow approached them. "Can Zach walk to school with us?"

Zach was slipping out of his seat already.

"Hold up a minute, buster," Lorine said, tapping her cheek.

The little mirror of his mom lunged for her with a hug and smacking kiss. "I love you," she whispered into his ear, then called a cheery, "Have fun," for the rest of the world to hear. Jaden wanted to think if any of her lives had been different she could have been a mom as in tune as Lorine.

The women cleared the table and carried the dishes to the kitchen window. "So why'd you run away?" Jaden asked when the chatter of the dining hall was behind them.

"It beat the alternatives."

Jaden respected the non-answer. "So what do you do for Denny's Dairy?"

"I monitor the robotics. Make sure they don't screw up and put more than one slice of cheese in each wrapper. Stuff like that. Can't have the masses tempted into overindulgence."

"Heaven forbid."

"It's not brain surgery, but the pay's good."

Jaden thought she knew the answer, but asked the expected question anyway. "So why start smuggling?"

"Two reasons. It gets Zach into fresh air and better schools faster. And," she winked, "it's pure bonus to undo my uncle's attempts to control society."

Pretty sharp for twenty-ish, Jaden thought, smiling.

"Should I assume I'm next, since you're so interested in me?"

Maybe too sharp. But Jaden feigned nonchalance. "I considered tailing you covertly. Now I'm glad I didn't."

"Why?"

"Because you'd realize you were being followed. That could've been bad news for both of us."

They stepped out into a bright spring morning complete with balmy sunshine and clear skies. A day that could only be better outside of the city. The wide variety of fruit and flower vendors teased her nose and for the first time in ages, Jaden could've been talked into taking a day off.

But as they approached the el platform, her good mood went sour. The monstrosity above cast oppressive shadows on the street and her spirit. She'd swear she could feel the coffee she'd called breakfast eating a hole through her stomach. Maybe conversation would make the trip more tolerable.

"So what's with Zach's dad?"

"For starters he resembles my uncle." Both women laughed as they passed through what Jaden had once known as turnstiles. Now it was a narrow plastic arch armed with a laser eye. She didn't trust those much more than the actual train. She silently and forcibly chanted a reminder that technology was her friend.

"You don't look like a technophobe."

"What?"

They pushed their way toward a free space near the middle of the train full of commuters.

"You just seem pretty into modern e-life."

"I've got nothing against technology. It's a beautiful tool."

Lorine stared her down, an extraordinary feat.

"Fine, I confess. I hate this elevated train crap."

"Gotcha."

Jaden searched for a way to get back on topic. "So where's your drop?"

"I've already made one. The next is on the job."

Having completely missed it, Jaden replayed the past few minutes. "Oh, the brush at the scanning checkpoint. Very smooth."

Lorine smiled. "I've done all right. Micky's a good teacher. So are you."

"Thanks."

"I hold the practice take-down record on my floor. Mine's the next stop," Lorine said, through the current jostling exchange of people.

Jaden did her best to keep the relief hidden and knew she failed when Lorine grew too interested in the blurred scenery. She wanted to dance with joy when her feet touched solid ground, but the moment was marred by the man shadowing them.

"Keep moving," she said to Lorine. "Don't turn back or slow down for any reason."

"Gotcha. You can take him, Ms. Michaels."

The girl was full of surprises. "If you ever tire of supervising machines, come see me."

Jaden moved closer, and pretended to take something from Lorine. Then she turned into the next alley and waited for the shadow to make his move. Was he after the woman or the product? Either way, he was damned slow about it.

At last, he slunk by the alley and Jaden knew he'd been sent for Lorine. Rather than let him take her and follow, Jaden opted to intervene before he could lay a hand on the bright young mother.

Later she'd take time to evaluate if she was turning soft.

Unable to help himself, Brian strolled through the caffeine packing room, under the guise of looking for Jaden. His daylong searches into Kristoff, Albertson and Ms. Michaels herself had been more than informative. He wanted to discuss his findings with her, but she'd gone missing in action.

Around him grinders spun, infusing the air with the unmatched scent of fresh, pure coffee. How could anyone consider this a crime? His years as a cop had him evaluating the working women. They looked happy enough, chatting amidst the noise of grinding, measuring and sealing for tomorrow's deliveries. They were all in better condition than the occupants of any brothel or sweatshop he'd busted.

How did Micky maintain such a tough street rep with clean, content women running his routes?

"Bull--" The rest of the incredulous voice was lost under the louder grinding. Brian tried to lip read, in vain. "It's an act," burst forth when the grinder stopped.

"It's not. But catch this. When I tell her I saw the tail on us, she offers me a job!"

"Get real, Lorine. If it pays enough, I'll see things too."

"I wasn't seeing things. She acted like she took a drop off me, and then disappeared."

"You been reading too many fairy tales to that boy of yours."

Brian decided the women were discussing the 'legendary' Jaden. He switched gears from slow to snail's pace to pick up the details.

"Sherlock Holmes is not a fairy tale. My point is I peeked."

"Huh?"

"She told me not to, but I did. I looked back. She was whaling on him big time. I was almost late to work."

"That's her job ain't it?"

More grinding, though lips continued to move.

"An elbow to his jaw and he went down. Just like she showed us."

"So I'll pay more attention next time."

"Then she shot him."

Brian gave up the casual eavesdropping. "Who did Jaden shoot?" And how'd she get a gun? He'd searched her stuff and discovered her penchant for knives. And Micky wasn't stupid enough to stash guns in the guest suite.

The younger woman blinked up at him. He could

practically see the scales as she weighed the risk of talking with him. "I don't know his name."

"Description?"

"Short, bulky, bald. Really beat up fake-leather jacket and faded jeans."

"Walking or driving?"

"Walking. Followed us off the train."

"The elevated train?"

"There's another kind?"

Brian shook off surprise and came back to the point. "Jaden thought he was a threat to you or the product?"

"Don't know." The girl shrugged. "She faked an exchange then–"

"Fell back to find out," he finished for her. Standard procedure. "And her conclusion?"

"I hope she'll tell me when she gets back."

Brian waved the other woman away and took the place beside Lorine. "She didn't meet you at your day job? She didn't escort you back here?"

The girl shook her head and was offering to organize search parties when her name clicked in Brian's memory. "Lorine, right? Lost niece of health chairman, Kristoff."

Her chin came up. "Not so lost." She resumed grinding in a clear dismissal.

"No. You escaped the family biz with a wild fling."

"Anyone can read a file."

"True. But only you can fill in the details."

"If I don't, you'll report me found?"

"No." The last thing he wanted was Kristoff raiding Micky's place. Caffeine-deprived citizens would riot in the streets. Hell, he'd gladly lead them. He applied his most charming, good cop smile. "I'm too selfish to turn the good stuff over to your uncle."

Her face softened and her fingers toyed with a stray coffee bean. "I wanted choices. I thought Zach's dad did too, but as a medic he turned out to be as bad as Leo when it came to juicing. I'm not sure they weren't in it from the beginning." Her eyes flashed as motherly instinct barreled through any lingering grief. "I won't let my son become a freak of nature. Juicing's not like immunizing against disease. Every study shows it consistently backfires."

Brian stopped her tirade with a raised finger. "Every study?" If she could prove it, they were talking a whole new level of government fraud. And a whole lot of motive to support Jaden's theory.

"Every true, double-blind study, yes."

"You know this how?"

"The family biz, as you put it." She stuck out her hand as if they'd just met. "Lorine Sheraton, graduate, magna cum laude, Harvard Medical School." She grinned. "Harvard because of dear Uncle Leo. Magna cum laude because I'm a perfectionist."

"You're the prodigy."

"I'm a *natural* phenomenon." Her cheeks burned. "I double checked my DNA on my own when I was thirteen. I refused to use any genetic fabrication to my personal advantage."

"I meant no offense. Does Micky know?"

"Should he? It doesn't affect my work here."

"It will."

Lorine jumped to her feet. "It will not!"

Brian yanked her back down before she could cause a scene. He dumped beans into the grinder and punched the button for cover noise. "Shut up and listen. I'd guess you're smuggling to save up for another move. This time completely out of reach." He took her widened eyes as confirmation. "A few days working for me and your funding will be complete."

"You don't know how much I need."

"Doesn't matter. I can get the money. Hell, I'll help you move. You in?"

"What's the job?"

"Strictly in-house stuff. No physical risk. What's your answer?"

"I'm in."

Brian kissed her coffee-scented hands. "I'll clear it with Micky." Hot damn, his own personal medical expert! With the expected results, he could press charges. And with the connections he'd found today, he could force Albertson to give up his seat on the bench.

Maybe not the exact justice Jaden sought, but she wouldn't have to resort to murder. And he wouldn't have to delve into his personal mysteries her claims brought to light.

Flying high on the day's progress, Brian strode off in the direction of the suite, only to freeze in front of a security monitor. A woman was struggling to enter at the back door. A woman with Jaden's hair, clutching her hip and wearing a familiar, though horribly damaged, cow-safe jacket he'd once called his own.

He shot down the hall like a bullet.

Jaden took a slow, measured breath, gripped the panel and tried again to enter the god-forsaken code correctly. The door opened on a rush of air and Brian's cursing voice. He pulled her inside and though she wanted to blame the pain, it was his presence that sent tears of gratitude streaming down her face.

Tears twice in two days. She *was* going soft.

She pushed at him, in defense of pride if nothing else, but it only added insult to the injury. Feeling small and incapable didn't suit her. She pushed again and he merely murmured soothing nonsense.

"Shut up." The raspy voice was hers. How appalling.

"What hurts? What's happened?"

"Hip," she growled, pointing to the obvious injury rather than the invisible agony of another victim crying a river inside her head.

She paused, felt him take a peek at the bleeding wound, then tried to move along. But he swept her up into his arms and she cursed the part of her that wanted to sink in and stay there forever.

She'd never needed help before and now seemed much too late to break a perfectly good habit. "Put me down. I can make it."

"Sure you can," he agreed. "I just want to get to the infirmary before dawn."

"No infirmary. Suite."

"I am sweet, but we're going for professional help."

"No... Oh!" Jaden started at the slither of a silk scarf across her knees. Except it wasn't *her* knees she was feeling.

The current object of Albertson's perverse attention was a young girl. Her blindfold impaired Jaden's vision as well and prevented both of them from bracing against the evil torment attacking her.

The intensity of the connection eased with Brian's touch. Her vision wasn't back to normal, but the gradual relief of terror allowed her to begin thinking clearly. "Somehow he knows," she explained. "Albertson knows they can connect with me." She heard a door open and close, then voices and shoes moving closer. "I said suite."

"Overruled," Brian said. "I'm setting you down now."

To her shame, she clung. "Don't let go."

"Just lay back and let them get a look at that hip."

Her free hand searched for clues to her surroundings. Hard, narrow surface, cool to the touch. Definitely the infirmary. Why wouldn't he listen? "I want to take care of this on my own."

"Stop wasting energy arguing."

New hands touched her and she flinched, cowering into Brian. Oh, how she hated this! She'd worked for years to master involuntary reactions. But the child's new terror amplified her own memories making her feel like a fragile victim once more.

Unknown voices swirled around her. Hands she couldn't see to anticipate kept landing on her clothing and skin, kept delving into the wound. Oh, God! She'd be crying again soon, or worse, vacating her body. Then what would happen to her? To the poor trapped little girl?

"Make them stop," she begged. "Make them stop."

Silence.

Praise God!

She felt nothing but the table beneath her.

Hallelujah!

Then a flurry of movement and she was cradled in Brian's arms, his hand smoothing her hair, his lips brushing her eyes.

The horrible connection to Albertson's victim faded to the barest level of awareness. A level she could handle. Jaden tried to feel guilt instead of relief. The blindfold prevented any location clues, making a rescue impossible. And the damage had been done. Only time could help the child now.

"Better?" he asked.

She blinked and filled her gaze with the carved beauty of

his face. "Getting there." She reached up to trace his jaw. His eyes were dark, his brow furrowed with...worry?

"You were screaming."

Her hand fell. *Whoops.* "Sorry."

"You will be," his voice rumbled from his chest, "if you claim that was a headache."

"Not here."

"Fine." He shifted to slide an arm beneath her legs. "Hang on."

She obeyed, making an effort to not enjoy it too much when he stood up, clipped out orders for supplies, and left the infirmary.

"I can see why you made chief."

"Flattery won't get you off the hook," he growled.

"You're just mad because I got blood on your jacket."

From her intimate vantage point she caught the hint of a smile teasing his mouth.

"My jacket's a lot better than this rag you're wearing."

She joined his effort to lighten the mood. "Then why's your name in the collar?"

He rolled his eyes, but his mouth curved. "Open the door." She did and he carried her straight to the bathroom, setting her gently on her feet. "Can you strip on your own?"

She could, now. Did she dare ask for help anyway?

A voice from the door announced the arrival of the medical supplies.

He questioned her with only a compelling look, then went to deal with the delivery.

The moment alone seemed unbearable. She wanted him nearly as much as she wanted to run from him. She knew better than to mix it up like this. Their situation was precarious enough already.

"What caused the cut?"

She appreciated his understatement as much as his brisk tone. Sex didn't challenge her–sex with someone who mattered did. And Brian, whose touch restored her balance, mattered a great deal to the success of her mission.

"Hello? Are you zoning again?"

"No. I'm good. I'm here." She eased out of the jacket and peeled the torn clothing away from the wound. Then she took her first real look at the gash making an angry red highlight over the crest of her left hip. "I caught on the edge of something in the alley."

"Ya think? This sucker's ragged. And nearly bone deep."

"Ya think?" she echoed. "Hand me the Biosan."

"We'll sanitize that in a minute." Brian punched buttons on the shower control panel. "Soap and hot water first."

His surgical removal of her clothing stifled her protests about waste and necessity. Of course the heat of his hands pushing her under the delicious fall of real water, real hot water, made her positively giddy.

She couldn't recall ever feeling giddy.

Not even the brutal sting of water sliding over open flesh dimmed the thrill.

"You're a saint," she moaned.

"Hardly."

Oh, God. He'd climbed into the shower with her. His broad palms skimmed rich lather across her shoulders, down her arms, then back again. Her body responded with a hot, wet surge that had nothing to do with water.

"You've seen your share, haven't you?" he said as he washed her back.

She felt his gaze on each of her visible scars from various blades and bullets. Different battles, some practice, but all for and from the same root: protect, defend and destroy evil.

"I mean to achieve my goal." She didn't have to add 'with or without you'.

Those big, warm hands turned her, tipped her head under the spray to work on her hair. Her lids drooped in rapture, but she studied his face from beneath her lashes, then let her gaze wander lower.

He'd been formed by a masterful sculptor, she decided. Though the gorgeous expanse of torso showed evidence of his own close calls. She followed a crease of a bullet's path along his ribcage, pleased with his reactive twitch. "Why'd you let this scar?"

"Chicks dig it."

She snorted, then hissed as soap bit at the wound she'd put out of her mind.

He snatched her close, and the magnificent press of breasts to hair-roughened chest dulled the pain. She fused her mouth to his, teasing those firm lips open with her tongue. Between them, his powerful erection pulsed its primal invitation.

"Let's fix you up," he said, drawing away.

"Um. Sure thing." She licked her lips, savored the taste of him, unsure if she should feel relief or despair. Did it matter? The moment was gone thanks to the man's astonishing control. Accepting the towel he offered, she began to dry off.

"Think Micky charges extra for trashed towels?"

She glanced down to where her blood still oozed from her hip. Watched as Brian applied tender pressure. "It happened in the line of duty, so he'd better not."

"Word in the shop is you really 'whaled' on the guy."

"I was pissed," she admitted.

"Why?"

"I like Lorine."

"Me too. And?"

"She has a cute kid." She couldn't believe him. Them. Clad in thin towels, after the best shower of all her lives, medic and patient conversed as if her world wasn't spinning off its axis.

"And?" he prompted again.

She sighed. "And he was wearing what's left of your jacket."

"Remind me to thank you. Ready?"

She nodded and set her teeth against the assault of antiseptic. The first half of the Biosan treatment didn't hurt and supposedly contained numbing agents. She'd decided long ago the numbing thing was a marketing placebo to boost Biosan sales. The second phase burned like hell itself. She swore.

"I'm impressed."

"With?"

"Your creative use of the language. Expressive and to the point." He stood up and kissed her nose. "Though I worry that you eat with that mouth."

"I do other things with it too." The seductive purr hung between them in the steamy air.

"Oh, yeah?"

That he needed to clear his throat charmed her. Who the hell had invaded her body and ripped out her ability to think rationally?

"Well," he continued, "those other things can wait until you put this back together." He skimmed a finger just above the wound.

She closed her eyes at the mixture of bliss and agony, then took a deep, bracing breath. "All right. Let's get to it." She found a laser similar to the one she'd used on Katie on the tray of supplies he'd brought into the bathroom. Uncomfortable, yes. But a huge step up from the archaic method of stitching skin together. She handed it to him. "Go for it."

"You want me to do it?"

"You've got the better angle." She hoped she sounded casual. Not like a woman ready to slap on a band-aid and jump the nearly naked hunk in front of her.

"I don't want to hurt you."

"Aw, you are sweet." She smiled when he grimaced. "But I can take it, really."

"Then take it on the bed."

She felt her mouth drop open.

"Better angle," he said coolly.

"Right." She stretched out the word since it was the only one she could think of. Then she stretched out her aching body, keeping all her more important parts covered with the towel.

To her further surprise, he draped her with a blanket before he began sealing the gash. "It's set to infuse a tetanus booster as we go."

Brian watched her jaw clench against the process and he forced himself to continue. Bruises were blooming all over, marring the silky perfection of her skin.

"You took a beating," he said, more to himself than her.

"Other guy's worse." The strain scraped her voice.

He was making progress, but it was slow. Even slower over the deep parts. The area closest to the bone would be the worst. He searched for a distraction. For both of them. "Lorine said you shot him. I didn't think you carried."

"His gun."

Steady. "You kept it?"

She nodded. "Prints. Ow!"

"I know. We're over the bone. Don't talk. Just listen." He concentrated on knitting her flesh. "About earlier. I found a medical expert to contradict the juicing tests. I don't juice. Never have." He stopped and pulled his brain out of his raging hard-on. They'd dodged that bullet, barely. The woman didn't need sex, she needed to heal. On a variety of levels. He tried again. "I found some useful dirt on Kristoff and Albertson."

Her body sagged as the laser moved beyond the bone. He'd never known anyone to stay conscious through a laser treatment of this duration and delicacy. "All down hill from here. We'll look at the research tomorrow on the way to Gary. It might serve your purpose." *And solve my dilemma.*

Her eyes were closed, her brow smooth and her breathing even. Finally.

She needed rest, so he moved to clean up and think through the options. Rested, she might be more receptive to his news, though she'd likely argue more about taking the el.

He came to the bedroom doorway. Her peaceful sleep gave him hope there was a softer side of her in there somewhere. He wanted to believe she'd settle for Albertson behind bars rather than Albertson in an early grave.

Ah, hell. He might as well want to believe in reincarnation.

Chapter Ten

After three days, searchers found the body of missing nine-year-old Michelle Patterson in a shallow grave behind Lincoln Park. At this time, police have no suspects in custody and details regarding the cause of death are being withheld. Memorial services will be held at First Presbyterian Church on Friday. Michelle is survived by her parents, John and Louise Patterson and her sister, Nicole.

–Obituary from the Lancaster Ledger, 1952

In the twilight between asleep and awake, Jaden rolled to find the solid, sexy, warmth of Brian. And swore viciously as her injured hip brought her back to reality.

He wasn't in the bed. Hadn't been in the bed. It had all been a triple x-rated dream. Well, thank God for dreams. Especially when the live performance would derail all her goals.

Gently, with the support of the bed, she began stretching all the tight spots from yesterday's ordeal.

"Sleeping Beauty wakes?" Brian asked from the door. "Feeling better or worse?"

Both! "I'm fine, thanks. I'll be ready in thirty minutes."

"No rush. I'll go make coffee."

"My hero."

She would've taken hours if possible. The el all the way to Gary would be a challenge. She'd spent more time on that train these past days than all her lives put together.

She sent a glance toward the door and carefully climbed out of bed. With a clarity only granted to the desperate, she realized her rant over the train was a poor disguise for her distress over the man who planned to accompany her.

Last night's near miss should fall into the 'blessing' category. Instead, her traitorous body wanted to go out there and beg if necessary. She should thank Brian for his phenomenal control, rather than spend time contemplating how to undo him.

She knew it was dangerous to even fall into a rhythm resembling partnership. By degrees, that meant friendship was out of the question. And sex—well that shouldn't even be on the galaxy map.

No matter how broad those shoulders, how steady that heartbeat, how comforting his touch, she couldn't trust him. Not a thousand years ago. Not now.

The bathroom mirror offered proof to the contrary. She trusted him to fuse an open wound while she lay naked on the bed. Her fingers traced his exceptional work. Any scarring would be too faint to count.

She returned to the bedroom and quickly found a dark micro fiber tracksuit. Shadows and flexibility would help when poking around Albertson territory. She strapped her daggers into place and was pulling on the pants when she heard knuckles rapping on the open door. She turned her head and saw Brian filling the doorway, coffee in hand, mouth slack.

"Um. Excuse me."

She decided to be flattered. "Oh, you've seen it all before," she said, trying to laugh.

"Really?" He shook his head. "Last night, right?"

She tied the pants at the waist, and then met his quizzing gaze. "Starting to believe me?"

He had the grace to look away. "I just didn't peg you for the thong type."

The laughter felt wonderful. "Best-ever correction to women's underwear."

"And I suppose you were on the design team."

She zipped her jacket and took the jibe, or compliment, in stride. "Sorry to disappoint you." Though it was more disappointing when he kept dashing her fragile hope.

Belief was the trickiest element of humanity. You couldn't force yours on anyone and you could never be certain what fired another's blood.

She took the coffee mug and drank deeply. "You know you can't have it both ways." He frowned, so she elaborated. "You can't think I'm a loon out to harass your buddy and give my story credit at the same time."

"I know."

"Then what'll it be?"

"For now," he linked her arm in his, "You're a unique and beautiful woman who's quite possibly confused. Therefore you require my guidance and protection." He led her toward the kitchen table.

"How chivalrous."

"Isn't it? I guess that old picture wore off on me."

She enjoyed the light banter. Too much. Reining in her emotions, she broke the silly mood. "Did you mention a medical expert?"

He refilled his coffee and joined her at the table. "She says she can prove all the tests about the safety of juicing were altered."

Jaden's mug hit the table with a small thud. "By whom?"

"Kristoff and some other key players."

"Side effects?"

"They knew and buried the information."

"Control freak. Names of the others?" Watching him, she caught the barest flinch. "Albertson."

He nodded. "He may have provided test subjects."

"May have?"

"I'll go as far as probably, but that's it until I see real evidence."

The coffee turned bitter in her mouth.

"Cheer up." His voice became a caress. "This might send him straight to a cozy cement cell."

"Doubting Thomas." She softened the accusation with a smile. He couldn't fight the instinct to protect any more than she could. Without memories, she couldn't blame him for not getting it. Unseating the judge wouldn't cut it. Even from prison he'd run operations to exploit women. The imperative task, her ultimate purpose, was to put a final end to his relentless streak of terror.

Brian stood and extended a hand. "Feel up to a field trip?"

"I'm fine." She made the effort to evade his touch.

They exited Micky's headquarters into another beautiful day. The sunshine streaming down gave even this area of town a glow of spring. As they walked, she tried blocking thoughts of being a normal woman out for the day with her lover. A useless exercise. Premature. They weren't lovers yet–and wouldn't be, she amended.

She had a job to do and getting twisted up over a romp in the sheets with Brian wouldn't get it done.

"How much time will we have?"

"None, if I can't get you on the train."

"I'll get on the train."

He jerked a thumb over his shoulder. "That was the second platform you've stomped by."

"I'm not stomping." To prove it, she eased her stride until the next platform came into view. It took every ounce of will, but she climbed the stairs without hesitation, glaring at him as she stepped through the security scanner.

"Nicely done."

"Oh, save it," she snarled.

The train settled and the doors split. She moved quickly to the nearest seat, steeling herself against the nagging worry that this would be the time it would all collapse.

"Are you afraid of anything else?" Brian asked, dropping easily into the seat beside her, legs stretched, ankles crossed.

She hated him for it on multiple levels. "No."

"So why this? The magnetic upgrade to the el is state of the art."

"The upgrade's wonderful."

"Cut me some slack," Brian urged. He slung an arm around her shoulders and squeezed. "Just tell me already."

"Fine." She crossed legs and arms, aware of the defensive body language, but too unnerved by the discussion to care.

In one big breath she spilled the major points. "I watched this monstrosity go up in the 1890's. I saw the workmen on the build. I listened to the designers."

"And you knew better."

"It's bizarre, ugly and loud."

"Not anymore. That's why they upgraded."

His steady practicality irritated her. Hell, her irrational fear irritated her, but she'd tried everything and it refused to leave her psyche.

"As far as I can recall, Chicago is the only place I've lived twice."

"And that's significant to you."

How swiftly he moved from comfort to condescension.

"Drop the shrink act, Brian."

"That transparent, huh?"

"Put it this way: you make a better woman."

He laughed, his arm curling her into his side as the warm sound spilled over her. Wouldn't it be nice if just once she could be a normal woman content with love and life?

She wriggled, to escape the impossible, wayward thoughts.

"What are you hoping to find?" he asked at last.

"I could ask you the same thing." Another thought vied for brain space. She could get used to him. Correction–she could get used to a man like him. A man who, though he didn't understand all of her, accepted the more inevitable aspects. Like being wounded in a street fight. Or breaking into an abandoned steel mill owned by an evil entity posing as a judge.

Lord, she sounded crazy to herself.

Brian stood and offered his hand. She planned to dodge again, but somehow her fingers knit with his. When the doors swept open at the only platform in Gary, it was Brian's nudge that got her off the train.

"Penny for your thoughts."

She shielded her eyes from the angle of the late morning sun and looked closely at what had once been a thriving mill. "Abandonment looks sad, even on buildings. Why does the train even run here anymore?"

"So people can appreciate their history. There's a steel museum and everything."

She turned a full circle. There was plenty of nothing for miles. "Define 'everything'." But she loved museums of any variety. Maybe if she lived, she'd come back and check it out.

"The building in question is this way." Brian said, taking the lead.

He didn't have to tell her. She'd figured it out from the window patterns the moment she'd seen it. What did she hope to find? Well it would've been too much to catch the bastard in the act of terrorizing children and women. But maybe he'd gotten sloppy and left something incriminating behind. Something to give Brian a legal reason to put him away.

A girl could dream, right?

"Front or back?"

He'd lost her. "Huh?"

"Which entrance?"

He was testy, not a good sign on a cop. "What do you know about this place?" she asked pointedly.

"Nothing at all. Never seen it."

"But you found it."

His eyes hit the dirt. "I remembered a passing comment when the Judge bought it. I knew where to look."

"And you didn't wonder why he needed an out-dated mill?"

"Guess I forgot to quiz him in the course of living my life."

"Lives," she corrected, insistent now. And impatient. She didn't care what he knew, researched or forgot. She just wanted to see the latest hell of Albertson's creation. And take it down with him in it.

"Keep walking. Think tourist." Knowing both her enemy's tactics and standard security, Jaden spotted the discreet guards on the second level.

Brian turned a full wide-eyed, out-of-towner circle and spoke a little too loudly. "Isn't this somethin' honey? Can't you just see it all in action?"

"Sure, babe." Acting wasn't her strong suit, but she gave her best whatever the task. She figured a woman on this trek would be disinterested at best, irritable at worst. "Is there a restaurant at the museum?" she whined.

He grinned with approval and she told the butterflies swirling in her gut to settle. Then he whispered in her ear and she grounded all further flights of fancy. But when his arms banded around her and he nuzzled her neck, she gave up and sank into the feel of him. He guided her off the path and she found herself caught between old cooling pipe and lean, sexy man. His mouth a breath from hers, he whispered, "Doing great, just hang in another minute."

Damn. She'd gotten lost in the act. Stupid! As if he'd dared her, she leaned in, taking over the kiss he'd been about to plant on her. Who's acting now? She wondered, reveling in the tremor that shook him.

She pressed against him, realizing he was pressed against a side door alcove. They were out of sight and for the moment, out of danger.

Pulling back, trying to breathe, she took her fill of the view of his full mouth, the marvelous feel of his hard body under hers. His hands gripped her waist, keeping her from moving in or away, careful of the laser-healed site.

"Another time, another place, we'll finish this."

No other words could douse her fire so quickly. Complete memories aside, she knew better. There had never been a time or place for them.

"In your dreams."

He mumbled something unintelligible and her focus returned to the task. Aside from the guard, there didn't seem to be any further security. Wireless or otherwise. But the ability to simply stroll in put her senses on high alert.

"Well sec-tech, what's the delay?"

"This is too easy."

"Don't look a gift horse in the mouth. Why would anyone bother with real security in a ghost town?"

Jaden tuned out the rest of his commentary. Closing her eyes she stilled her mind and just listened with the sort of sixth sense she'd developed for Albertson.

Behind her, Brian shuffled impatiently. "The docket's only half full today. We're either in or out. You're wrong or right."

The man could push her buttons like no one else. Silently, she pushed through the door into the cool, vast space of the abandoned mill.

The pain hit her like the el she despised. It wasn't the urgent bite of the young, terrorized girls. Nor was it the bone-deep ache of innocence lost. This crushing weight was the accumulation of untold suffering.

Oh, how she'd failed each one of them.

Then, as abruptly as it hit, the pain subsided. Jaden found herself on her knees, her palms full of hot tears. Brian's voice in her ear, his arms around her created the blessed reprieve.

She could deny Cleveland's opinion no longer. She needed a partner. She needed Brian.

"Can you stand?"

She nodded, not trusting her voice.

"What is this? What comes over you? No more delays."

"Later." The weakness disgusted her. "I promise."

She pushed further into the mystery of the mill, testing doors, lighting up passages with her penlight.

The third door in the second hall held the answers. She felt it, even through the filter of Brian's touch. Opening the door, she reached and found the control panel. Lights came up and trios of long narrow windows filled with artificial sunlight and fluffy clouds. Just like she'd seen through the girl's eyes before her warehouse blew up.

One hand in Brian's, she began flipping the next series of switches. A refitted electric chair from the early 20th century elevated from the floor. Behind it a table appeared spread with everything from feathers to a bullwhip. The silk scarf from last night was folded neatly in the middle. She ripped her gaze to the left where a wall slid away, revealing a bank of flat screen monitors.

"The better to terrify you, my dear."

"Jaden?" Brian's voice echoed the bewilderment she'd felt on her first encounter with this madman.

"Little Red Riding Hood. Big bad wolf. You've gotta remember that. The better to see you with, the better to hear you with, the better to eat you with."

"This can't be Albertson."

She gave herself points for not caving to the temptation to strap him into the chair and *make* him see the truth.

"You expected a handwritten, notarized letter of confession?"

"Woulda been nice."

She counted to ten. By two's. A little calmer, she tried again. "As a cop, tell me what you see."

"First glance? A sex gym. You've got bondage, voyeurism and sadism all available at a whim."

"And?" She jerked her chin to the windows.

"Atmosphere?" His face fell as flat as the joke. "That might provide a false time line for a person forced to be here."

"Might?"

"Come on. The way Gary smells? Blindfolded, bound

and gagged, a person would know where they were."

She wanted to cross her arms, but didn't risk breaking contact with Brian. She didn't care to imagine how debilitating she might become in here without him. It rankled, but at the moment it was a fact she couldn't dispute.

"It doesn't smell like old steel processing in here."

He sniffed and moved toward the back wall. She stayed close, summoning her fraying patience.

"No." His grip tightened and he groaned. "No."

She looked around him, understanding immediately. "That's his mark." She refused to tremble at the sight of the infinity symbol at the end of a short branding iron resting on a cold grate. "If you live, you live without threat of a repeat. A very civilized and relatively new development."

Brian blanched. "Albertson has a ring like this."

"Nice of you to notice. Proof enough yet?" Maybe at last justice would be served and she'd live to see the world free of a demonic presence.

But Brian shook his head. "The connection's weak."

She had her own, more colorful thoughts on weak at the moment, but he held her fast.

"Listen. It's circumstantial. Anyone could've commissioned that thing." He nodded at the branding iron. "A fraternity, a cult–"

"Getting warmer. He's a demon."

"Uh-huh. Does Albertson know he's possessed?

"It's more likely he doesn't know he's human."

"It's still not enough to single out Albertson beyond any doubt."

"Then I'll handle it myself."

"I thought that hadn't been working."

The accuracy of the barb stung. "It'll be fine when I find

the right weapon. If you're not able to help through legal channels, I can deal with the fallout."

"Can you?" He raised their linked hands. "You said there's more to this than simple abuse of power and molestation."

She nodded. The unanswered questions hadn't stopped circling through her mind. "He's escalated from simple depravity, past despicable right into deranged."

"By all appearances he's as sane as they come."

"Is that supposed to be acceptance of my tall tale?"

"No. I'm cautiously exploring a theory."

Had she honestly expected more from a man unaware of the depth and span of his life? "He knows something I don't. Or something I haven't recalled. And you're involved or he wouldn't have tried to kill you. Cleveland said I'd need a partner."

"Is Cleveland like...you?"

"Only as alike as a scar can make us." She peeled back the fabricated skin, exposing the old scar behind her ear. Then she reached for the branding iron. "Match it up."

He responded with a restoring brush of his lips to her hair. "I'm believing all I can, Jaden." Setting the branding iron aside, he kissed the scar.

And put a chink in the armor surrounding her heart. "You can lead a horse to water..."

"Shouldn't that be my line?"

A familiar sound interrupted her, but she couldn't place it. "What is that?" She dragged him away from the horrifying chamber, not bothering to return it to its original condition. Better that Albertson know she was close.

"A train," he said. "This way."

They worked their way through the dim passageways to

the back of the building. Above them, footsteps pounded.

"Guards?" she hissed.

He pulled into a shadow. "You said there wasn't any security."

"There isn't any visual or auditory set up." She paused. "But they're not searching. Hear that? They're all moving to one place."

He concurred and they continued until they reached what had once been a loading dock. She stopped and backpedaled, keeping them out of sight, when chains rattled and groaned to raise the rusty metal door.

Sunlight streamed in, a sweet contradiction to the black purpose of this hideaway.

To her astonishment, a three car train pulled by an old diesel engine squealed to a stop.

"What the hell?" Brian breathed.

Doors on the cargo cars opened and suddenly the loading dock was full of chained people. All female, all slumped with defeat.

"They're just kids."

"No," Jaden contradicted. "But he likes the young look." She ducked back further into the shadows as the cars were loaded. She had to think of a way to help them.

Brian opened his mouth and she saved him the trouble. "I know. Still no damned proof this is Albertson. It's probably some diligent squatter who started up a slave trade without consulting the owner of such a fine establishment." She rolled her eyes at the temper brewing in his. "Whatever. We need to get on that train."

"Hell, no."

"You've got a better way to find out the destination?"

Brian fisted his free hand. How to make her see reason?

"Let's find the office and confiscate the records first."

"Okay." She lowered her eyes, but he wasn't buying the sudden submissive routine. He knew her brain was shifting gears faster than the old style dragsters his grandfather talked about.

"Proof's essential for conviction," he reminded her. "You do want your nemesis to spend more than a couple years in lockup."

The meek nod of agreement worried him more than her continued unexplained collapses. "Well?"

"We could at least tag the train."

Brian sympathized. He didn't want those poor girls hurt anymore than she did. But in his opinion this rescue was a close second to preventing more victims. If Judge Albertson was behind this disgusting mess he'd have an office and meticulous records. That meant evidence and evidence meant irreversible convictions.

He tempted her. "I bet the records name the destination."

"If there are records."

The sullen tone he chalked up to being overruled. He had to admit, defeat didn't look so good on her. "Trust me, Jaden. We'll figure it out."

She gave a last wistful look to the tracks, then fell in behind him, hand still linked.

Brian followed his instincts, shadowing the footsteps of the guards on the floor above. He was counting on another access, something suiting the powerful orchestrator of such horrible acts. And no, he still couldn't completely wrap his mind around Albertson in that role. But they'd know soon enough. He smiled at the sight of a narrow, spiraling staircase. No way it could be the Judge's access, but good enough for two not-so-dead investigators.

Beginning the corkscrew climb, he heard the distant grind of steel against track and the slow pulse of the train gaining speed.

Then he heard nothing but Jaden's scream as she tumbled down the stairs. Lights bloomed around them. There'd been cameras, at least sensors of some sort and he'd bet she'd known all along. Hell, he should've known all along. A voice from above told him to freeze–and he obeyed, praying Jaden would do the same. But when guards closed in on him from below, he realized she'd disappeared from the radar.

Some partner.

Chapter Eleven

The neighborhood grieves today over the loss of Mr. Harold Blair. Known as the grandpa-in-residence, he shared candy, time and wisdom with two generations of children on Gregg Street.

Preliminary police reports say he died of a gunshot wound to the heart. His foster son returned home during the attack, fatally wounding the assailant, an unnamed woman, while she tried to escape.

–From the Lancaster Ledger, 1962

Jaden couldn't let herself look back. She might try to help him. The women on the train needed her more. This is what she should've done at the museum: let the doubting Mr. Thomas take care of himself. He'd contrive some reason for his presence in his buddy's secret torture hideout.

The thought bolstered her as the mill threatened to drain her and she moved at top speed toward the sunshine–and the train undoubtedly destined for a thousand hells.

Neither the shouts nor the gunfire on her heels stopped her. She was a woman on a mission. It felt good to be working solo again.

Putting Brian out of her head, she ran to catch the old diesel, swinging herself up onto the junction of the second and third cargo cars. Letting her body adjust to the rolling rhythm of the train, she found she preferred the smooth ride of the el. Brian would revel in the irony. And there, before she decided how best to derail the Judge's delivery, she said a prayer for Brian.

It seemed most expedient to free the prisoners, rally them to revolt and take over the train. She set out to assess the threat. Reality was depressing, at least as far as her innate desire for battle was concerned.

Cursory surveillance proved only the engineer and one other armed man stood in her way. Easy enough, she thought, slinking up and into the engine compartment, feeling like an actor out of an old black and white western.

"Howdy," she said, humoring herself.

Both men turned, gaping like landed fish. Before the armed man could swing his gun into position, Jaden kicked and disarmed him. With the butt of the gun pressed into his larynx and her knee to his chest, she let him contemplate suffocation while she found the rest of his weaponry.

"Afraid of the chained women, are you?" In addition to the rifle at his throat, the man had a pistol, two knives and a taser. She used the taser against him and then casually pocketed the rest. The women on board had gained a small arsenal.

Approaching the engineer, she drew her favorite dagger from the sheath at her back. Emphasizing her advantage she sent a hair-skimming stroke down the length of his arm. The ensuing pat down revealed nothing noteworthy.

"Weapons locker?" she asked.

"You just disabled it, ma'am." He cocked his head toward the guard.

"Where are we headed?" she asked in her best syrup-soaked tone.

"Chicago, ma'am. Hammond Street docks."

She appreciated his immediate and full cooperation. Maybe extreme violence could be avoided.

"Then what?" she asked.

"Routine transfer to the ferry. I'm not used to overseeing that, ma'am. Not sure if they'll approve."

"'They' who?"

"Guards like him handle the ferry."

"You're separate from his crew?"

He nodded.

"Where does the ferry go?"

Engineer shrugged. "I just drive the train."

"The ETA?"

He blinked, then understood she wanted the estimated time of arrival. "Oh, about another hour. This ol' girl's dependable, but slow."

"Fair enough." She'd have to hustle. "If anyone calls for your pal back there, tell them he's sick. It'll be true enough if he comes around too soon."

With that, she snatched the keys from the guard's belt and began putting her plan into action. She began to think Brian's wisdom was the better part of valor when she couldn't get Cleveland to answer his phone. She checked the time. Forty-five minutes to single-handedly save about forty women with a plan B.

And what was plan B?

It started the same as plan A: first free and then rally the prisoners. But it needed a different ending without Cleveland to back her up at the docks.

She moved into the first car behind the engine. As she released the women from their shackles, she asked questions, but received only exhausted, wounded stares. If they'd been drugged, she didn't see obvious evidence. No needle tracks, glassy eyes or hypo-spray patterns.

She pushed open the second car to find conditions the same.

Her reassurances earned no reaction from the captives, but the silence spoke volumes about their lack of confidence in her and themselves. None bore Albertson's mark, but several willowy blondes wore braided sterling armbands in an infinity pattern.

"Take those off. I'll keep them for evidence." Slowly, they obeyed. "Where are you from?" she asked the waif nearest the door. But the pale shadow of a woman merely shook her head.

Jaden mentally crossed her fingers that car three would give the forming plan B a chance. She stuck the key in each binding presented, wondering how to rally the downtrodden troops into decisive action.

A firm hand touched her shoulder. "Ms. Michaels?"

Jaden looked up, straight into the distorted face of Maria. The woman had a black eye, a brutal handprint on her neck, and a lopsided, mile-wide smile.

"It's good to see you." She embraced Jaden with remarkable calm.

"I'm glad you're okay. I thought–well by now–"

"The worst. I know. When the guy snagged me, I was certain you were right behind him, ready to pounce. I'm glad I never gave up on you."

Jaden noticed their conversation had sparked other women to begin talking. So far, she didn't recognize any voices from attacks she'd been linked to. The knowledge gave her no comfort.

"I–we had to prioritize. A young girl was also at risk that

night."

Maria waved it off. "No explanation needed. How can I help you?"

"Sit them down and let them know we're going to escape. I'm going for water, and then we'll work out the details."

Jaden turned back toward the engine when a dark, nagging question demanded an answer. "Have you seen any deaths?"

Maria nodded soberly.

"What happened to the bodies?"

"The woman who died in my cell was hauled away by a guard. He muttered something about ballast or filler. It sounded like nautical talk to me."

Jaden nodded. "Do you have any idea what's going on?"

"We've all been tested one way or another. Not all of us have been sexually assaulted. But the guards kept track of who was naturally blonde."

"Yeah. They're all one car back." Jaden paused to think. "I got the feeling he was capturing women with a specific look. Besides young," she finished.

Her mind raced over possibilities and concerns as she wove her way back through the first two cars of prisoners. What riddle did this train solve? And what new questions did it raise?

Albertson had women kidnapped from Chicago and brought to Gary, only to head back to Chicago for a ferry to who knows where. But where were the younger victims? Where were the innocent girls whose weeping haunted her every quiet moment?

She struggled to keep her balance as she relived the engineer's comments. A 'routine' transfer of this sort could only mean slave trade.

She fumed at her obtuse ignorance. Albertson had been

supplying the black market slave auctions from docks in her own back yard. And she'd been so distracted by day to day assaults she'd missed the bigger picture. She swore viciously.

How many women had been sold into slavery because of her failure to accomplish her mission?

Just one was one too many. She would *not* allow these thirty-eight to join them.

Jaden steeled herself for the pending battle.

Brian let the guards haul him roughly into a huge office and dump him into a chair. With one eye swollen shut, the lack of depth perception created an interesting challenge to his observation skills. He shifted, and received a painful reminder of the billy club cracking his ribs. These guards didn't smile on visitors.

He focused his good eye on the man by the door. "Got an ice pack around here?"

"We got nothin' for trespassers."

It didn't seem likely the Judge would hire help like this personally. That gave Brian hope that the man he'd held up as a mentor for most of his life might still be worthy. Anyone could use an infinity symbol. Albertson didn't have sole rights to it.

To distract his body from the pain, he let his eye rove. Dark wood furnishings gleamed under brass fixtures. The lavish civilization was an obscene contrast to the torture chamber downstairs, but that wasn't what made his stomach pitch. No, that sickening feeling rolled over him when he spotted a burgundy leather cigar box embossed with an infinity symbol.

Anyone could use an infinity symbol.

The denial sounded foolish even in his head.

He reached out, willing it to be illusion, but his hand was shoved away before he made contact.

"Keep yer mitts off," the guard rumbled.

Brian nodded, unable to take his eye from the gift he'd presented to Judge Albertson when he'd graduated from the police academy.

On the off chance the Judge was being manipulated, Brian asked, "What is this place?"

The guard snickered. "A finishing school for the less fortunate."

If only. "Run by?"

"Shut yer trap. Ye'll know what the boss-man wants yeh to know soon enough."

Brian used the silence to review his options. Damned few. Fight or flight were the only answers his brain provided.

The guard drew a genuine Cuban cigar from the humidor on the credenza and made a show of lighting it for his half-blind prisoner. The flame jumped and flashed off a unique ring on the man's right index finger.

"Nice ring," Brian said.

"Gotta earn it, son. Yeh wan' in?"

"Maybe."

"Turn over the girl and I'll put in a good word." The guard came to hover over Brian who fought not to gag on the stench of bad breath. "An' don't waste my time playin' coy. I've been lookin' for that dame. I mean to find her."

The guard pressed a button on a remote and the paneling slid away to reveal more monitors. The feed was live from various cameras around the mill.

Brian knew somewhere, someone else watched him.

"The girl, huh? Then we're on the same team. Albertson wanted her delivered. Seems I held up my end, but you'll have a devil of a time explaining how you chased her away." His reward was miniscule, but satisfying, when the guard pinched his thumb in the hinge of the old fashioned lighter.

"You 'bout had me, son. But we don' know no Albertson. Better just come on clean."

"Fine. I followed her here."

"Film says otherwise." He pressed more buttons. "Lookie here. Y'all showed up together."

"Her idea. I'm just playing the devoted boyfriend."

"Fancy yerself some undercover hot shot do yeh?"

Brian bristled, calculating the effort required to fight his way out of the mill. Stamina or skill wasn't the issue. Time was. So far, none of the monitors showed anything about Jaden. Concern threatened to derail his concentration. When did it get personal? Sex, or near sex, was one thing. But when did she start to matter on this deep level? Unfortunately, he thought he knew.

"Well, boy, what'll it be?"

"Huh?"

"Better listen when I speak, son."

"Oh, for heaven's sake, Jackson, leave the boy alone."

Brian whirled at the sound of the rotund Judge and regretted the move immediately.

"Go get some ice." With an imperial wave, the Judge sent the hick packing. "Not the sharpest knife in the drawer, but loyal to a fault."

Brian caught the tone-setting statement and hoped to keep this battle to words only. At least until he had the answers. "Some finishing school you've got here," he began, accepting the single ice pack. He applied it to his face to shield any telltale expressions from the Judge.

Albertson laughed heartily and settled into the chair

behind his desk. "Ah, you can't believe everything you hear. Or see." He paused. "This little venture caters to an eclectic clientele, Brian."

"A clientele you feel the need to satisfy?"

"Now, now. Don't go judging the man on the bench."

"You've commended my judgment in the past."

"True enough." He steepled thick fingers under multiple chins. "But we both know how this town works. How the wheels of power must be greased. Believe me, no one comes to real harm here."

Then where? Brian shut his good eye. "You're the real power in this town."

"From your lips to God's ears." A chuckle rumbled from the barreled chest. "It pays to know the weaknesses of men."

"Which are?"

The chair creaked in protest and the judge shifted forward. "In your case. The underdog."

Brian opened his eye, met the narrow gaze of the judge and decided he resembled the dark side of Buddha. "I believe innocent until proven guilty."

"Yes, yes." The flabby face relaxed. "But you're a sucker for a sob story. I blame your mother, really." He flipped off the monitors. "That girl you're with in the film? That's the Michaels woman. She's not what she seems."

"Not a security specialist?"

"Watch your tone. I sentenced her to house arrest."

"Her house no longer exists."

To his credit, the Judge put on an effective look of surprise, and then softened it to relief. "Until recently I thought you no longer existed. It's good to see you alive and well."

"Thanks."

"The services for the officer lost at the museum are this

afternoon."

Brian hadn't known. And wondered where this new prickly path would lead.

"Tragic, tragic." Jowls swayed as Albertson shook his head in pity. "Responding to the museum call, right?"

"Yes."

"The Michaels woman was there."

"Yes."

"She can't be trusted. Whatever lies she's told you, she can't be trusted. She's a thief. And a stalker. She'll do anything to discredit me."

"Why is that?" Brian set the melting ice aside to stare at the infinity ring on Albertson's finger.

"She's a fanatic. Claims I don't respect women. Don't protect them. For heaven's sake, I don't write the laws, I just uphold them."

"Interpret them."

"Naturally. It's the job. If women would just make an attempt to understand and respect their men. All these false accusations are a detriment to society."

"Juiced men can cause a great deal of damage."

"So can a woman. The juicing is essential to maintain our military superiority and peace."

"Peace?" Brian stood and came closer to rest his palms on the desk to scan the papers there. "In the world maybe, but not in our homes."

"She's gotten to you," Albertson accused.

"No. I'm just playing devil's advocate. You told me never to juice myself. Why?" He pushed back, ignoring the ache in his ribs and stuffed his hands in his pockets.

"You were perfect as is. The supplement was not."

"But it's been in use since–"

"You didn't need it, strong and big as you are. And you were never headed to the combat zones anyway."

The message was clear: he should be grateful. Gratitude breeds loyalty. Time to pay the toll. And lie like a dog. "I'm thankful for your protection and support all these years. I'd like to think I've shown it."

"You have, son, you have." But his smile lacked the usual warmth. "How'd you get tangled with this fanatical woman?"

"Pure chance. I recognized her on the street. Knowing you were interested in her activity the other night I endeared myself to her to find out more."

The Judge gave a knowing little snort. "Endeared. I like that one. So what have you learned?"

"What you already know." He shrugged. "She's a fanatic about your 'archaic' decisions and vehemently opposed to juicing."

"How did that bring you here?"

"She heard some tests had been done out here and wanted to explore. Naturally, I couldn't let her come alone."

"Naturally."

Brian smothered a snicker over Albertson's irritation. "When and where is the funeral?"

"South side." The Judge came to his feet. "My driver's downstairs. We'd better get moving. You'll want your uniform."

The picture of propriety, Brian agreed. Following the Judge into the private elevator he wondered at his stupidity. How had he underestimated the danger of Albertson's calculating tendencies?

Brian dropped regret in favor of noting placement of cameras, security panels and guards along the route out of the building. He wouldn't underestimate the danger again.

* * *

"Where are they taking us?" Maria asked as soon as Jaden reappeared.

Together they moved down the line, rationing a bit of water for each woman. "Hammond Street docks to meet a ferry. After that, I can only guess."

Maria's hand gripped Jaden's arm. "Canada?" she whispered.

"Then the world." Jaden looked around. The percentage of blondes, redheads and brunettes was pretty even. "It has to be a slave order."

"No! That's ridiculous."

"Have you heard anything to the contrary?"

Maria shook her head. "I've heard lots of crying."

"Were you beaten frequently?" Jaden gave her a closer inspection.

Maria shook her head and pointed to her eye. "This happened during the snag. Not knowing what's next is the worst. Though I'm not a big fan of this little number." She touched a stamp on her arm.

Jaden smiled at Maria's snarling. Attitude like this was a good sign from a woman who'd soon be an integral partner in the rescue. Then she frowned over the small tattoo on Maria's upper arm. It may as well have been a UPC code from the 20th century.

"What the—"

"Yeah, that's what I said. I get snatched sneaking a smoke and figured Micky knew I was skimming. No biggie, it'll come out of my tips. But then I'm shoved into a van with a couple other broads and it's lights out. I woke up in a cell with this un-fashion statement and four other chicks who could be my sisters."

"Be happy they're not. Are they here now?"

Maria shook her head. "They disappeared two days ago."

Steeling herself against the bitter taste of failure, Jaden outlined her plan to Maria. Then she tried again to reach Cleveland. Still no service.

With only ten minutes to the docks, she left Maria to explain the plan of attack to the other women and returned to the engine. The guard was coming around, so she subdued him once more and discussed the engineer's options. He seemed like a decent guy caught in the wrong web.

"How'd you land this job?"

"I went for the wrong paycheck."

Bingo! "Tell me how and who. You've got 5 minutes to give me a reason to let you off this hook."

"I'm working my butt off pulling doubles on the el maintenance crew to keep the roof over my wife, baby girl and my sister's heads. This guy comes on site and offers me side work. Like I don't spend enough time away from home. But the gig means enough money so I can drop to only one shift and on-calls."

"Driving this get up."

"You got it." The engineer shook his head. "At first I didn't get it. But when I asked a question, they made it clear. Keep making the runs or they'll add my family to the cargo."

"It is a slave trade."

He nodded. "I've heard guards talk about the underground market just over the Canadian border."

And a demand overseas for beautiful Americans.

"Help these ladies out and you can relocate. Safely. Just give me your family info cards and I'll get them to you, wherever you decide to start over."

"Cute lady, but I ain't stupid."

"Then take the offer. I can get you cash enough to set yourself up. It's your best shot for a clean start." She waited, damned near an eternity, for him to conclude she was his best option. Finally he nodded and dug into his wallet for his dependent ID cards.

"You won't regret this," she assured him. "The women are going to commandeer that ferry once I give the signal. Then you're going to pilot them to safety. Got it?"

"Where is safety?"

Good question. One under heated debate both in the rail cars and her own head. "Lansing," she decided. "Get the ferry into Grand Haven and find a ride into Lansing."

"Me and what truck line? This group'll draw attention."

"He won't find you. If we play this right he won't even know anything's wrong for another day, maybe two."

"You've got a vivid imagination."

"Oh? You going to tell him?"

"Hell, I wouldn't know who to tell." He tipped his head to the man on the floor. "That's where I get my orders." He began to apply the brakes. "He's scary enough."

"But the threats?"

"Came in writing to my house. And on my email."

Jaden didn't have more time to talk. She climbed out to hang on the side of the engine, waited for the train to slow, then jumped. Lord help her if Maria or the engineer lost courage now.

Jaden rolled to her feet and jogged with the train for a few more yards until she found cover in a cluster of containers going to rust on worn-out trailer cars. Her heart thudded in her chest when no ferry awaited them. Had the Judge been notified of intruders and changed the plan? Her dark thoughts turned thunderous as she envisioned Brian turning her in.

Then a soft horn sounded from beyond the lakeshore, soon answered by two answering calls from the engine's whistle.

So far so good.

She studied the ferry's deliberate pace and psyched herself up to interrupt the exchange. Behind her the cargo doors creaked open and the chains held by the prisoners began to jangle with their movements.

Jaden let the first three guards, one for each car she presumed, walk by without incident. They were for the women to handle. The next man out—wasn't. Jaden blinked. This guard was all woman. Over six foot and built like a porn-site feature model, the ebony-skinned beauty headed for the engine with her scanner on her hip.

Jaden left her fate to the engineer and strolled up onto the ferry as if she'd been sent by the Amazon herself.

"You're new," another burly male said in greeting.

"And you're finished," she replied, with a swift kick to his balls. When he doubled over, she was ready with a two fisted drop against the back of his neck, sending him face first into the decking. Blood seeped from his prone form and she left him for the newly freed prisoners to clean up. Jaden swiftly searched the pilothouse, kitchen, upper and lower decks and the engine room before the agreed signal sounded.

"Ahoy the ferry!" Maria's voice carried from the dock.

Jaden grinned, popping back up from the engine room to the main deck. "One success and you're Captain Nemo."

"I'll settle for not swimming with the little mermaid. All clear?"

"Welcome aboard." Jaden helped Maria get the women situated on the upper deck. Once assignments had been handed out for kitchen duty and comfort detail, Jaden pulled Maria aside. "This is a rough picture of what the GPS should look like. If he starts pulling you off this course, take him out like I showed you and take over. Unload everyone in Grand Haven, then send the boat west into the lake and scuttle it."

"Scuttle?"

"As in sink."

Maria groaned. "And ride back how? On Jonah's whale?"

"The automated system is working fine. Set the new course, set fire to the engine room and wave *bon voyage*. If the automated system fails, put it into the current and then start a fire in the engine room and row back in the life raft."

"Jesus, Jaden."

"I don't think it'll come to that. The engineer is solid enough. I just want you to have a back up plan."

Jaden and Maria returned to the gangplank to haul the unconscious guard into the train engine with his cohorts. The sight visibly bolstered Maria's confidence. The engineer held two guns on the others–though they were tied well out of reach from one another. And three were unconscious.

"Impressive," Maria beamed approvingly.

"Thanks," he said. "We ready to sail?"

Jaden found a beat up messenger bag and loaded it with the weapons confiscated from Albertson's crew then caught up with Maria and the newly commissioned captain.

"I'll do my best to have transportation waiting in Grand Haven." She fumbled with the cell card, but still no service. "Once in Lansing, feel free to split up, but email me on my secure site so I know how to reach everyone." She handed over the electronic address. Then Maria and the engineer-turned-sea captain were pulling away from the dock and waving like kids at a circus.

Jaden watched until the ferry became a speck on the horizon, periodically attempting to will cell card service into existence.

It didn't seem possible that less than four hours ago she was scoping out the dragon's lair and drawing some critical conclusions.

Taking her first real look at the Hammond street dock, she sighed. It was a long walk back to Chicago. And she still had four hard-core monster underlings to depose of before she got started.

"Wake up!" The shout of a female voice tore through the deserted dock. The Amazon.

Jaden stepped up her pace when the second outburst was accompanied by stomping and struggling inside the engine. Jaden opted to listen first in the hope of avoiding a messy and time consuming interrogation.

"That was her! You let her slip past," the Amazon accused in a voice straight from an island vacation.

"No way. We blew her up," a groggy male voice replied.

"And the horse she rode in on," another man chuckled.

"Transport officers are disposable."

"Worthless fools," Amazon ranted. "That was her! Judge A will give us all injections when he discovers she's alive."

It was exactly the information she could use to her benefit. Jaden opened the door with a lethal smile on her face. "What the Judge doesn't know will hurt you." She set her dagger spinning between her two index fingers, watching the prisoners watch her. She might have the mobility advantage at the moment, but they weren't caving. "Let's play truth or dagger. You talk truthfully, we've got no problem. But silence or lies and you win a little private time with me and my pointed pal."

The guard she'd tased en route squirmed and crossed his legs. Fear was beautiful on the face of the enemy. She pinned him with a look. "You first. Where are the children?

"Silence is not golden," Jaden deadpanned when he refused to answer. She pretended to look away, giving him ample time to consult the Amazon, clearly the senior officer of this wretched crew. "Don't worry about her. She's no threat."

"You don't know her," one of the guards from the ferry blurted. He got a snarl from the Amazon for his trouble.

"And none of you know me. So I'll fill you in. I'd gladly kill you all–slowly–just for this slavery thing. Sending the pieces back to your boss in tiny boxes would really improve my mood. But I'm short on time and more interested in what else you know. Work with me and we'll have no problem. Work against me and you'll suffer."

"You are nuthin'," Amazon said, her accent sliding quickly downhill. "Ya got no hold here."

"To the contrary, dearheart." Using the Judge's favorite pet name put an ounce of fear into her black laser gaze. "I'm the only thing. I hold all the cards."

Amazon spat on Jaden's shoe.

"Impressive. Now help or shut up."

To emphasize her point, Jaden lashed out, pulling the punch just millimeters shy of Amazon's nose. Catching the minute flinch, Jaden called her tactic a success.

She turned back to the tasered guard. "What do you know about the children?"

This time he spoke up. "They're in a subbasement in Chicago."

Under her nose. She gritted her teeth. "How many?"

He shook his head. "Don't know."

She eyed Amazon, then the others in turn. The wiry fellow who looked as if he'd piss his pants any second gulped and stammered. "Fi–Fif–fifty-two at last count."

"And when was this last count?"

"Shut up ya fool," Amazon growled.

He thought about it, took one more look and Jaden and spilled his guts.

"M–Monday."

"His acquisition rate?" Jaden asked despite the Amazon's swearing and thrashing attempts to break free. Mr. Talkative didn't pretend to misunderstand her.

"A few. Three to five" he clarified, when Jaden glared. "A–a week."

She didn't know there were that many vulnerable children on the Chicago streets. Even with the conservative stats she'd seen, that sort of disappearance rate should've been noticed.

"Not all l-local."

The Amazon surged again to fight the bindings and wield threats. Jaden put a bullet into the wall an inch above her head. She stilled.

"You were saying?"

"The ac-account–"

Mr. Talkative was drowned out by the blood-curdling cry of the Amazon breaking free of the wall. Interrogation over, Jaden switched to self-defense as she found herself wrapped in mortal combat.

The handcuffs weren't much deterrent to the Amazon's fighting skills. She'd turned them into an asset, and Jaden had to work to avoid immediate strangulation.

She spun, bringing their faces so close Jaden could smell the copper on her breath. She was in deep with this one. Buying an ounce of time, she snuck her fingers between the Amazon's crushing arm and her throat. Gulping air like a drowning woman, she made a dive to the floor.

Pressed between steel floor and juiced Amazon, Jaden didn't have the luxury of strategy. She whipped her head up and back. The crack of bone to cartilage, the squish of blood, the Amazon's outraged shriek blended into a sweet symphony. Jaden tucked her chin and rolled, escaping the shocked Amazon and shooting to her feet.

They squared off, each re-assessing the other. Blood dripped from Amazon's smashed nose, but her eyes still glinted with relentless determination.

When she lunged, Jaden was ready.

The dagger slid neatly between Amazon's ribs, her momentum pushing her body onto the blade. Her lung pierced, she choked on her own blood as she bled out at the feet of her men.

She steadied herself, wiping the blade on her pants before sheathing the knife. Her hands were steady, though her soul quaked with the burden of taking a female life for the first time.

"Okay." She came back to Mr. Talkative. "You were saying?"

"A better egress," Brian said to his reflection. They should have planned a rendezvous time and place. His mind roamed back to the recent hours in the suite.

How quickly things change. Only yesterday he'd itched to return here, to his home, and all the comforts that implied. Today, with Albertson waiting out front, he thought he might suffocate from the familiar. Or be crushed by the weight of his formal uniform.

He tucked his cell card into an inside pocket and was halfway to the door when a better idea occurred. If even remotely possible, she'd be at Larry's funeral. If she knew about it. A lot of ifs. He turned back anyway and gathered his best tracking equipment from his secret stash. Then he went to resume the charade of a man mentored by greatness.

Sliding into the judge's car, he had to wonder at the irony of attending a funeral with the devil himself. If he could only have one more night with Jaden in that damned suite. One more night with her anywhere. If she lived through whatever she was doing on that train, he'd tell her everything.

Everything.

Chapter Twelve

Time Stamp: 1826

The sheriff halts between me and the lifeless body on the floor. I can feel his suspicions as if they are my own. Can't blame him. Who wouldn't suspect a female able to remain upright in the middle of such a horrifying sight?

A purpled, strained face and a vivid red ring above the clerical collar leaves no room to doubt the cause of death. Strangulation. The strap in my hand leaves no room for defense.

"Death was too good for him."

"No, Sarah! Take it back. He's a man of God. He founded this orphanage."

The sheriff's plea is lost on me. As are the growing voices crying out for my hanging. They don't understand what he was. Is. He fooled them all. All but me and the little girl cowering in the pantry.

"Hanging suits me fine."

The sooner the better. I already know my fate and my failure. And I don't want to be so far behind this infernal race next time.

By sheer will, Jaden continued to put one foot in front of

the next. Her hip ached and was seeping blood again. If she ever saw Brian again, he'd be ticked she messed up his fine work.

If she ever saw Brian again.

The sound of that rib-cracking blow echoed in her ears. She'd left him to deal with the beating on his own. It was the only choice, she reminded herself. The women had no one else. Brian was a big boy. Capable. Inventive.

To keep her sanity, she tried reaching Cleveland again. Finally he answered.

She explained her location. "Can you pick me up?"

"Sure. Hang tight."

As if there were options. She used the time to link up with trustworthy security contacts in Michigan and Illinois to assist the escapees and the engineer's family. The to-do list complete, she tried to empty herself of the sensory overload.

"Someone call a cab?" Cleveland asked upon arrival. He brought her to her feet and opened the door for her.

She looked up into his face, kissed him full on the mouth and then slid into the passenger seat. Cars were still cars, but this was a treasure. "How'd you rate a 1957 Chevy?"

He smirked. "I like the classics."

"Must've cost a fortune to replace the old gas engine."

"Worth it. You know about cars. About history," he added cryptically.

"And you know a lot about the street," she dodged. "What can you tell me about disappearing girls? Under twelve."

"Chicago streets are riddled with underfed, disadvantaged folks of all ages who go missing all the time."

"Cleve," she pleaded, "everyone trusts you. Talks to you. Help me out."

He slowed to accommodate the heavier traffic funneling

into the toll lanes as they neared the city.

"I wouldn't hold out like that from you."

"You've never mentioned your home. Or this cool ride."

"They call it bitter for a reason, girl," he teased. "About disappearing kids...there's not much to be heard." He paused while the machine scanned the tag on his window. "What've you been told?"

"There's a standing weekly order for girls under twelve. A guy dubbed 'the accountant' runs supply and demand numbers. All outgoing shipments originate in Chicago."

He moved through the barricade and resumed cruising speed. "That's myth-quality bullshit. No one could keep that quiet."

"Girls are snagged from all over."

He shook his head. "Still. They have to come in. Someone would notice."

"The Judge could pull it off."

"Y'know, I've always been a history buff. A sucker for a good legend. When my sister died—when I was branded, those events made me curious."

She wondered if Brian had been right and Cleveland was repeating life till he got it right. She wondered when she'd get it right.

"My curiosity got me into trouble. My wits got me out. Out of trouble I had more time to research the things that satisfy my curiosity."

"And," she demanded, impatient and tired.

"I searched the infinity symbol."

As had she.

"I found an interesting correlation in several not so recent crimes."

As had she.

"It seemed like Albertson was copycatting older criminals. Then I met you and things you said, reactions you had made me—"

"Curious," she finished for him. "And you researched me too. Found correlations that shouldn't be there."

"Nope. I just rifled your place a couple times." He winked. "I only lifted the one picture. You should keep better track of your secrets, girlfriend."

Jaden shifted in the seat, needing to see his reaction. "You believe in reincarnation?"

"In a few select instances. I don't know how or why, but I believe *you* are different. Your police chief too."

"You might mention that to him next time you meet." Why deny it? She was too tired to fabricate any sort of believable disclaimer anyway. "Why did you suggest a partner?"

"Everyone can use help. Even you."

She studied her hands, feeling mulish. "Brian makes me feel stronger." It even sounded stupid to her ears.

"See?" He smiled gently. "You're used to being the urban legend. The tough broad no one gets close to." A block from his home, he turned into a dilapidated parking garage. "If a person knows how to unravel it and weave the ends together. There's been three entangled in this battle for a long time."

"I know that," she snapped.

He continued blandly. "The third wasn't me." He posed a pout. Then winked. "I wanted you to keep an eye out."

"So you must know what I've been doing wrong. What I can't find."

"Best I can tell, seeing how I've only lived once, is you're bitter."

The Judge had said as much. But bitterness kept her

sharp, kept her focused and enabled her to kill when needed without hesitation. And the judge would never give her anything helpful.

"I don't think full victory rests in your weapon searches. I think the key's in you. What's the only thing you've never done?"

"How should I know? I have memories, but can anyone truly have full recall?"

"Bitter," he pointed out.

"Annoyed," she corrected. Exhaustion threatened and she gladly climbed out of the car. If she could sleep, she'd be out for hours. But it wouldn't be restful. It would be hours plagued by the nightmares of little girls headed to doomed lives, or worse. Little girls in need of saving. "I don't need riddles, I need answers. I have to find them Cleveland. And then I have to stop him."

"You will. After you're rested it'll be easier."

"If I could get a location, make an ID, they'll have to put him away."

"Will those other women come forward?"

"They'll speak with one of my connections and he'll hold the record until needed."

"Larry's funeral is today," Cleveland said as they entered his apartment. "Graveside service at sunset in the Southside Cemetery."

Jaden shifted her aching body. Laid her fingers over the bruising imprint of the Amazon's hand on her neck.

"Thought I missed it," she replied, shifting again to stare out the window. "Where are the kids?"

"Game room. Quit dodging. We'll go together."

"With the kids? Dressed like this?"

"Clothes don't matter and a couple more hours alone won't

faze Quinn and Katie, they're safe here."

"How's that working out?"

"I love it. I think they're happy. It's great to have someone to share all this."

Someone ought to be happy, she groused. She'd given up on the golden family at the end of her rainbow. Hell, she'd given up on rainbows. But she said, "They're good kids."

Cleveland combed through her hair with his fingers. "You've been through hell and back. We'll skip it."

"Drop the reverse psychology crap. We'll go."

"You'll be recognized unless we disguise you."

"No more disguises." Jaden made up her mind. "It's past time to commune with the living. A few of them should be there." She had a question or two about the legalities before she brought kidnapping charges against the judge for the women on the train. Maybe the threat would scare him enough to tell her where the young girls were stashed.

"Forget I brought it up. The cemetery will be crawling with cops. You'll get hauled in for violating the house arrest order."

"No house, no arrest?" she offered.

"Too lame."

"We'll just stay in the background. I'll just jog by–"

"Jogging in a cemetery?"

"Less traffic. More people should try it. Give me a ball cap and I'm set."

Cleveland grumbled, but he knew when not to argue with her. "Fine, but no fighting. You've been through enough today."

"Yes, Dad."

"Clean yourself up and we'll go."

Cleveland called a cab service, in the interest of keeping a low profile and respecting her revulsion of the el. After a brief word with the kids, they met the cab and headed out.

"You okay?" Cleveland asked at the cemetery gate.

"No." She croaked and swallowed a sob. "But I'll manage."

"It's natural to miss him, but you didn't kill him."

"Didn't I? He was responding to an alarm *I* set."

"Oh, that's right. The man only did his job, only took real risks when you were involved."

Jaden felt a shaky smile curve her mouth. "I can always count on you for perspective." Her legs finally moved willingly, carrying her to the people milling around at the graveside.

Larry's will specified no viewing, no wake, no visitation. Music began soft and subtle, then grew into a livelier tune. The faces around her began to smile. It was perfect music for reminiscing about a man people thoroughly enjoyed.

Jaden stayed on the fringe, much as she'd lived so many of her lives. Closing her eyes, she tipped her head toward the one white puff of cloud in the wide sky. *I miss you. I'll probably see you soon.* Well, with her record, probably not.

"Well look at this. I've never seen so many bodies come back to life at a funeral."

Loomis.

Prepped for the worst, she had to try. "I wanted to talk with you."

"Get the hell outta here."

She blinked and stepped away, swallowing her own sharp grief. "I'm sorry for your loss."

He just kept bearing down on her. "Get out before I haul you in."

"For what, surviving a hit?"

A stirring in the crowd behind Loomis caught her eye. The scene put a tight cap on her horrendous day. Brian, in dress blues and all his glory as Chief of Police, came into view.

And stood at the right of the Judge.

She couldn't breathe. The betrayal suffocated her.

Loomis gripped her arm above the elbow and turned her away from Larry's mourners. He shoved her across the neat lawn as if he wanted to force her to stumble. She wouldn't let it happen.

"Ease up Loomis," she growled.

"As soon as you get what you deserve," he growled back.

At the street he gave her a rough push. "This is a private party, you'd best keep running."

Okay, the man had lost his mind. Grief could do that. Jaden didn't bother with further protest. Legal routes had never worked before, why think this time could be different. If she couldn't even get Brian's help when he was a cop, the answer to ending the vicious cycle of her lives wasn't in a law book.

That left weapons. And the best tangible resource was the museum. With a sigh, Jaden headed off. No one could keep her from a private memorial for Larry at the scene of the tragedy.

Brian knew the jogger had to be Jaden. The slight favor in her stride, the swinging braid, and the fury shimmering around her. There could be no doubt.

Except in her mind, if she'd seen him here.

He eased away from the Judge, knowing the man noted his every move as he carried on politely with the other mourners. Maneuvering randomly took a great deal of planning, Brian mused, patiently waiting to exchange sympathies with Loomis.

Brian suppressed a satisfied smile over the smooth transfer. Now that the tracking device was in place, he'd always know Jaden's whereabouts.

Assuming she didn't throw it away when she found it.

Jaden ran, letting go of her grief with each jarring footfall. Grief from each previous life. Grief for parents, for innocence. For her friend, Larry. For the only woman she'd ever killed. For her only sister, murdered by the same demonic entity that currently wore judge's robes.

She caught a cab to Lakeshore Park and ran until her lungs burned and her hip insisted she slow down. Easing into an achy walk, she blamed her watery eyes and runny nose on the lake wind buffeting her. For lack of anything better, she wiped her face with her sleeve.

And froze.

Then swore, loudly, into the device attached to her sleeve. Loomis wired her–but why?

She began stretching, or rather, pretending to stretch while taking inventory of the people around her. She'd run for miles, lost in her mournful and useless thought. The lakeside greenway was as meticulously designed as the cemetery, but with happier people. None of whom appeared to care about her.

She worked the dime-sized disk off her sleeve and walked until she found an empty bench in an equally deserted clearing. She couldn't go anywhere she wanted to until she'd disabled the device. Slumping into the seat, she wished for the jeweler's loupe in her tool kit. But that was tucked safely away in the suite in Micky's warehouse and she wouldn't go *there* until she knew who wanted her tracked and why.

Loomis had to be working on orders from higher up. But

whose? Jaden found herself wishing for something, some*one* else she should've left in the suite: Brian.

With an eye out for the likely tail, she rolled the edges of the flat tracking button between her thumb and fingers, jumping when a tiny holographic recording filled her palm. She'd not seen an upgrade like this.

"Keep this close. I'm on your side," Brian said on the wispy recording.

He was in his formal uniform, officially resuming his previous life. The life he missed terribly. The life that put them on opposite sides of the justice versus vengeance issue.

She tried to be happy for him and just couldn't muster the energy.

She played the hologram again, listening for vocal clues. And again, to study his surroundings. But there was only the striking image of him speaking those few words.

She got to her feet and continued on to the museum, pocketing the tracking communicator.

I'm on your side.

She wanted to believe it. To believe he agreed with her than Albertson must die. But that would mean a leap of faith she's not sure she could make in his place. Brian and the Judge had history, good history. It was unreasonable to expect him to throw it aside easily. Unreasonable to expect that killing the judge wouldn't hurt the orphaned, doubtful Brian.

She didn't want Brian to hurt.

Dammit, she wasn't *going* soft. She'd bypassed soft and dissolved straight into a squishy puddle of emotions. With a final look at the hologram, she cocked her arm and pitched the tracking device into Lake Michigan.

Brian scowled at the dark van sitting across the street. He

hadn't ordered the extra protection. And he didn't need the invasion of privacy at the moment. Which meant someone else with enough clout to waste the manpower had ordered this extra watch.

Albertson.

Over a dinner the Judge insisted upon, they'd discussed the good old days. The continued message of loyalty hadn't flown over Brian's head, he just didn't care. The good old days seemed stained after the nasty discovery at the mill.

He walked through his house, nursing a beer. It didn't feel like home anymore. Nothing was obviously disturbed, but Brian understood dinner had been a delay to allow Albertson's men time to search the place. He was sure they'd wired him for sound too.

He checked the receiving unit on his wrist that showed Jaden's location. She was either still in Lakeshore Park or she'd found and dumped the tracer. Had she found the hologram? He tried tapping into a sixth sense, to *feel* her.

Nothing.

He scoffed at his overactive imagination.

He ached that she'd been right about so much regarding the Judge. At the funeral, he found himself mourning the effective loss of a man he considered family. No more. It was like being orphaned again, only this time he counted it as a blessing. She'd been right about it all. The man was a monster.

A monster in league with a power hungry scientist. He'd like to kill them both for their destruction against humanity and the tragedies on the horizon. The vigilante attitude went against everything he thought he believed about right, wrong and justice. But he felt it to his soul anyway.

Brian needed to get back to Micky's place and see how much progress Lorine had made. If the lady doc could prove

Kristoff's fraud, the sting would require precise timing. But he wouldn't risk leading the boys in the van into the safe haven the smuggler had created.

Draining the beer, Brian pressed a button to draw the privacy screen across his front windows. He heard the el whisper by and checked his receiver again. The transmitter still hadn't moved.

Well, it was way past time to find out why.

Jaden slipped into the museum and cooled her temper in the massive marble foyer. Her nerves frayed from the day, she took a moment to pull herself together before heading to the weapons gallery. The missing piece of this millennia-old puzzle had to be here. She'd find it and use it to destroy the evil still running free in this world.

She refused to indulge in any more tears. She'd failed. Past tense. It *would* be different this time. Entering her favorite gallery, she walked toward the scabbard and etched sword of a warrior from the 15th century. It was a narrow, lighter blade, but just as deadly as the heavier broadswords wielded by mail covered men.

Her hand reached toward the case, longing for another touch of the elegant steel. This had not been hers. Her sword had been broken in front of her face as a broadsword split her back for treason in battle.

Jaden closed her eyes and recalled the singing of steel through air, the perfect match of hilt to palm. It hadn't been treason, but justice, if anyone had bothered to inquire. Ah, well, a little late to dispute facts now.

"Reliving the glory days, dearheart?"

Jaden didn't acknowledge Albertson immediately, nor did she open her eyes. She savored the memory of disarming him and running him through.

"Ah, yes. You cheated if I recall," he continued. "Waiting until I was spent to turn on me."

She sighed and faced the Judge. "And still you laughed all the way into your next life."

"You can change the future, dearheart."

She scoffed, turning away to view a model sized suit of armor. She recognized the coat of arms, recalled the captain she'd admired for his compassion.

"I'd settle for salvaging the mess you've made of the present." She viewed a painting of a gauntlet and felt as overwhelmed as the young man facing the challenge. "Where are the children?" she demanded.

"Safe." He held out a hand, a peace offering she supposed. She happily envisioned breaking each of his fingers. "You and I merely look at life and its options differently. Humanity spouts claims of tolerance, acceptance, and celebration of differences. Yet you refuse to keep up with society."

"No society wants what you're offering."

His laughter bounced off the marble, glass and steel. "Don't lower yourself with false stupidity. If they didn't want me, I wouldn't be here."

She hated it when he was right. Purging the world of those he poisoned was impractical if not impossible. If he was right...maybe it was time to give up. What was the point of continuing a losing battle?

"Reward yourself, dearheart," his whisper swirled around her. "Take hold of your life. Let go of the past and embrace the life you desire."

The gallery faded away and her view filled with green grass, a dog barking and happy giggles of children. Her children. She could see her own green eyes reflected in cherubic faces framed with their father's dark waves of hair. She gazed into the face of her husband and her heart stuttered with the weight of the love they shared. Real. Soul-deep. Forever.

Yes, her mind cried. *Yes*, her heart echoed. This was the prize she craved. Each life she'd been denied this irrefutable beauty, this most basic element of human nurture.

"It's yours, dearheart. Take it and live it." The words caressed her skin as smooth as silk.

Could it be that easy? Could simply accepting make it truth?

Yes. Her answer pulsed within her bloodstream.

She reached for her daughter in her husband's arms. Called to her sons. She would claim this happiness as her reality. She would let peace and love rule the remainder of her days.

"No." Her own voice sounded hoarse and unused. She struggled for air and tried again, "No!"

Then she felt it, the scarf around her neck. A scarf she'd not been wearing moments ago. She wriggled and it tightened. She threw an elbow back, but it got lost in the rolls of fat of the monster that'd used her own dreams to seduce her into complacency.

Anger surged within her and spilled over, empowering her. She dropped to her knees, startling Albertson into loosening his grip. She shot for freedom between his legs. On her back she raised both feet and kicked mightily. His bulk did the rest, carrying him into a case of catapult remnants. The display shattered under the assault and Albertson screamed as shards of glass and history cut into his fleshy form.

Jaden made a clumsy dash for cover as feet pounded

toward the noise and mess. Her head felt too heavy, her legs like lead and her mind fuzzy from the blurring of truth and reality. Desperate, she put all her dwindling energy into escape.

Albertson cursed violently, knowing the incompetent men tending him would blame his injuries for the foul words and attitude.

He'd almost had her! Never had he been as close as today! He didn't bother to assess where his illusion had broken down. Just knowing he'd mastered a connection this clear told him he could get to her any time. She couldn't stop him now. She'd lost her tough edge and would soon lose their perpetual battle.

So close to over, he could taste it.

Absently, he licked his lips and cursed the tang of his own blood. She'd cost him dearly by diverting that slave shipment, but it was only money. She'd killed his best lieutenant and left the other guards to fate. He'd ordered a bullet into each lacking brain. Incompetent people were as disposable as money.

Hands dabbed at his face and hands. "Enough!" he roared, lumbering to his feet and out of the hall. He left the gibberish of apologies and promises in his wake.

No, she'd lost the battle already. He could feel her strength fading. He needn't worry about the completion of his plan. She'd never find the girls. This time he'd win. She was merely the last loose end. And he knew just how to clip her off.

Chapter Thirteen

"I say: Know your enemy and know yourself; in a hundred battles, you will never be defeated. When you are ignorant of the enemy but know yourself, your chances of winning or losing are equal. If ignorant both of your enemy and of yourself, you are sure to be defeated in every battle."

–Sun Tzu

Brian's vision still reeled with the sight of Albertson strangling Jaden. Why remained a mystery, but his greater concern was what would've happened if he hadn't found her in time. He'd been ready to jump in, to do anything to spare her, but it seemed just his presence restored her enough to escape.

Then he'd lost her, of course, in the chaos of people trying to assist the Judge. He shook his head at the stubborn independence that made her toss the tracking device into the lake.

But he had another one. When he found her, they'd talk about why she would wear it. But she wasn't in the suite. Or Micky's office. According to security, she hadn't been in the building since leaving with him this morning.

This morning! It seemed like a lifetime ago.

Brian found Lorine in the impromptu research center she'd carved into a corner of the library Micky provided his mules–girls, he corrected. The thought the smuggler put into their comfort continued to surprise him.

"How's it going?" he asked, keeping his voice low as Zach slept in her arms.

"Good enough, I suppose," she muttered.

"Trouble?"

"Confusion. The data's encoded."

"But I retrieved it all from public record."

"Yes," she agreed impatiently. "And the layman doesn't know how to interpret a urinalysis, much less a statement of hormonal impact."

"Does that mean you've found a negative indicator from juicing?"

Her mouth twisted with the irony. "We could use my life as exhibit A to prove that." She kissed Zach's hair, then looked up at him and gasped. "What ran over you?"

He touched the tender fullness under his eye. "Colorful?"

"To put it mildly." She shooed him away. "Go put something on that. I'll get a hold of you when I have what you need."

Brian nodded. What he needed was to know if Jaden was okay. He'd settle for enough to nail Kristoff until then. "Oh. Almost forgot." He removed his jacket and separated the lining from the shell. With a last once-over he handed the copied letter to Lorine.

She scanned it and blanched. "Oh, my God." Her eyes met Brian's. "Is this for real?"

"Yes." His reaction had been similar. The infinity letterhead was one more tie to the Judge, but the brief content was the most damning. Albertson's words praised Kristoff's discovery of an intriguing mental side effect of juicing and how to use it to accomplish their individual goals. "Will it help break the code?"

Lorine mumbled, stood and handed Zach to Brian. "Take him to the day care. I've got to figure this out."

He didn't question her further, timing was everything and they were quickly running out of it. He delivered the sleeping boy and returned to the still-empty suite.

Scooping ice into two packs, he eased his tired body onto the couch to wait for Jaden. With one pack on his face, one on his ribs, he considered just how many more lies it would take to find the truth in this bizarre case.

Albertson said the right things to effectively separate himself from the grotesque chamber in the Gary mill. But Brian found Jaden's claims ringing truer than his mentor's. Especially after his covert review of the Judge's calendar. He knew he'd lost a degree of objectivity to the pull of Jaden's sexuality, but he didn't think another detective would come to a different conclusion: the Judge was up to his eyeballs in some very nasty stuff.

Fraud at the least. Abuse of power. The illegal litany continued as his body gave in to the hellish day.

The nightmare came fast and hard making his heart pound in his chest. Beneath him, horse hooves pounded the earth. He struggled to see into the trees, searching for a sign. At last, he saw broken twigs. Marred with blood.

Agony speared him, stealing his breath, but he slid from the horse and pressed into the thicket on foot. The sight made him quake.

A woman hovered over the prone body at her feet. A body dressed in the colors of his lord. Blood seeped into the ground. "No!" he cried, rushing forward.

She turned and soul-shattering pain tore through him. He closed his eyes and cursed the gods. It could not be her. Anyone but her.

"I would not have done so only for me."

Her voice. May he never hear again.

Around them, his men approached. Nowhere for her to run or to hide. He struggled to free his sword. The murderous act must be dealt with, and swiftly.

"Mercy? A final word, Captain?" Her hand reached out.

He ran the blade through her heart.

Brian came awake with a jolt, sending ice packs flying.

This wasn't the first dream of its kind. And he'd accepted that the face of the woman in his dreams matched Jaden's. Exactly. But this was the first time he'd dreamed through to her death. This was the first time he truly understood it probably wasn't a dream at all.

Jaden rested in the quiet sanctuary of Micky's security office. She would've preferred an hour with her antique punching bag, but it was vaporized and this was a close second. Around her, monitors offered silent testimony of everything in Micky's domain, but her mind played other images for her torture.

Impossible images of husband, children, family. A sledding hill in winter. She shivered.

What had Albertson done to her? How had he crawled into her mind and tapped the dreams she kept buried. Dreams she enjoyed vicariously through others.

Again she reviewed and compared the cycle of her lives. Albertson abuses her and she learns the greater danger. She survives the incident and strives to spare others similar pain. She hunts him and, eventually exhausting all other options, she kills him.

Vigilante, Brian called her. Brian, the final link, the man who'd snuffed out her every life.

But this life had taken a detour from the pattern. Previously, she could only speculate about his attacks on new victims. Now, each new molestation played out with full sensory experience in her brain. Was this anomaly what enabled Albertson to wield his manipulations right inside her head?

"Hell yes I'm bitter," she confessed to the panel of monitors. "How many lives were lost because of my failures?"

"How many saved because of your actions?"

Brian's voice washed over her, but she didn't turn around. He was just another illusion and she wasn't going to get into it with another illusion tonight.

"Nearly forty on that train today. Forty lives saved because of you."

Maybe she would argue with her imagination. "And dozens more lost before they started because he's too clever."

She flinched at the sound of crying in her head. Turning, she dared to hope Brian might be real. Had the monster become so good as to layer the illusions?

Brian saw her expression and felt the grief like a weight on his chest. He crossed to her in a single stride. She'd suffered more than enough for her and the others.

He sank his hands into her hair. "This will help," he said, running his hands down and across her shoulders.

He pulled her to her feet and pressed her to the full length of his body. He brushed his cheek over her head, then tipped her chin up to seal the contact with his lips on hers. But her mouth remained immobile.

"I thought touching me helped."

"It makes me want..." She tried to pull back.

He held her in place. "What?" He could pray they wanted the same things.

"Things..." her voice cracked. "Things that can't be."

"Try me, Jaden. We're more than unlikely partners. We're connected. Trust me. What disables you like this?"

"Your Judge."

He cringed at the phrase.

"I hear the victims he attacks. I feel what they feel."

His heart broke for her. But he'd matched the Judge's unaccounted time pretty evenly with her 'headaches'. "Unless you're touching someone?"

"No. Not someone." Her tongue darted out, wetting her lips, whetting his appetite. "Just you."

He'd never let her go. Never let that infinite bastard win. "Let me in, Jaden. Let me help."

She slumped down into the chair, but didn't shrug off his hands on her shoulders. She reached into her pocket and pulled out a cell card. "The contact number is listed under 'floral delivery'. All the evidence you need to convict the Judge of a variety of crimes against women."

"That won't be enough for you." It wasn't enough for him anymore.

"It has to be." She bit her lip. "Vengeance isn't so good for my health."

A residual chill from the recent nightmare trickled down his spine. "Because of me."

He was finally starting to get the whole picture. Letting the Judge survive, even behind bars would eat at her. Sure, she'd live through the confrontation and conviction, but what kind of life would it be? And he wouldn't be party to anything that ended her life or made her miserable.

"And if there's another way?"

"That is the other way."

"What about together?"

"No." Her head fell into her hands and she began to shake. "They're here. In Chicago. And I can't find them."

"Who?"

"The girls he's been 'training'."

The shaking turned to more violent quaking. Shock? Fear? His or hers? Uncertain, he warmed her icy hands between his. "Is this from a current victim?"

Her teeth chattered so hard she couldn't form words to answer. He'd had enough. Hauling her into his arms, he headed for the privacy of the suite.

Maintaining the physical contact, he wrapped her in blankets and snugged her into the bed, tucking himself behind her for support.

"What is this?" he asked, when her teeth slowed down.

"Overload." Her eyes fluttered closed. "Happened to my sister once."

"You have a sister?"

"Once." Tears slipped through the lashes resting on her cheeks. "Only one in all this time. His abuse killed her. She just gave up. Died in 1952."

"Jaden that's—"

"Impossible. I know."

"No. Horrible." He took a deep breath. He'd sworn to tell her everything. "Can you hear me?"

She nodded, eyes still closed.

"I believe you. Not just here and now. About then, too. All the other times." He sounded like an idiot. How to get it out?

"Why now?"

"I found records in the Gary office. He's been supplying Kristoff with test subjects and eliminating Kristoff's critics. I saw him attack you in the museum."

She shook her head. "Not enough."

"I know that now. We have to kill him Jaden. There's no other way."

"No. Death doesn't stop him and I'm too tired to meet him again."

"Then rest. I'll kill him this time."

"No. That's my job." She struggled to sit up. "The key is living through it. Check the diary. The opal."

"Later."

"Now."

Brian decided if she was bossy enough to give orders and try to elbow him, he could leave her for a moment.

"Here." He pressed book and opal into her hands when he returned. "You've got more color."

"Cleveland says I'm bitter."

"Nice. Stronger voice, more attitude." He nestled into the bed once more to stroke her hair. "You're making fast progress."

"Cleveland mentioned taking a partner." She leafed through the fragile diary pages like a speed-reader.

"You've got one."

"Inner fire. Conviction."

"You've got plenty of both," he observed easily.

"Not me. You." Her gaze lifted and struck him with the intensity. "I missed my own clues. Too bitter. Stress and time turn coal to diamonds."

"What makes an opal?" He leaned in to read the diary.

She frowned and snapped it closed. "My fire. In here." She held the opal pendant over her heart. "Your conviction. Belief. If we're united, he will fall."

"He deserves more than a fall."

"I've been so blind! He knows. You. Me. That's why he

tried to kill you."

"He just spent half the day with me. Why aren't I dead?"

"What does he believe?"

The question startled him, but he followed her thought process. "He believes I'm undercover. That I'll bring you to him."

"What do you believe?"

"That I'll do anything to spare you this crushing pain."

She smiled, weakly, but it lit up her face. He kissed her mouth and now she kissed him back. The fire sparked.

He took them deeper, blending tongues, tastes, breath. He felt her hand in his hair, felt her need and revealed his own.

"You're too weak for this." He thought he might be too weak for this too.

"No. I need this. Need you. We may never get this chance again."

"In your next life."

Her eyes fell. She pushed him away. "I only ever wanted one life. One with you. He robbed me of my innocence, my family and you." She curled, burying her head in the nearest pillow.

He rubbed her back, toyed with her hair. "I've hurt you in the past. I'm so sorry, love."

She rolled back, her eyes bright when they met his. She was stronger than a moment before. It was a heady sensation to witness the depth of his effect on her.

"No if."

"Huh?"

She sat up, tucking her feet under her, dragging him along. "No *if*. You really believe me. Since when?"

Everything. He wouldn't torture them both by pretending any longer. Why deny the bizarre when he recognized the reality in it? "I believed when I saw your face over two dead bodies in your apartment." He took a breath and spilled it. "Your face has haunted my dreams and nightmares since I was a kid." He kissed her cheeks. "I chalked it up to imagination. To the sci-fi and real crime books I read.

"But these eyes have reached across time, haven't they?" His lips floated over each eye. "You've cried for the impossible." His mouth found hers, brushed and hovered. "Now celebrate the possible. Our time. Let's take it."

For a moment, Jaden simply stared at him. Possible or not, she'd waited a thousand years for this. She launched herself into his arms and let time fall away as her mouth fused to his.

If they only had tonight, then she'd make damn sure they both remembered it into the vast expanse of eternity.

She tugged clothing out of her way, desperate to get her hands on his skin. Warm and firm, she traced the lines of him, burning it into her memories, etching it into her senses. In a thousand years there had only been this one man for her.

His scent made her high, his eyes scorched her, his desire clear. His hands raced over her body and he rolled until he pinned her to the mattress. She laughed, pure and simple, for here was the joy she'd longed for.

I'm yours, she chanted, surrendering her body and soul. She gasped, when his mouth found her breast. Arched when his hand teased its mate. And scarcely breathed when he explored lower.

His mouth drifted across her center, his tongue circled and teased. She bucked, crying his name. His big hands anchored her as he sent her flying at will. She pleaded shameless, ecstatic, until she soared free.

Floating, she delighted in the feel of his body brushing

against her every nerve as he stretched out beside her. In the glow of loving, she let her fingers explore him slowly. His jaw, the muscled chest beneath crisp, dark curls. She traced the lines of his abs, trailed lower and smiled when he tensed. Oh, yes, this was the man of her heart.

You're mine. She claimed him with her mouth first, thrilled by his approving growl. Then she straddled him and teased them both with a hot, wet slide over his engorged length. Not enough.

Mine.

Yours.

"Now." He gripped her hips and settled her onto his shaft with one smooth, marvelous, deep thrust.

She arched, savoring, before the timeless need ripped though her. Here, at last, was the only union she'd ever wanted. The only man who made her *feel.*

She rocked, stoking the fire slowly, until his hips pumped beneath her. She matched his primal rhythm, driving them both toward the crest. Looking into his eyes, she saw all that mattered. The climax splintered her senses and the wall around her heart exploded in a brilliant rainbow.

"Got a cigarette?" Brian asked when he could speak again.

Her satisfied chuckle was as seductive as anything she could've said.

She stretched like a cat. "I bet I know where to find one."

"Micky probably stocked 'em around here somewhere."

"*Mmm-hmm.*"

"He's thought of everything else."

"*Mmm-hmm.*"

"You don't care?" He slid his fingers up and down her spine, savored the tremor.

"Nope." She propped up on an elbow and nuzzled his

neck. "You really want nicotine?"

Her tongue was doing crazy things against his neck. "Nope. I want you."

Her smile was all cat-in-the-cream. "You've had me."

He paused, mid-kiss. "I have." He tucked her hair behind her ear. He'd had her and thrown her away too many times. He'd be a fool no more. "This time I'm not letting you go."

Chapter Fourteen

Excerpt from Confessions of a Brothel-keeper as told to W.T. Stead, reporter for the Pall Mall Gazette, 1885:

Maids as you call them, fresh girls as we know them in the trade, are constantly in request...I have gone and courted girls in the country under all sorts of disguises...I bring her to London to see the sights...giving her plenty to eat and drink. I offer her nice lodging for the night: she goes to bed in my house and then the affair is managed. My client gets his maid, I get my...commission and in the morning the girl, who has lost her character and dare not go home, in all probability will do as the others do and become one of my 'marks'. Another very simple way of supplying maids is by breeding them. Many women who are on the streets have female children. They are worth keeping. When they get to be twelve or thirteen they become merchantable.

Jaden woke sated and renewed. Who knew a night of such little sleep could be so refreshing? Reaching for Brian, her fingers brushed a note card instead of his hair. He'd gone to the library to see Lorine.

Playtime was officially over.

Jaden rolled from the bed to clean up and go find this

mysterious library.

A woman who'd only lived once might be jealous. A woman who'd lived repeatedly, well...she might be jealous too, Jaden realized, grinning at her reflection in the bathroom mirror.

Her eyes drifted over her body, recalling each nuance of last night in Brian's arms. At her hip, eyes paused. He'd done a fine job mending and later teasing the still-sensitive area. No, there was no room for jealousy when a woman gave her trust to a man like Brian.

Jaden's grin faded and she turned away from the mirror, hoping to turn away from the darker thought creeping up on her. Only one thing could come between them. The one thing that had always come between them.

Albertson.

The judge knew Brian was the key to success for both of them. As did she. If Brian stood with her, the judge would be sentenced to hell. But if Brian harbored any doubt, if he sided with the judge, Jaden faced the daunting task of starting her quest once more.

She thought again of Lorine and her beautiful toddler. It seemed there was a case for jealousy after all.

Brian flipped open the Trident II palm sized monitor he'd purchased after confiscating one like it during the arrest of a jewel thief. The gadget was cutting edge, able to monitor up to four wireless cameras or signals simultaneously. The company claimed a maximum range of a two-mile radius, but Brian found a hacker who knew how to piggyback cell signals and didn't like behavior modification needles. They'd made a slightly unethical deal and now Brian's Trident had a ten-mile reach.

Just enough reach for what he had in mind.

Currently, camera one showed the van, still watching his empty apartment. Camera two had been re-programmed to receive input from Jaden's new transmitter. And camera three was about to record the small-screen debut of Dr. Lorine.

"All set?" he asked.

She answered with a satisfied smile. "Anything to knock Uncle Leo off his high horse."

And maybe take a certain judge with him, Brian thought. And when that bastard was in a cell with his own personal attitude-adjusting needle, Brian would personally oversee a lethal overdose.

"You okay?" Lorine interrupted his dark fantasy.

"Yeah. A lot on my mind."

He felt like a volcano ready to blow at every turn. The handwriting analysis proved he and Byron shared an uncanny likeness in penmanship as well as names. Jaden's 'memories' were documented tragedies throughout history. And he'd fallen in love with the object of a professional investigation, which had been personal from the beginning.

He pushed all but the juicing issues away for now. "Let's run this like a deposition. Start with your name and credentials please."

She did. Lorine epitomized the professional witness as she ran through the studies, the results, and the discrepancies between actual findings and reported findings.

Apparently once she'd broken the code, the false front Kristoff had painted for the public fell away to reveal the truth.

Lorine continued to prove the case against her uncle. As she spoke, Brian wondered at the audacity of Kristoff and Albertson. To use the finest soldiers in the country as guinea pigs was bad enough, but then to apply them to a personal power agenda? He shook his head.

Appalling how they'd exploited the unexpected side effect from juicing: the vulnerability to mind control. He took notes on the timeline Lorine provided. He'd run a thorough search later into the secure database and see just what chaos Kristoff had inflicted in America or elsewhere.

Brian lit up the laptop and checked his own draft record. He'd served the two mandatory years plus a third before turning his interests to protecting his close community rather than the world community. Within moments his personnel and medical files were available. It may have saved his life. Though he'd stayed away from the original juice, at Albertson's request, he'd missed the service-wide obligatory administration of the new juice.

"While human growth hormone has been used as a performance enhancement for our troops," Lorine intoned like a tenured professor, "this new formulation adds a dangerous level of serotonin and invariably results in an impairment of a soldier's ability to reason and discriminate logically."

She continued tearing apart each previous study, showing how the results were compromised.

She'd earned her new life. And she'd need it. If her family didn't care for her earlier choices, they'd sure be furious that she tore down their connection to influence.

As Lorine wrapped it up, she made a passionate call for Kristoff's resignation. For everyone's sake, Brian hoped the man listened, because his life was about to get ugly.

"Good job, doctor." Brian stopped and saved the recording.

Lorine shrugged out of the lab coat they'd used for staging. "I used to crave that title."

"Not now?"

She gave him a glowing smile. "Now I prefer 'Mommy'. And am I ever ready for a nap."

"You want a new bank account? New ID?"

"Will this play for the masses?"

He shook his head. "Don't think so, but I can't promise it won't get leaked to the media."

"Then just use plain old me. If Uncle Leo crashes and burns, I'll be the least of their worries."

"But your research brought him down."

"My family disowned me four years ago. To hunt me down means I exist. Trust me, they won't bother."

The Trident II beeped and Brian swiveled the angle on his home camera. The van was gone. *Even idiots catch on after awhile.*

Curious, he checked the status on Jaden. And smiled to see she was still in the suite where he'd left her. Safe, within reach, and oblivious to the tag he'd attached while she slept.

She considered meeting Brian at the library, but that smacked of checking up on him. So she sat at the table with her coffee, the diary, and a Chicago map. Occasionally, she toyed with the setting on her watch that revealed Brian's current position in the northwest corner of the third floor.

She smiled. Two could play the tracking game. Oh, she'd accepted, even understood, why he'd asked Loomis to plant the device on her at the funeral. And she might've felt a twinge of regret over tossing good equipment to the fishes.

But in the misty hours before dawn, she'd tagged him with a device of her own and she had every intention of keeping him in 'sight' until she disposed of Albertson.

A hand rapped on the door.

Jaden couldn't abandon her security habits. She got up to

check the peephole and her heart leaped to see Leigh, the young girl hurt so terribly by Albertson. She owed this girl plenty, just for surviving enough to put her hot on the Judge's trail.

"Come in!" she said, opening the door and her arms.

Leigh blinked, and then her mouth curved into a cautious smile. "Hi. I wasn't sure...the girls have said all kinds of things."

"Girls usually do." Jaden gave her warmest smile. The girl was still so fragile. "You look better. Want some coffee?"

"Sure. I just wanted to thank you personally." Leigh followed Jaden to the kitchen and accepted her coffee mug with steady hands.

Much better. The first time they'd met, the girl couldn't keep anything down. Jaden hadn't been sure Leigh wouldn't take her own life during those desperate days.

"I–I -" She gulped the hot coffee and started over. "I came to offer my services."

She directed Leigh to take a seat, shoving the diary and map aside. "What kind of services?"

"Anything you or the Chief need. W–without you both I wouldn't be here."

Jaden felt her brows shoot to her hairline and composed herself. "You don't owe me or anyone else. You've been through a horrendous experience."

"And I'm useless if I can't overcome it." She swallowed and chewed her lower lip. "I still haven't been outside. But–"

"Healing takes time," Jaden interrupted. "There's no schedule, Leigh. You can't rush it."

"You've done it."

Jaden nodded. "I've had more time." *What an understatement.*

"I'm gonna get the brand removed. To hell with his 'insurance'. If I ever see him again, I guarantee he won't live through a repeat performance from me."

"I hear you."

"You can't understand all the shame."

Jaden kept quiet, knowing the importance of having someone listen without offering unwanted solutions.

"I didn't tell you all of it." Her voice had lost the bravado. "I'm sorry." Tears welled in Leigh's eyes. "I just couldn't bring myself to say it out loud. I saw the little girls." Leigh's hands began to shake and the coffee sloshed.

Jaden reached out to guide the mug safely to the table. She nearly bit through her tongue as she waited. And waited.

"He blindfolded me."

"The Judge."

"No. The other guy. Bobby or Benny or something."

"Billy?" Jaden knew it had to be Brenda's ex.

"Yeah, that was it." Leigh twined her hands. "He shoved me onto a bed. The only light was over that bed." She shivered. "Oh, Jaden, it was like some bizarre cavern theatre."

"You were underground?" She had to be sure, knowing how Albertson liked to tweak the settings.

Leigh nodded emphatically. "It smelled damp. Like the basement in my dad's old house."

"What about the little girls?"

"I couldn't see too many faces." Leigh choked on a sob. "Just a few near the front. Those eyes. I thought they looked like zombies from a bad movie."

"Performance." Jaden recalled Leigh's earlier choice of words. "You performed for these girls?"

"You didn't go through this? Oh, I'm so embarrassed." She was crying freely now. "I knew it. I'm so stupid."

"No," Jaden soothed. "This wasn't your fault. You did what you had to do to survive. I know that well."

As the words sunk in, Leigh took a ragged breath and continued. "It was awful. I thought it was finally over when the Judge tossed me at B-Billy. He promised to let me live, let me go, if I did everything he said."

"An education," Jaden muttered to herself.

"He made those girls watch...watch..."

"Forget it," Jaden interjected to save her reliving the brutal memory. "I'm sure they were drugged."

"Maybe."

Jaden drew the map closer. "Micky said you just showed up. How did you get away and back here?"

"He just let me go. Catch and release, he called it." Leigh caught her lip between her teeth. "After he finished with me, he blindfolded me again, tied my hands and sat me on an electric cart."

"How could you tell?"

"The sound of the motor. And the feel. It was small, but quick. And no fuel smell. Just a short ride on that, then into a closed room. An elevator, but a big one. The damp smells faded as it climbed. Then I was back on the street."

"Blindfolded and tied up."

Leigh shook her head. "Someone took my arm, guided me for awhile, and then knocked me out. When I came to, the cuffs and scarf were gone and I was a few blocks from my normal route."

"Scarf?"

"I'm so sorry about not telling you the whole thing."

Jaden reined in her impatience. "Show me where you came to."

Leigh pointed to a corner two blocks north and one block

east of the el platform she used to take to work each day.

"The street was empty?" Leigh nodded. "And you just walked back here." Another nod.

Elevators, damp smells, electric carts. The new facts rolled around in Jaden's brain, bouncing in and out of several possible scenarios. The most likely of which was a subway system. A failed city plan that very few people alive today would know about.

"I'm sorry I kept this from you. Can you forgive me?"

Jaden's cell card chirped and trembled in her pocket. She answered it instead of Leigh.

"Michaels," she answered.

Cleveland's voice filled her ear. "Katie's gone."

"When and how?" Her stomach began to churn as Cleveland explained. Not with a new victim's fear, this time with anticipation. If she timed it right, she could catch the Judge in the act and take him down. Forever.

"We'll be right there." She disconnected her friend and turned to the quaking girl by the door. "You're coming with me," she ordered, grabbing a jacket from the closet.

"I–I can't."

"There's nothing for me to forgive. You survived. You said you'd do anything. Now's your chance."

Leigh was chewing her lip again. "Outside?"

"Yes." As gently as possible, considering the urgency, Jaden said, "I need you to walk me back through your escape."

With any luck at all, she'd find a back door into the subway system Albertson had cultivated for his vile intent.

In the library, Brian polished up the raw feed of Lorine's report and attached documentation. Calling up the website of the National Health Commission, he emailed the presentation directly to the Health Chairmen of New York City and Dallas, just in case the National Chair was also compromised by Kristoff.

Taking another moment to compose a more detailed message to the Commandant of the Marine Corps, Brian said a prayer. His father's oldest brother had deserted the family over an issue that couldn't possibly be important now. Hopefully sending the information to the public email box, with a modified last name would assure that he'd read it and take action.

Brian figured the officer's death had been bartered between Kristoff and Albertson to hurt Jaden. An order like that would only be executed by a juiced assassin. Brian was hoping his uncle would be able to help find the saboteur.

The Trident II beeped a notice that Jaden had left the suite, heading toward the dorm section. He cleaned up his gear and dashed off to fill her in.

He didn't find her before his cell card rang with a ridiculous alarm. It had been so long since that specific ring had sounded, he scrambled to read the display showing the badge number of the officer calling.

Loomis.

Brian hesitated. He wasn't back on duty—and didn't plan to be until Albertson was dead—permanently.

"Yeah?" he said, finally answering.

"I'm on my way to a B&E call at your place," Loomis grumbled. "Guess you're not home."

Brian stormed the security office and unfolded the Trident II. Camera two had begun to record when motion tripped the newly programmed sensor. His front door stood open to the world. He used his thumb to move the camera around. Two men, formerly of the van he'd bet, were ransacking his place.

"Ready or not, here comes round two."

"Huh?" Loomis asked.

"Nothing." The transmission from Jaden's tag showed she'd just left the building. Running off without him again. Would she never hold still? "Look," he said to Loomis, "forget the official call. Divert to the warehouse district and meet me at West 16th and State. We've got bigger fish to fry."

"Right boss."

He entered the suite to stow the computer and grab his gun. "This is off the record, Loomis."

"You got it."

Brian disconnected and slid the card into his jacket, only to watch it fall to the floor. "Stupid to hang on to the past." Wasn't a fresh future what he wanted? A chance to make his city safer? Tossing the abused jacket, Brian plowed the closet for the next best thing. He found a supple leather duster and donned it, stocking it with his preferred weapon, a .38 pistol, and a long reach taser in case he felt generous.

Next, he dialed Jaden's cell and waited as it rang twice, three times, then four. Unheard of. Worry nipped at the edges of reason.

"Hello?"

Not Jaden. "Who is this," he barked.

"L-Leigh."

"Put Jaden on." He'd find out details later, right now, he just needed to hear her voice. To let her know how he'd pushed Kristoff into a corner. To share his ideas for taking down Albertson.

"I can't, sir."

"Don't sir me, hand her the phone."

"She's–"

"You're outside." Just days ago she'd been terrified of the

street. He softened his voice. "Congratulations, Leigh. What's going on with Jaden?"

"She seems to be in pain."

"Can you put the phone to her ear?"

"Jaden? He's attacking someone?"

A gruff sound he took as affirmation came over the earpiece. "You don't have to hang on to track him."

"Yes," she groaned. "Ka-tie."

"Breathe, babe. I'm on my way." But Jaden didn't reply. Brian looked at the scanner. They were headed in opposite directions. Not for long. "I've got a van coming."

"What the he–"

"Hang on, babe. I'll be right there."

He heard her gasp, then the connection died.

Swearing a blue streak, he didn't wait for Loomis to stop before jumping in. Consulting the Trident II he guided Loomis to Jaden's location.

"There!" he pointed through the windshield to the women in the shadows of an alley entrance.

Loomis stomped on the brakes and Brian ran to help Jaden and Leigh into the van.

"Just take a seat in back," Brian instructed Leigh on his way to kneel by Jaden. "Nice day for a walk."

"Shut up and touch me."

He stroked a wisp of hair off her forehead. Her next breath was visibly better. "You know where we're going?"

"Sort of." She gave a wan smile. "Do it again?"

He cradled her face and kissed her full on the lips. "Better?"

"Yeah."

He helped her to her feet, knowing she'd happily beat him up later if he carried her. "I set the sting for Kristoff."

"I hope he's allergic."

The humor did more to ease his mind than anything. "You armed?"

"And dangerous. We need to hustle. Katie—"

"Are you sure?"

She nodded. "Cleve called."

"Damn." He should've killed Albertson when he had the chance. Should've torched the whole damn mill instead of looking for legal recourse.

"It's not your fault." Jaden stroked his fist until his hand relaxed. "Albertson's the bad guy here."

"Did you just read my mind?" Brian asked.

"No, your face." She kissed his open palm. "You didn't let me hang on to the blame. I can't let you."

Before he could say the words burning in his throat, before he could promise her the world, the van lurched forward.

"Where to?" Loomis boomed from the front seat.

"Wacker Street platform," Jaden said.

Loomis whipped the bulky vehicle around and floored it.

Jaden and Brian strapped in, with a glance of shared regret for Larry between them. As if they'd partnered for years, they set to separate tasks. She opened the cell frequency scanner while he scanned the emergency channels.

Brian reached over to help Leigh with the safety restraints on her seat. She was pale, but hanging in. "You made it outside," he observed. "Way to go."

Leigh studied the floor.

"She can show us how to get inside."

Brian looked from Jaden to Leigh and back again. "Inside where, exactly?"

"Wait until Cleveland gets here."

"He's coming with us?" But Jaden didn't get to answer because Loomis came to an abrupt halt. Brian saw Cleveland and Quinn waiting under the platform stairs. He threw the door open and urged them inside.

They'd officially breached safe capacity of the evidence van. Leigh moved into the front seat, and to Brian's surprise, Quinn took her place in front of a monitor, while Cleveland tucked himself onto the floor at Jaden's feet.

"Check this, Jaden," the kid said enthusiastically, sliding a clear mini-disk into a drive.

A glance from Jaden kept Brian quiet. He settled for watching the three of them in turns, wondering what he'd missed this time. Wondering if their respective plans would collide or compliment.

"Cleveland's got the best library access. D'you know that?"

"Sounds right," Jaden replied. "What'd you find?"

The monitor came to life and a map bloomed across the modest screen. As if he'd been born in an evidence van, Quinn manipulated the picture, highlighting and zooming in on what he wanted to present.

"You're a natural, kiddo," Brian said, impressed.

Loomis grunted. "What is that?"

"The Chicago subway system," Quinn declared.

"Chicago doesn't have a subway," Loomis made the point before Brian could.

"It wanted to," Jaden interjected. "On several occasions contractors tried to move away from the el trains into sub trains. They lost the fight, but not before digging the core tunnels. How'd you come across this Quinn?"

"Why?" Brian asked.

"I've been poking around since...well, since I heard crying

in the gutters one day. I haven't found the access..."

"I have that!" Brian exclaimed.

All heads turned.

He took an electronic marker and drew an infinity symbol over the map. "I just didn't know it," he clarified. "Head to the el maintenance hub, Loomis."

"Wait," Jaden said. Loomis stilled with his hand over the ignition switch. "What are you looking at, Chief?"

She studied the cryptic notation, but couldn't see what excited him. She gave up. "What's the infinity symbol tell you?"

"That we have to break it." Brian traced it again. "The hub is where the line meets itself. The top swoop right heads toward the lake, the docks. Go from middle, up and down left and you're aimed at Peoria. Or you can circle around, back to the hub or continue on toward Gary."

"So?"

"The hub is a center. Peoria is where several of Kristoff's labs are. Gary is the mill and torture chamber."

"But the girls weren't there. The transfer guards denied it. Maria didn't see children. Leigh saw them, but she wasn't at the mill."

"The elevator!" Brian and Jaden said in tandem, causing a confused uproar from everyone else.

"Leigh says they're underground," Jaden clarified. "She knows a back entrance. Let me out Loomis."

"Hold on a minute," Brian stalled. "We'll go together."

"If we both go under he'll escape up top."

"And the reverse would be true," Cleveland concurred, contributing for the first time. "There are a few more of us here to help."

"Then you take the subway," Brian said to Cleveland.

"No," Jaden contradicted. "How's a guy like him gonna hide among young girls? Leigh and I will go in the back way. They might be scared of men."

She had a point.

"They won't be scared of me," Quinn offered.

Brian ruffled his hair. "Let's not scar you any more than necessary, okay?" He traded speaking looks with Cleveland. "Can you deal, Leigh?"

She gave a weak nod. "I'll do what it takes."

"Then here we are. Loomis and I will take the el to Gary. You," he frowned at Jaden, "and Leigh will go in her way." Another assessment of man and boy. "You two are in charge of monitoring the progress from here. When they get the girls up and out, you can get them to safety."

"We'll do it," Quinn said.

"Whatever it takes," Cleveland agreed with a proud look for the boy.

"Let's get to it," Jaden stood. "We'll celebrate over his fat body in a couple hours."

"You mean his dead body," Brian grumbled.

"No. You kill him and your career's over."

"I'll smoke the pervert," Loomis offered.

"His blood's on my hands and it'll stay there," Jaden stated in a tone that stopped the argument.

"All right, all right." Brian kept his eyes off Jaden and moved closer to Quinn, popping open the Trident II.

"Cool!" Quinn exclaimed.

"Yeah, I'll get you one when this is over. For now, note this frequency." Brian wrote down a few numbers. "Keep track of it and let me know if anything goes haywire." He'd be too far away to track Jaden without the van's help.

Quinn called up the software and entered the info. "Says

it's in the van with us."

"Um, yeah. Just a test I suppose. Let's rock," Brian moved to open the doors.

"Not so fast." Jaden was hanging over Quinn's shoulder. She shot a smug look at Brian. "Keep an eye on this one too."

"Hey, it's right here, too."

"I bet. What's it say now?" She moved to Brian and wrapped herself around him, smacking his lips with hers.

"They're right on top of each other."

Brian smirked. He didn't know what to think of her easy acceptance of his tag or the realization that she'd tagged him without his knowledge.

"Great minds think alike."

"Guess so."

He hopped from the van to the pavement and helped her down. "Be careful."

She tilted her smiling face up to him and puckered her lips. "Load me up, big guy. It might be awhile before I can touch you again."

He gave himself to her through their mysterious connection. Touching her, kissing her, sharing his breath and heartbeat. He wanted her to have all of him. His strength as a shield from the perpetual drain of the Judge.

"Promise me—"

Her hand stilled his lips. "Don't ask what I can't give."

Though it went against his judgment, he let it drop. He would just get there first and finish off Albertson before the Judge could destroy them both.

Brian kissed her one last time, reluctantly releasing her when Leigh joined them. He wanted to send armored cavalry with them and knew his thought would annoy Jaden.

He watched them go.

The ultra-capable, big girl warrior setting off for another epic battle. It didn't seem so painful when it had only been theory. When he hadn't know it was his soul mate dashing off to finish a thousand-year war with evil incarnate.

Chapter Fifteen

"It is an old maxim of mine that when you have excluded the impossible, whatever remains, however improbable, must be the truth."
—Sherlock Holmes, of Sir Arthur Conan Doyle.

Jaden watched Brian's back ascending to the el, refusing to regret the unspoken words. Spilling her guts wouldn't help his concentration. If they lived, they'd have a lifetime to talk.

Hopefully.

"You guys take care," Jaden called into the van.

"Seems things are better," Cleveland observed dryly.

Jaden just grunted.

"They're a mess of gross mush." Quinn made gagging noises.

"You guys are unbelievable. Katie's scared out of her mind, who knows where, and you're talking about my love life?"

"I'm not worried. Cleveland says you're the link. You'll find her. You'll save them all."

She eyed Cleveland over the boy's head. "Some bedtime tales you tell."

"Legends and quests are the best," he countered pointedly. He turned his penetrating gaze to Leigh. "Guide her well. She'll bring you home."

Leigh only blinked watery eyes.

Cleveland smiled and then closed the van doors. Jaden knew he'd done it on purpose, making sure the last image in their minds was that picture of his ultimate confidence in them.

"This way," Leigh said.

An effective tool, Jaden thought. Leigh's shoulders were squared and her stride steady as they moved toward the scene of such recent horror in her life.

She followed, sensing at the edge of her consciousness that Albertson knew they were closing in. How would he spin it? What tricks would he pull out to stop them? She hoped her infusion of strength from Brian was enough to ward off any additional mental attacks.

"Leigh, if I, um..." She tried again. "If I zone on you, punch me right here." She pointed to her solar plexus. "Just like I showed in class." The girl's eyes went wide. "Kick if you have to."

"Why?"

"The Judge, well, he's been able to get in my head and make me see things. If he gets a hold, pain will pull me out. You can do it. And I probably won't fight back."

"Probably?"

The single word weighted with such vast doubt made Jaden smile. "It's the safest way to get me back on your side."

"What is this really about?"

"Conquering evil. No more, no less."

Leigh nodded and guided them around the corner.

Jaden's thoughts wandered as they neared the target. There had to be a way to take down Albertson legally. Regardless of Brian's rash words and fiery sense of justice, death hadn't worked so far.

Turning the police chief into a vigilante didn't sound like a positive solution. For the little girls now and the female population in the future, what they needed was a positive, permanent solution.

Brian loved Albertson; at least he'd loved the man he'd known until recently. Jaden understood first-hand the choking vine of mixed emotions. The churning tension of hating someone you loved. If she could spare Brian that pain, she would. He wouldn't like having a family friend behind bars with two needles a day, but it had to be better than having your lover kill a friend outright.

Jaden pulled a digital hand-cam from her pocket. "If I'm out of commission, take this and film all you can. Make copies, hide them and get the original to Loomis."

"The to-do list is sure growing. You're gonna have to do that yourself. I suck with cameras. I always cut off heads."

Jaden smiled at the rambling. Leigh was doing whatever she could to keep herself moving forward when she clearly wanted to run like hell back to Micky's safe house.

"I appreciate the escort, Leigh."

No answer. She'd frozen like a statue in front of an unremarkable doorway.

"This is it?" Jaden prompted.

A jerky nod was all the confirmation Leigh could give.

"I'll take it from here then."

"No. If I stop now he wins."

Jaden began to protest, until she recognized the glittering determination in Leigh's eyes.

"Good for you." She turned on the camera, unsnapped the strap on her dagger and flipped the safety off her pistol. "I'm ready. Lead on."

Brian stood with Loomis on the Gary platform. Loomis used binoculars to assess the guards on patrol. "Nothin'. This place is deader than a doornail."

Naturally, Brian understood the phrasing. Taking the opportunity, Brian checked in with Quinn and Cleveland. "What's her status?" he asked via his link to the van.

"We just lost her signal," Cleveland replied. "She must be underground."

Shit. He didn't think of that. "There might be a way to boost it." Did Cleveland hear his desperation? He had to get a grip on this or Albertson would win easily.

"Give me that," Loomis lowered the binoculars and held out a hand for the communicator. He relayed instructions for boosting the signal, waited, then returned the device to Brian.

"There she is!"

Quinn's happy voice eased Brian's worry.

"Any fallout on Kristoff yet?" he asked Cleveland.

"Not that we've picked up. I'll let you know."

"Fine." Not willing to delay any longer he signed off. "We're going in."

They strolled toward the abandoned mill as if they owned it, instead of a morally bankrupt judge.

"What's your plan?" Loomis asked.

"Go in, subdue the guards, release any prisoners. When we find the Judge make him beg for his life."

"You'll let him live?"

"Hell no."

"But Jaden said–"

"She's wrong. He'll never stop unless we, I, take him out."

"Whatever, boss." Loomis shrugged and pulled his gun from his shoulder holster.

They loped across the open area without incident. Either the mill had been cleared out, or the orders were to hold fire.

"Too quiet," Loomis groused.

Brian agreed. "Get set then."

They offed the safeties on their weapons and kicked in the front door. This room Brian had never seen. It rivaled the entries of grand estates, down to the sweeping, marble staircase.

"Welcome, boys," Albertson boomed.

They looked up to see the Judge in all his glory at the balcony, surrounded by armed men, with weapons at the ready.

Brian lowered his gun, but didn't engage the safety. "Had a report there was trouble. You okay, old man?"

He saw the Judge flinch.

"Just protecting my interests, son."

"From what threat?"

"Come in, come in, and we'll talk. What report alerted you?"

"Squatters draining an energy source," Loomis improvised.

"Oh, yes, of course. All handled." He lumbered down the wide staircase. "Just decided to step up the security. Can't be too sure who's who and what's what with the visitors I'm expecting. You're not in uniform."

Brian ignored the reference. "More unsavory associates?"

The Judge nodded. "With wicked tastes."

The Judge was baiting him and Brian kept his irritation to himself. "Well, keep 'em happy. If you're okay, we'll be going."

"Information is the key with allies and enemies. Know their weaknesses. Know when to use those weaknesses against them." He tapped a fleshy finger to his grayed temple.

They were discussing Jaden. He knew she was coming. Enough was enough. He pulled his weapon and aimed at Albertson's black heart. "I'm not her weakness. Why don't you give your boys the day off and show us around your playground?"

Albertson chortled. "Love is a many splendored thing. But she doesn't love you, son. She can't. She's as far from human as I."

He wouldn't let the words bother him. It was crap and he knew it. Just more of the mind games he'd applied to Jaden in the museum.

"Hand over the gun." The guards descended on Brian and Loomis. "Think on it. Then we'll talk again."

Taking weapons, the guards hauled them away. Upstairs, Brian realized. He shot Loomis a look to just play along. If they were going up to the cells, he'd lay good odds they wouldn't be confined for long.

Jaden clipped the camera to her waistband and set it to record as they walked into a narrow hallway and descended a steep half flight of stairs. At the landing, Leigh turned in circles.

"It was here. The elevator was here."

She wouldn't insult Leigh by asking useless questions. Instead, Jaden moved to each wall in turn, looking for a hidden trip of some sort.

Leigh found it first and gave a small cry as the elevator door slid back. They stepped into the car and Jaden pressed the lowest button on the panel.

"Smell right?" she asked as the car began to move.

Leigh nodded. Her breathing was shallow, her eyes wide with fear.

"You're doing great. We'll be out of here in no time."

"Sure."

The door opened, and to her benefit, Leigh's fresh terror

made her stall. The hesitation saved her from a man's boot to her jaw.

Jaden shoved her back and leaped forward, dagger at the ready. The man finished the arc of his kick and faced Jaden with a sneer.

"Billy," the women said in unison.

"At your service." He bowed, just out of Jaden's reach. "Well, hey there peach," he addressed Leigh. "Back for more Big Billy, huh?"

"Pig!" Leigh screamed, launching herself at the man who'd degraded her so terribly.

Jaden followed the skirmish into a dank, brick alcove. It was best for Leigh to do as much damage as possible. Healing. Not many victims had the opportunity or courage to attack their abusers.

Billy shrieked like the girls he guarded when fingernails raked at his eyes. Foul names poured from his mouth, several interestingly new to Jaden's seasoned vocabulary, but so far he held back from causing Leigh real bodily harm.

She let them go until he tripped Leigh. As the woman went down, Jaden threw herself into the brawl before Billy could complete the damaging stomp he had in mind.

"Deal with me." She waved the dagger. "I'll go easy on you."

"Bitch!" he snarled and faced her. His lip was already swelling and blood oozed from the rakes Leigh had inflicted.

"I'm past the name calling." Jaden aimed an elbow at his jaw, let him dodge the diversion and with a swift duck and spin, she reached around to slice at his hamstring.

He dropped to the floor, howling in pain.

"That was for Brenda." She raised her knee, much as he had over Leigh and brought her foot down hard enough to crush the kneecap on his good leg. He passed out from the pain.

Sheathing the dagger, Jaden looked to Leigh. "Is this the easiest way to get the girls out?"

"Yes."

Her strong voice pleased Jaden. She'd make a full recovery. "Good. Then we'll leave him here and let them each take a shot on their way out."

Leigh's smile showed her wicked delight in the idea.

Oh, yeah, she'd get over this ordeal. Jaden searched Billy, stripping him of his communicator, taser and a small pistol she found in an ankle holster.

Jaden took the lead, gun ready, not willing to waste any more time. She kneecapped the first guard they encountered. He willingly spilled the names and locations of his only two associates. Taking his taser, Leigh agreed to divert the next man in line.

Jaden gave him a debilitating shock, cuffed him, and stuffed him in a corner. The third guard sat at a desk, oblivious to the plight of his crew. Jaden clipped him with a bullet to the shoulder and got his attention.

"Keys," she demanded, as he gaped in shock.

He reached for his weapon and Jaden shot it out of his hand.

"Keys," she repeated.

"Here," he groaned.

Jaden stepped closer, gun to his head, while Leigh approached from the opposite side with the taser in hand. They found the three electronic keys on a ring at his belt.

"Thank you," Leigh said, taking the camera from Jaden before running off to free the girls.

"Yes, thank you." Jaden moved a donut box and perched

herself on his desk. "Now, what can you tell me about the subway?"

"Nothing."

She slipped her gun into her waistband and removed the dagger. "I'm very good with this. Ask Billy to tell you all about it sometime." She toyed with some paperwork, picking up the one with medications specified. "Drugs for the girls?" She didn't need him to answer; his pained look said it all.

Behind her, she heard Leigh encouraging the girls to move.

"Leigh," she called without taking her eyes from the guard. "How many girls?"

"Fourteen."

"And how's Katie?"

"She's here. Just a little groggy."

"Trade ya." She held out the paper and accepted the return of the camera. "Cleveland will know how to get them feeling better."

"Got it." Leigh hustled off.

"Leigh?"

"Yeah?"

"Good work, girlfriend." Then she put the rescue behind her and focused her significant energy on the guard. She tossed the knife in the air and caught it just before the blade landed in his crotch. "Let's try this again. What would you like to tell me about the subway?"

"You can't trust her, son," Albertson's voice came over the speaker in the cell. "Who's stood by you, watched out for you all these years?"

Brian wondered how he hadn't seen the truth of this bastard before now. Must be that blocking thing Jaden accused him of.

"Now, you think you're in love. But you can't trust what you see. She's got powers to fool you. Every woman does, but she's not just a woman."

"Does he ever shut up?" Loomis groused.

"Be grateful he doesn't know your weakness."

A grunt was the only answer from somewhere down the hall where Loomis had been locked away, out of Brian's sight.

"She's a little demon, I say. No white wings on that one, son. She's not your salvation. Think back to who's been there for you. Me. What lies has she fed you?"

Brian threw a pillow at the speaker. Then struggled to move the prison-like cot. Using the cot as a stepstool he tried to pry the speaker off the ceiling. No luck. He jumped down and began using the cot to knock the speaker down.

And still Albertson's voice droned on. "What kind of a woman spouts nonsense of past lives? She needs psychiatric help, son. You'd be helping her by bringing her in."

"Stop the damned banging, Chief," Loomis hollered. "You're letting him get to you."

Brian stopped. "No. I just want out of here."

Loomis stepped up in front of Brian's locked cell. "Then let's go."

The bars slid back as Brian gaped. "How?"

"These locks are old. Any one with a few years on the force should know how to slip past 'em."

"I've got more than a few years on the force," Brian pointed out irritably.

"He's not yanking my chain, sir."

Brian stared into the young face of a guard. "And you are?"

"Provost, sir. Undercover from the Central Region

Investigation Authority." He offered his hand. "We've suspected Albertson of facilitating the trade of missing children."

Brian wanted credentials and knew it was stupid to ask, especially when the man was returning his weapon. Here was the gift horse, the legal way to bring down Albertson. But he knew it wouldn't be enough. The Judge had to die.

Jaden may worry for his career, but he worried for her soul. And what good was a job when a man like the Judge could breathe the same free air as honest citizens?

"Shall we?" Provost urged them out and down the hall.

"What's your plan?" Loomis asked.

"There's a subway access. You can escape that way."

"No. Not without the Judge in custody. My custody."

Loomis and Provost gave Brian equally dumbfounded stares.

"I assure you, Chief, we'll be making an arrest today. We have enough documentation."

"Gary's been annexed by Chicago. My city, my jurisdiction."

"Begging your pardon, kidnapping is a federal crime."

"He's kidnapped plenty of the locals."

Loomis put a beefy hand on a shoulder of each man. "Enough with the pissing contest. Isn't putting the bastard away the point?"

Brian bit his tongue. He'd make his move when Jaden showed up. If she showed up. No, he couldn't think that way.

She was fine.

She had to be fine.

"A disturbing report, son. She's destroying evidence."

Brian whipped around, but it was merely Albertson on the speaker again.

"I told you she couldn't be trusted. What sort of law-abiding official can love a woman who's–"

Brian didn't hear the rest. He was too busy laughing at the Judge's paradox. Yes, what sort of law-abiding official could love a person capable of such atrocities as destroying evidence or destroying people?

"Lead the way, Provost. It's your case."

They descended to the hallway outside the torture chamber without encountering a single guard. A fact that set Brian's teeth on edge. The Judge wouldn't just give up like this. He had to have the place wired six ways to Sunday.

Brian was about to break for the Judge's office when crying erupted from inside that horrible room. The men decided with only eyes and hand signals who would go in and how.

First through, Brian went low, gun drawn. Loomis backed him and Provost followed. The room was empty, the crying coming from the girl depicted on the panel of monitors.

"Again, I say welcome." This time the Judge was real, his rolling gait closing the distance. "I've sent the boys on an errand. It seems a dear friend has run into a bit of trouble."

"Then he shouldn't be alone in the boat," Brian sneered, raising the gun to the Judge's head. "Trouble's found you too."

Provost protested the aggression, to no avail.

Loomis didn't bother.

"I pray you'll soon realize you're under her negative influence. Put that away."

Brian held steady. "I'd think praying wouldn't be your favorite hobby."

"I have other interests, true." He waved an arm to indicate the whole room. "Why interfere with Kristoff's good work?"

The sorrowful tone didn't fool Brian. "He's juicing men

for mind control. A unit here and there, soon an army. For what? World domination?"

"Such melodrama." The Judge laughed, but Brian could see he continued to calculate. "Put the gun down, son. Killing me won't stop the cycle. Ask your lady love."

"Finally the truth. What are you?"

"Only what I am." Laughter, sadistic and cruel bounced off the high, metal ceiling. "As eternal and evil as they come."

Brian felt Provost and Loomis shrink back.

He stepped forward. "My 'lady love' isn't pulling the trigger this time. Shall we see what difference I make in this circular equation?"

They were close enough, Brian could see the minute widening of Albertson's eyes. "The way I see it, I'm the one who must choose who to believe. The choice I make determines your fate, right?"

Any possible answer fell away at the rumbling beneath their feet. The Judge smiled, even winked. "I'll be going now, son. Take care with your life and don't forget your duty."

Brian cocked the gun and fired, but the shot went uselessly into the rafters as Provost tackled him.

The two men wrestled, shouting obscenities and legalities at each other while the Judge hauled his bulk into the electric chair elevator and disappeared into the floor.

"Show me the other access!" Brian demanded, earning the advantage over Provost at last.

"Hell no! We need him alive."

Brian rolled over and roared in denial. He'd failed her. With 'Protocol Provost' here, even if they killed the judge, one of them would get the death penalty for taking a life. He scrambled to his feet.

It would be him. He'd take the lethal injection, not her.

That would be the change, the catalyst to allow her to live, just once, a full life.

He scrambled for the elevator, searching the floor for an access panel. Finding it, he overrode the circuit and recalled the chair.

"Hold him," he ordered Loomis to restrain Provost. He heard the officers scuffle and then looked up to see his own man had prevailed.

"Here it comes." Brian pulled back the hammer and waited for his shot.

But when the chair came into view Jaden stood behind it, her gun trained on Brian.

"What the hell are you doing?"

"Saving your life." She lowered her weapon. "There's a Federal officer on site."

Seeing the Judge was bound in the chair, Brian lowered his gun too. "Loomis found him." His heart leaped at her smirk when she caught sight of the cop sitting on the undercover officer.

"I've got it all on tape," she said. "The whole nasty set up."

The Judge started spouting vile threats and nonsense. Jaden walked over to the table, picked up the scarf and returning to the Judge deliberately gagged him with it.

"Statements from guards too," she continued. "I've wired a copy to Cleveland."

"Knock out Provost there and let me kill him," Brian snapped, glaring at the Judge.

"No. Legal's the only way." She took a step toward him. "You were right. It's our time. Let's not continue as prisoners of fate."

"Oh, Jaden." He opened his arms and she fell into the

embrace. Closing his eyes, he rubbed his jaw over her hair and just savored the miracle of her.

Then the gates of hell opened.

Loomis shouted a warning as gunfire erupted around them. Provost rolled and scrambled, leaving Loomis alone and bleeding.

Brian's first shot, hands full of Jaden, only nicked the Judge, who'd freed a hand and was punching the panel of the chair-elevator. The chair began to sink into the floor.

He fired again, but the bastard only smiled. A smug, immortal expression that turned Brian's gut inside out. He loosed his weapon on the chair, disabling the electronics and slowing the Judge's escape.

Slowly, he trained his weapon on the Judge's brow, envisioning the end result. Positive. Permanent.

He pulled the trigger.

"No!"

Someone screamed. Jaden? The Judge? He wasn't sure.

Jaden launched and felt the bullet tear through her side. More gunfire and voices erupted, the sounds popping and ricocheting from every angle. She wouldn't let Brian kill the Judge and with him, their chance for life. Pain blinded her, but it beat the tragic frustration of knowing she'd have to live again. Knowing she'd face this damned demon again.

Just once, she'd wanted the normal life of those around her. The regular, mundane aches and pains. It apparently had been too much to hope for.

Her vision clearing, she saw the Judge circling her, a long, familiar blade in his hand.

"That's mine," she hissed, coming to her feet with a grace born of a thousand lives as a warrior.

He laughed, morphing into his true demonic form: tall and

muscled with leathered skin smelling of sulphur and death. "Come try and claim it."

The change fueled her. She recognized this would at last be the true and final battle. Everything fell away. Her pain, spectators, victims. Nothing mattered but winning.

They engaged in the fatal dance and she let him get cocky. He taunted her, inviting her to meet hate with hate. He lunged, she blocked. He speared, she dodged. He had the advantage of reach with the longer blade, but she had two daggers, agility and a secret in her favor.

She alone knew who'd forged that weapon.

The sword slid past her face, splitting the air with a rush and leaving a fine line of blood in its wake. She smiled, sensing the beginning of the end and spun in closer, grazing his sword arm on the way.

Even the demonic would bleed and blood made for a loose grip. Furious, the demon attacked. Jaden lowered her daggers to absorb the lethal strike as she made her choice.

"I have chosen love."

It didn't even hurt. Just a flash of metal disappearing into her chest. An agonized scream and it was done. At last.

In the eerie quiet of the aftermath, she sensed a presence from her past. Comfort, concern and assurance all blended in the dark recesses of her mind. Her heart at peace, Jaden wanted to sink into the glory of it.

But someone was calling her name and she felt his touch.

Brian.

"Jaden? Can you hear me?"

Her vision hemmed by the darkness, she reveled in the strength of his voice. He was alive. "*Mmm*-hmm."

"Stay with me."

"*Mmm*. Touch me..." she managed.

He did. "Hang in there. Cleveland called reinforcements." His fingers combed through her hair. His hand pressed into the raw wound. "God, I'm so sorry."

"You shot me."

"Did not. You jumped into the bullet. And dropped your guard. Why, Jaden?"

True enough. "To finish." She felt different, free. "Won't lose you." Never again.

And that's what she'd never said aloud. She needed to tell him she couldn't bear to ever live without him. Someone came between them to dress her wound. She clung to Brian and tried again to get the words out.

"Shh. I'm right here. Let them help."

"You help more. I love you. More–" She struggled for breath. "More than I hated him."

Other voices crowded in on them, but she heard only his, felt only his hands. "I love you, too."

His lips found hers and the darkness slid back a notch. She could breathe deeply again. Vague, familiar warmth spread over her. Not the heat of blood leaking from her body. This warmth bubbled from her soul.

Happiness, she decided.

At last she felt more than today's hurts and the pains of battles centuries past. She felt joy.

True, timeless, joy.

"You failed."

The evil entity, which had most recently been a judge, stood mute. What could be said? What excuse offered? After a thousand years, the world had been his for the taking and she'd won the final battle. He still wasn't sure how.

"You allowed love to grow. You underestimate its

power."

The punishment would be severe, he knew.

"Away from me. There will be another way."

Jaden studied Brian's face as he lay next to her on the hospital bed. "So what did they decide?"

"Officially, it's cardiac arrest."

She chuckled. "Even without a body?"

"A minor technicality. Everyone present holds high level clearances. All trained for silence. I don't think anyone wants to discuss it anyway."

"That bizarre?"

He nodded. "I shot, you dove. The CRIA officers fired a suppression pattern." He shrugged. "I don't get it. He wasn't wounded." His brow creased. "The way you fought. Oh, God. You scared the hell out of me."

"I'm sorry. It was the only way. He had to think he'd win." She kissed the frown off his face. "It's past time to thank you."

The frown returned. "For shooting you?"

She laughed, free and clear and she liked the sound. "No. For making victory possible. You helped forge that sword for me, as a wedding gift...before our lives were so rudely interrupted."

"But how?"

"Love." She whispered the word against his lips. "Pure and simple. The sword carried it and I finally trusted you enough to open my heart." She kissed him soundly. "Love is the only thing evil cannot overcome. Thank you." She kissed him again. She couldn't get enough of him. "Thank you for believing, for loving. For my very life, Brian."

"See. I told you so," Quinn said pointing to Jaden and

Brian. "They're all over each other again."

Hovering near the door, Katie rolled her eyes. "Why is he so stupid?"

"He'll outgrow it," Cleveland promised.

Her doubtful expression made Jaden laugh. She patted the bed. "Come here, you two." They hopped up and she enveloped them both in a big hug. "How are the bravest kids in the city?"

Katie blushed and Quinn smirked.

"They're still intrigued with tracking two particular frequencies," Cleveland said with meaning. "Loomis gave them your Trident II."

Brian chuckled, removing the tag he'd planted on Jaden the day before. She did the same and handed them both to the kids.

When the new family departed, Jaden snuggled deeper into Brian's warmth. It may have taken a thousand years, but it was worth the wait. She'd found her way through victim, past survivor, to the brilliant reward in the arms of her soul mate.

Meet the Author:

Regan Black crafts her stories in the South Carolina Lowcountry where the rich history adds fire to her vivid imagination. Encouraged by her husband, children, retired greyhounds and numerous other pets, she savors the rare quiet moments when the words flow onto the page.

A voracious reader, she's often found with a book in hand, or at least nearby, as she taxis children and dogs to their respective appointments. She's pleased to credit her friends and critique partners with the successful leap from her blissfully boring daily life into the women's adventure market.

Visit
www.reganblack.com

Turn the page for the exciting first chapter
of
Invasion of Justice
Book Two in the Shadows of Justice series

By

Regan Black

**Coming
Early 2006
From
Echelon Press
www.echelonpress.com**

Chapter One

He forced the lock with a custom security card General Hawthorne would envy—under other circumstances. Pride swelled as the new idea formed. He'd guarantee admiration in the General's eyes before this night was over.

Each silent step brought him closer to the target. His pulse quickened and he paused until he'd harnessed the adrenaline. This was his proving ground and there was no room for error.

At the lab, he swiped the card again and then offered his eye, the modified one, for verification. He tucked the card away and paused to enjoy the soft hiss of the door opening, etching every moment into his memory.

A man only got one first.

He noticed the target's hunched shoulders, glasses pushed high on the forehead, eyes hovering over the microscope. Those cells in the dish were deadly, but not in the way the genetic engineers intended.

He slowed his breathing for the final approach. Damn, he could practically see the black death cloud. His lips curled. He could almost smell the blood. His fingers twitched in anticipation of the slick, sticky feel.

He struck the nerve center on the target's neck, sending him to the floor in a heap, leaving the priceless cells in their dish. Pulling a miniature hypodermic from his pocket, he drew the substance from the dish and injected it into the target. He pressed his fingers to the jugular and waited, counting the prescribed ten pulse beats.

Then, with reverence born of training, he unwrapped the sacred blade and began the fun part. A man should enjoy his work, after all.

Indianapolis, IN May 2096:

She came awake in a rush, her hands fisted and slippery.

"Lights," she croaked, terrified what the light would reveal. She sighed, her first deep breath in how long? Her hands glistened with sweat, not blood. It had been so real.

Too real.

She scrambled to sit up, bracing herself against the cool

scrollwork of her mahogany headboard. It wasn't the first time she'd been in the mind of evil and she knew what would follow.

Looking to the phone, a retro 1900's antique landline connected to her modern cell card, she waited.

And waited.

Long enough to wonder if it had only been a dream. She scrubbed at her face and decided the link had been too strong, too nasty to have been a mere nightmare.

When the clunky contraption rang, she jumped for it.

"Petra Neiman."

"Yeah, I've got a tangled mess for you," the caller stated.

That she knew. As if ritual evisceration could be anything less. She wanted the who and where of it.

The nameless voice who made these calls obliged. "Kincaid wants you in Chicago immediately. A dead Jane Doe is likely connected to a solid lead on two recent kidnappings."

She almost corrected him. It was a murder, high profile, with no secondary crime, in a seaside genetics lab. She'd smelled the humid tang of saltwater on the assassin's clothes.

The revelation startled her. Not even she maintained a sense of smell during a dream.

"Ms. Neiman? Are you there?"

"Yes. How long until the car arrives?"

"Thirty minutes."

"I'll call my assistant."

"Um...Special Agent Kincaid insists you come alone."

Special Agent Kincaid should get a hobby that didn't contradict her needs. "Then I'll need a videographer."

"He says whatever you need will be on site."

"Fine. I'll be ready." There was no point in beheading the messenger. She dropped the receiver back into the cradle and stared at her ceiling.

Yes, she'd be ready. But she knew she was only marking time until the call from the coast came in.

The flight into Chicago was uneventful, but Petra's talents were nearly overwhelmed upon landing. Almost as soon as the wheels settled, a heavy darkness pressed in on her. She had to disagree with her new assistant's opinion; having "evil radar" was not the ultimate asset.

In the government-issued black transport van Petra closed her eyes and opened her mind. The city vibrated with a nasty presence that didn't mind being known.

She shivered. Awareness at this level was a two-way street. The malevolence fueling the criminal Kincaid sought knew Petra was in town.

As the transport pulled up, she prepared herself for the known and unknown of the process. She would read the crime scene, interview witnesses, and gently tap their emotions for details they didn't often realize they'd left out. But even expecting to uncover the weird or surprising didn't always mute the shock.

"Thanks for coming," Kincaid said with a smile. The Special Agent in Charge of the Central Region Investigation Authority looked past her into the van. "Where's Kelly?"

Petra held her expression in neutral, but sent Kincaid a meaningful look. "Out tracking down real glazed donuts. Where's the videographer you promised?"

Kincaid's eyes narrowed, but he too reserved comment for later. "There's someone on site that can help us, I'm sure."

Petra nodded and took her first hard look at the area. The Hammond Street docks had once thrived with cargo train activity. Now, the prime location for loading and unloading boats and trucks was a deserted, nightmarish collection of worn and rusting parts.

Except the tracks. She walked closer to the original-style double rail and ties. The rails gleamed, even in the poor evening light. "I've heard of train collecting, but not true to life models."

"My thoughts too. This is some operation we've bumped into."

Petra looked at the old diesel engine sitting frozen on the tracks with three disconnected cars behind it. Petra walked inside the now empty area and just absorbed the lingering energies.

Fury. Fear. Survival. Salvation.

She took the electronic data pad Kincaid offered and checked his notes. Jane Doe was dead and three other men, all refusing to speak, had apparently watched it happen. Those three sat propped against the train wheels, awaiting her questions.

Mentally she ticked off her interview goals. She wanted to know which of them knew how to drive the antique diesel engine. She wanted to know the contents of the three cars. Evidence crews had found random hairs and prints and a half dozen sterling armbands in an infinity pattern.

"Need some help with a video?" a man's voice asked.

Petra whirled around, startled that anyone had slipped under her senses. She thought she'd seen him before, but couldn't put a name with the face.

"Have we met, sir?"

"Nope. I'm Gideon Callahan," he said.

She stepped back from the smile that didn't reach his eyes and the extended hand she couldn't accept. "A pleasure to meet you," she lied, through her most professional smile. "I'll pass on the video." She slid the data pad into her tote and withdrew a spiral notebook and pencil. "This'll do for today." She climbed up into the engine and opened herself to the residual feelings.

Gideon followed her. "So what the hell happened here?"

Petra began to put words to her thoughts and impressions. "This was quite a struggle. A battle for more than life." She crossed to the side wall where scratches marked the progress of the Jane Doe's attempt to escape her bonds.

Here was the fury. Complete and violent fury that the mission had gone off course.

"But whose course?"

"What?" Gideon asked.

She ignored him. "Two opposing forces determined to win. Why didn't the men struggle? Why didn't they help Jane Doe?"

"Cat fight."

"I beg your pardon?" Petra turned at last to study the man who wouldn't take the hint and disappear.

He had dark hair that would curl if not for the strict cut, straight boned features, a Van Dyke beard and deep brown eyes that didn't evoke warmth, but warning. She didn't need the warning from his eyes as his aura hummed with an evasive quality she didn't trust. And she'd never liked bearded men.

"Haven't you seen the autopsy report?"

This time she took personal blame for the irritation she felt with this man. She flipped pages, but couldn't find a hard copy. Pulling out her palmtop, she scanned the official email from the coroner via Kincaid.

"Give it up. The words don't do it justice. Take a look here."

Forcing herself to remain calm, she lifted her gaze to the holographic display open in his hand. The coroner's clinical voice detailed every injury Jane Doe earned in her final fight. Scratches, offensive and defensive, lacerations and the blade strike that ended it. Even in death, the woman looked wild and intimidating. Well over six feet with extreme musculature that made it easy to believe she'd been juicing.

"See," Gideon persisted, "cat fight. I don't know a guy that'll jump between two women out for blood. Especially juicers. Not sure I wanna see the bird who won."

I do. The thought came unbidden and nearly escaped verbally. She wanted, *needed*, to know more about the second woman she'd sensed here. The connection felt deeper than any other she'd felt before–including the link she shared with her only sibling, her brother Nathan.

"She fights but she doesn't juice."

"Not anymore." Gideon flipped off the hologram. "But women haven't looked like that since the days of the Amazon."

"Not the Jane Doe. The other woman." Petra stomped on her frustration. This issue could wait. "Bring in the witnesses, please."

"Okay, but they won't talk."

"I wish the same could be said of you," she muttered. His bark of laughter told her he had ears like a bat.

Putting Gideon out of her mind, she calmed herself with breath as she watched the witnesses file in. All three were nervous, but the first man was the target of hostile energy from the other two.

She didn't need them to talk as much as remember and feel. When she tapped those feelings, conversation would follow.

According to her notes, they'd been found less than twenty-four hours ago, along with the decaying Jane Doe. Men or not, she didn't think she'd have trouble getting a read on their emotions.

"The lady here wants to know why you didn't help your girl," Gideon blurted.

The men stared back at him with one surly expression in triplicate.

Petra knew her expression differed. If Gideon bothered to spare her a glance, he'd see the unruffled calm she practiced to perfection. But inside she plotted how best to remove him from the investigation–preferably in tiny pieces.

She walked, wishing she could swagger, to the testosterone-heavy end of the engine. "The lady here wants to know why the three of you are working on a decrepit railroad."

Reading the body language of all three, Petra quickly identified and mentally tapped the man the other two didn't respect. His sense of failure went deep and was mixed with a healthy dose of fear and insecurity.

Her prodding produced the expected result.

"J-just a job."

The other two groaned, but Gideon kept them from moving on the talker.

"We got nothing else to lose," he said to his associates. "We just h-hauled cargo."

"And where is that cargo now?" Gideon demanded before Petra could speak.

"W-we, I mean I, don't know. Just gone I guess."

"Drugs? Juice? Caffeine?" Gideon demanded. "That sort of cargo would need legs to just go anywhere."

"Women," Petra interrupted. "Girls and women." She felt Gideon turn to stare at her, but she kept her eyes on the three other men. "Hauling females to a slave auction." She sighed. Kincaid's instincts were right on target–as usual. Maybe they'd finally recover and close some of their stalled kidnapping cases. "Okay. Considering you're all undereducated, I can see the lure of the money here."

Beside her, Gideon shuffled and seethed. Well, he clearly needed a lesson in role reversal. It was past time for her shot at these thugs.

"But what happened? Who released your prisoners?" she continued.

The expressions on the two sterner faces flickered. And Mr. Talkative went pale.

"Sit," Gideon ordered the three men.

She saw the benefit. By sitting, they'd be closer to re-enacting the recent fright. She followed his lead. "A woman breaks free of the cargo hold and overpowers four guards?"

"Who was driving?" Gideon added.

Not one answered verbally, but Petra knew. And she knew her big picture was off. "None of you can drive this thing. The engineer went with the cargo. With the women. And you," she knelt in front of Mr. Talkative, "You're glad the Amazon's dead."

"'Course he is. She woulda killed him next," one of the others muttered.

Petra kept her eyes on the chatty guard. "Then I guess I owe someone my thanks. Who?"

"W-we don't know. She stormed in, took my weapons, and tazed me. When I c-came around we were all t-tied up."

Gideon coughed into his hand, but the expletive was clear enough.

"Think you coulda done better?" the biggest thug said with a clear challenge to Gideon.

"Yeah, I believe I coulda done better than the sorry group of you three combined."

"Awright. Come prove it." The third man surged to his feet,

snagged Petra's arm and spun her so her back landed against his hard chest. His thick forearm clamped over her throat, locking her in place and allowing her just enough air to stay conscious.

But the instant, unexpected physical contact provided a connection Petra never risked without preparation. And she wasn't anywhere close to prepared for the onslaught of this criminal.

It felt like being sucked into a whirlpool. His memories circled her, recent and not, and drowning seemed preferable to the rush of anger and fear washing off him and over her.

She heard strident male voices, but Petra couldn't sort out any actual words. If only she could latch onto one specific memory amidst the torrent and gain control. As if her thought and his actions summoned it, she seized on his recollection of the Amazon's last battle.

Here too was strangulation–the Amazon had the neck of a smaller blonde woman wrapped in the chain of her handcuffs. Petra watched, then mimicked the blonde's escape by pushing her fingers under the man's arm and letting her legs give way. The upward push combined with her suddenly dead weight threw her attacker off balance and she dropped to the floor and rolled out of the way.

Gulping air, leaning against the wall of the engine, Petra waited as the rest of the memory played out–all the way through the victorious slide of the blonde's dagger into the Amazon's ribcage.

And when the blonde turned to the man who owned this memory, Petra saw through the bravado to the pain hidden deep in the woman's green eyes. Here was the face that matched a dream she'd been having since childhood.

A sister. My sister. The knowledge bubbled up from a depth of awareness Petra had never known–not even with Nathan.

"Hey? You okay?" Gideon asked.

Petra shut him out, curling into a tight ball. She wanted to remain with the memory, to explore all she could of this new connection before dealing with the reality at hand.

"Stay back," Kincaid demanded, entering the engine. "Don't touch her."

Gideon sneered. "What if she's hurt?"

"I'm not," Petra said, putting an end to yet another pissing contest. They seemed to be Gideon's specialty.

"Can you lift your head?" Kincaid asked.

Petra obliged, raising her chin for his visual inspection, but keeping her eyes closed.

The men made noises about bruising and soft tissue damage, but Petra wasn't worried. "I'm fine." She'd learned years ago how best to heal herself. Opening her eyes to ease their concern, she asked about the status of the guards.

"All on their way to the city lockup," Kincaid replied. "Want a hand?"

"Thought we couldn't touch her."

"Actual contact is possible if I'm prepared," Petra explained.

Gideon's eyes narrowed. "Prepared for what?"

Oh, the temptation to shock him with his own ignorance. She managed to control herself. Barely. "Touch enhances my ability to read emotion." And memory, she left unsaid.

Gideon leveled his sharp gaze at Kincaid. "You hired an empath? It was bad enough when I thought she was psychic."

"She's been of great assistance to CRIA–"

Petra gained her feet and gave up on them both. "I'm going to the hotel to write your report, Kincaid," she called on her way out.

"Wait!" Kincaid jumped out of the engine after her. "You get anything on the victims?"

"They're safe. Escaped on a ferry headed up the Michigan coastline."

"Destination?"

Petra just shrugged.

"And the Jane Doe?"

"That was self-defense, not murder." Petra shook her head. "She was one scary woman."

"What about those arm bands?"

Petra sighed. "I don't know. Things went haywire before I could prod that out of them. If I'd been alone maybe I could've gotten more." She refused to look at Gideon.

"If you'd been alone, you'd be dead by now," Gideon said, joining them.

Petra looked at him, then away. But the docks weren't any improvement. The bleak, dismal view left an impression she didn't want to cloud her senses later. The very air smelled of disuse and decay. "I need to get out of here."

"I'll drive you," Kincaid offered. "We're at the Ritz downtown."

"Nice. But no thanks. I'll take the el." But as she walked the few blocks to the platform, her nerves got worse instead of better. Only after forcing herself through the security scanner and into the elevated train, did Petra realize the feelings weren't her own.

My sister.

Pushing aside the layer of anxiety, Petra smiled. Her sister hated the el. It was fascinating to discover such a detail about a person who'd been a figment of her imagination until an hour ago. Mentally, Petra reached out and waited for a reply. When nothing but emptiness returned to her, Petra sent out as much warmth as she could generate after the ordeal at the docks.

Once in her hotel suite, she wrote her first draft of the report and then ran through a brief healing meditation. When she felt restored, she put on her music and sent herself in search of the sister she'd never known.

The incessant summons of her phone brought her back before she'd made any real progress. But the distinctive chirp told her it was another CRIA call. Maybe they'd found the victim in the lab at last.

"Petra Neiman."

"It's Kincaid."

The tension in those words brought her to full alert. "Let me guess. Genetics researcher dead by self-evisceration. Pretty fresh scene, I'd bet. It got funneled to me—"

"And you didn't report it?"

"CRIA ordered me here. I haven't had a chance to re—"

"Just shut up a minute."

She did. This sort of impatience didn't match with Kincaid's normally temperate personality. Something was very wrong. "You're scaring me."

"About time something did. Meet me downstairs in ten minutes."

The connection died as Petra deciphered their emergency escape code. She had five minutes to meet him in the south stairwell on the tenth floor. Having not bothered to find the landmark when she checked in, she wasted two minutes getting her bearings.

Printed in the United States
26954LVS00001BA/184-207